I0567064

Apocalypse: Love with a Volumptuous Alien

By Victoria Veritas

~~~

ISBN number: 978-0-991-6448-41

Apocalypse

Love with a Voluptuous Alien

By Victoria Veritas

~~~ CHAPTER ONE ~~~

Mists shroud the majestic, mysterious ruins of the once powerful Mayan temple-city of Palenque, edged by dark, foreboding rainforest. Palenque was once a seat of power in a Mayan society that flourished thousands of years ago.

The soaring, jungle-swathed temples are Mexico's national treasure. Nearby modern Palenque is a sweaty, unattractive town, a jumping off place to visit the ruins of a Mayan city once revered for its ancient university. Today's city got its name about 200 years before nearby ruins were found in the 18th Century. It is the farthest west of all major Mayan sites and has a significant population of people of Mayan descent.

At dawn a Mayan chilam, or visionary shaman, Zak-kuk, 62, short, with gray-streaked long hair that hangs loosely down his back, piercing eyes and wearing a traditional white smock that reaches nearly to his feet, sits cross-legged. Next to him sits his son, 30, Katu-Quila, who has long black hair, flashing eyes, a beatific presence and wears a white smock like his father's. They bow to Palenque's Temple of the Inscriptions, a classic Mayan pyramid crowned by an elaborate comb.

The elderly shaman lights copal incense that flames and then smokes, giving off a pungent smell that fills the air. He chews the hallucinogenic Tenonanactl mushrooms, hands some to his son and their eyelids grow heavy and then close.

A vision unfolds in the minds of the two Mayans:

Before their eyes a scene of Palenque spreads out at a date far back in history, perhaps thousands of years ago. Light faintly illuminates the roof comb of Palenque's astronomical tower as the two Mayan astronomer-priests confer. The elderly shaman, Zak-Kuk, knows it is an earlier incarnation of himself and Katu-Quila, his son, as they observe the transiting stars and planets through an object that uses a giant crystal. His stargazing son records the astronomical positions in Mayan glyphs and says, "I have charted the heavens all my life. What is your wish, father?"

"To see the end of the fifth Mayan world."

"Is it worth devoting your life to charting the paths of the stars and the planets?"

"It would confirm my life, my son."

"It would confirm your work of many lifetimes, my father."

"Share my vision, my faithful son."

"The vision is clear, father. I bow to Palenque's Temple of the Inscriptions. It is …" His voice fades as the vision overcomes father and son.

The earth tips on its axis and its crust shudders, hurricanes sweep the jungle, and powerful waves of the Caribbean destroy everything before them. Mammoth trees, entangled plants and wild vines fly through the air, birds scream fiercely and are tossed about. A volcanic rain full of ash descends in a flash of violence as the earth heaves. Howler monkeys' screams are silenced by the cataclysm.

Central America suffers great damage as South America enlarges. In the United States beaches are torn up and much construction destroyed. Infrastructure crumbles. In Asia, coastal areas vanish, Australia grows in size, and African deserts are flooded. Some of Japan survives. Widespread damage hits the Mediterranean area. Islands rise in the mid-Atlantic and parts of the Caribbean. All is changed in the wink of an eye.

Then father and son disappear in the upheaval.

The vision fades abruptly and all is quiet as mists rise from the jungle. The shaman and his son slowly recover from their shocking vision in the pearl-pink light of dawn. The sound of a tour bus further interrupts their reverie. Soon, the day's first tourists will arrive.

CHAPTER TWO

High above the jungle surrounding Palenque a small prop plane circles as the pilot says, "For me, of all the Mayan ruins, Palenque is the most sublime. Fly over here in the morning as we are now when the fog shrouds the surrounding hills and luxuriant rainforest. It's obvious why this was a sacred place to the Mayan rulers. Palenque still has the feeling of a lost world that has been swallowed up by this vast, verdant jungle. This extraordinary city, more of which is being unearthed each year, might once have been the most beautiful city in Central America. Its temples and pyramids of white limestone are equal to the architecture of the Renaissance. I should know this story. I've flown enough experts in here, especially before Dec. 21, 2012.

"I had a hunch that the experts had the wrong date, 2012. I always thought it was later. The Mesoamerican prophecy identifies 2012 as the end of an age that they called the `Sun of Movement.' Sun means a Sun cycle, so we can look upon this as an Age of Movement or An Age of Change.

"It takes the Sun hundreds of years to completely cross the central cluster of stars in the Milky Way, but the Sun is aligning with this center portion of the Milky Way during present times that began during 1998. This change is gradual, not cataclysmic.

"Mayan inscriptions on stone tablets, or stele, state this age began on August 13, 3114, and ended on the Winter Solstice of December 21, 2012. These dates marked the beginning and end of a 5,125-year cycle in the Mayan Long Count Calendar, a course of 13 measurements they called "bactuns." Also, the Mayans foresaw a rare galactic alignment of our star, the Sun.

"They determined that the Sun would be positioned directly between Earth and the center of the Milky Way Galaxy on this date. This rare event occurs once every 25,800 years. This is the time it takes the Sun to pass through the 12 signs of the Zodiac, which are the star constellations Aries, Taurus and so on, but the Sun moves through them backward. Therefore, we are moving out of the Age of Pisces and into the Aquarian Age.

The pilot points to the ruins of the Temple of Inscriptions and says, "There, in an intact burial chamber in 1952, was found the skeleton of Pacal, the city's greatest ruler. The lone passenger dozes off and soon is snoring. He is Howard Mitchener, 34, tall, with dark, wavy hair, a lean, yet muscular body and a tired, amused look that often becomes a smirk. As he snores, he recalls the events of two nights ago.

It began in New York City at a party where he went to meet his boss, Mel Rothman, 38, editor at The New York Daily News and his longtime bar hopping buddy.

As he walks down the hall of a ritzy hotel, Mitchener hears a loud party, knocks and is warmly greeted with a kiss on the cheek. He introduces himself as a friend of Mel Rothman. The attractive hostess, tall, with long, dark hair and a well-shaped body in her late twenties, takes his hand, pulls him into the crowded room, pours him a full glass of red wine, smiles, and points toward Rothman, who is chatting with two brunettes.

Mitchener works his way carefully through the loud crowd. A stunning blonde with long curls, blue eyes, high cheek bones and a svelte figure taps Mitchener on the shoulder.

"How lucky to see you, Mitch. First time since, well, you left. You pretended to love me, you prick. Remember? We were real close. Too close for you, I guess. I could see the fear in your eyes when children and family were mentioned. You feared to commit, feared to stay with one woman, quick with an exit when things got serious. What bothered you? It wasn't sex, you loved sex. It wasn't my money, my looks. It was the fear of loving me. Too bad. I've moved on. We had good times. Thanks for a fun ride."

"The loss was mine Marsha, not yours. Remember that. I'm sorry."

"Bye, bye," she says and moves to the other side of the room.

Male company is never hard for her to find.

He wearily sighs, turns away, feeling ashamed and drained. I must look like hell. I feel like hell. She's a wonderful woman. I miss her at times.

In a daze, he finds himself introduced to Rothman's friend, who smiles, gives her name, and introduces him to her friend, Angelica, who has dark brown eyes, fine features, shining auburn hair piled high in big curls and tied by magenta bows. She is wearing black, horned-rimmed glasses. Her wide smile exposes bright, flashing teeth; her pouty lips hint at a quiet sensuality and he sees desire in her eyes as she looks at him.

Her trim Prussian blue dress is neatly cut, has a slight V-neck that highlights her throat, tempting bosom, and flows down her shapely hips and legs. She has a swooping curl that falls just above her right eye.

Mitchener smiles to himself at the childlike magenta bows and dark, horn-rimmed glasses that create an air of innocence. Rothman whispers in Mitchener's ear, "Isn't she gorgeous. I'm going to marry her."

The remark stuns Mitchener; it's so out of character for Rothman. Angelica looks at Mitchener, stirring something deep within him. Then some tipsy drunk trips and falls against Mitchener's arm, knocking Rothman's wine glass to the floor. Rothman reaches out to break his fall, hits the floor and screams as the shattered glass cuts into his hand. Blood streams from the cuts. When he looks up in anger, the tipsy drunk has pushed his way through the noisy crowd to the door and quickly disappears.

Angelica bends down, examines his hand and then races into the bathroom to get towels. After swabbing the blood away, she looks up and tells Mitchener "I'm taking him to the emergency room. Please take my friend home."

"I'll take Mel to the emergency room, Angelica," says her girlfriend. "The hospital is near my apartment."

"Thanks. I have to be to work early," says Angelica in a soft voice as Mitchener eyes her cleavage as she kneels on the floor.

In the car, an exhausted Mitchener follows Angelica's directions and then says of Rothman, "He has liked and loved many women. Has a lot of charm. But he never mentioned marriage before to me."

"He never mentioned marriage to me either. I just met him."

"Honestly, I was shocked when he told me," says Mitchener.

"So am I. I have no plans to marry him or anyone else."

Mitchener, starts to doze off, recovers and negotiates the turn into Angelica's apartment parking lot, hits a curb and bangs his head against the steering wheel and falls asleep. Angelica smiles, lifts his face gently in her hands, notes his closed eyes and whispers to herself, "You think that you found me, but I found you. My pulse rate is rising. Remember, Mitch, the universe is vibration like in the song, Good Vibrations. This resonance can occur between two people without them knowing it. You resonated with me, but didn't know it. I resonated with you and knew it. Love is exchanged and energy is created. I feel it and I just met you. Loving continually is the secret of happiness. Love and gratitude."

She kisses him lightly and whispers again, "You were attracted to me at my first glance."

"What?" says Mitchener slowly opening his eyes.

"Come on up for a moment. I don't trust your ability to drive." Angelica takes his hand as they climb the stairway and make their way to her apartment. He follows obediently and says, "All I can think of is crawling into bed for a good night sleep."

After entering her apartment, he heads for the couch and collapses. Angelica leaves the room to wash the last of the dried blood from her hands and pours herself a glass of red wine. When she returns, he's deeply asleep and snoring lightly. She decides to let him sleep while she sits on a nearby chair, sips her wine, gets another glass and leaves the room.

Just as she starts to doze off she decides to return to the couch, remove Michener's socks and pull off his jacket. She removes one sock, pulls hard on the other, while Michener remains in his dream world. Next she undoes his tie and unbuttons his shirt and slides it off. Her soft fingers then unbuckle his pants, which easily slip off.

Angelica's finds her heart is beating faster and her breathing comes quicker as she bends foreword and kisses his nipple. Then she looks at his gray shorts, which have risen to form a tent. Her forefinger touches the cloth-like tent cautiously and she laughs at her daring.

Should I? She thinks, and slips off his cotton gray shorts, re- vealing his manhood. She breathes faster, decides that he is resting comfortably, but will need a blanket. When she returns, she imagines he is slightly smiling. She kisses it gently, then circles it with her warms lips and reluctantly decides to let him sleep.

In her bedroom, she perfumes herself, dons a sheer night gown but can't fall sleep. She rubs a fragrant lubricant onto her two fingers and softly slips them between her thighs and into her body. She strokes deeper as her breaths come quicker; she moves her fingers faster and she moans, her hips quiver, her back arches and she sinks into a swooning bliss.

On the couch, Mitchener slips into an overpowering dream: A finely featured ancient Egyptian priestess of Hathor, the Egyptian goddess of music, dance, love and sex, glides toward him in her temple. The Temple of Hathor is dedicated to the Goddess Hathor, and the stars of Hathor, the Pleiades. In this temple, a marvel of man's beginnings can be found. A star clock, carved millennia ago, celebrates the Pleiades, the vastly great sun around which our solar system revolves, taking 25,827.5 years to complete one revolution. Called the Procession of the Equinoxes, the clock of stone has survived the ages.

The graceful, elegant priestess has shining black hair, piercing dark eyes and tawny skin. Her legs are perfect and she has a mystical air. An iridescent energy surrounds her.

She smiles and bows. A pleated robe of semi-transparent linen hangs over her voluptuous body. She wears simple leather sandals. Her fingers and toenails are dyed with henna. Golden sandals accent her painted toes. Lapis lazuli, turquoise and gold dust sparkle on her eyelids.

A religion has developed in Egypt satisfying its people even if they do not always adhere to its principles. There is a happy sense of cosmic unity. Man, or plant or animals all shared godhood. This belief in the sacredness of all that lived made for a serene present and perfect hereafter.

The priestess touches his head gently between his brows, sending him into a deep, trance-like state. He feels a powerful current of love pouring from her hands and senses she is from another dimension, a transcendent Being of Light.

The pupils of her eyes sparkle and dance. Music of the lyre floats on the air as her energy surges into his loins. She caresses his response with her fingers and then kisses his lips, his face, his hair and pulls him to her, lightly running her fingers over his flesh as his hands caress her curves. Soon he is within her and their bodies rise and fall in rhythm. A cloud of fragrance descends as he feels spasms about to overtake his body. Then she holds his body so tightly he cannot achieve release. Her spirit quiets him and he slides into a deep, cleansing sleep.

In the morning, Mitchener awakens slowly, notes he has been disrobed, smirks and then remembers his dream. Angelica, wrapped in a loose fitting white bathrobe, pulls him to a sitting position on the couch and hands him a cup of steaming coffee. Her white bathrobe falls open, giving him a quick peek at a pink nipple on a milky white breast. Angelica laughs and quickly pulls her robe tighter.

"Sorry."

"Never apologize for your beauty."

Mitchener sips his coffee and says, "I dreamed I made love to a lovely Egyptian priestess. I feel somehow it was you. Was it you?"

"Yes, of course," says Angelica. "You think time is lineal, but it is not. Time is spherical. The future has already happened; it is also possible to return to the past as you did in your so called dream. Was it a dream? Yes. Was it me? Yes. Only direct experience will change you forever when you discover the reality of time."

Moments later she rushes back and says, "Got to run. Sorry to ask you to leave. I want to thank you for last evening. We shared only a few moments, but you say you shared other moments with me in your dreams."

She hands him a slip of paper with her name, Angelica Haas, her address and telephone number.

"Come to dinner at 8 p.m. sharp."

She kisses his cheek lightly, motions him toward the door, opens it, pauses briefly, and says, "Don't forget my face. Take two minutes to memorize it."

Surprised, he starts to say something, but she adds, "Take a day off. Take this soft, pink pillow. Sleep on it. Enjoy its perfume and think of me. I have a passion for myrrh. Maybe, I'll come to you in your dreams again?"

She laughs and adds, "Here's another tip. Make yourself a part of the energy field, the cosmic energy that flows around you. Feel yourself slipping into the vortex of that energy, above, below and around you. Feel yourself becoming a part of it. Draw it into your body. Recharge yourself twice a day with this universal energy. It takes practice, but it works."

Mitchener starts to say something, but she puts her finger to his lips, silencing him.

"Remember, the entire cosmos is energy. It's not made of energy, it is energy. We're part of the cosmos, so we're energy too. Recharge yourself as I told you. You'll feel younger and more vital. I'm younger than you. You'll need all the energy you can get with me."

~~~ CHAPTER THREE ~~~

Mitchener asks for a day off, and goes back to his apartment. Soon, he's fast asleep over his gift from Angelica, a small, pink pillow drenched in her perfume. Its pungent aroma recalls the scent the priestess was anointed with in his dream. It isn't a problem to get a day off. He'll soon be on a plane to the jungle ruins of Palenque in the south of Mexico near the Guatemalan border. His assignment: Update his article on 2012 when last he visited Palenque.

Mitchener is packed, refreshed after catching up on his sleep and has his plane tickets and arrangements made. And, he has purchased Angelica a large bouquet of red roses, an expensive red wine from Burgundy, and, a surprise. Women love surprises, Mitchener thinks. I don't mind good ones myself. Take Angelica. Now there is a surprise. With her, tonight's date won't be routine.

Mitchener is not an amateur at seducing women, but Angelica's beauty, charm, grace and magnetism create in him a new emotion. He decides to dress casually, a button-down azure shirt, dark blue trousers and white tennis shoes. Why, not? He thinks, tomorrow night, I'm off to Mexico.

That evening he knocks on her door and rechecks his watch. It's exactly 8 p.m. Then the powerful scent of her perfume momentarily transports him when the door opens and Angelica smiles. Before he can react, she slips a blindfold over him.

"Describe my face."

"Well, you had dark brown eyes, high cheek bones, auburn hair pinned up in big curls on the back of your head and tied by magenta bows. You wore black horned-rimmed glasses. Your wide smile exposed bright, flashing teeth. Your face reflected a softness, a contentment; your pouty lips reflected sensuality."

"Now my dress."

"It was a dark blue dress, with a slight blue V-neck that high-lighted your throat and neck. You had a tempting bosom under a dress that flowed down your hips. You had great legs."

"Bravo! How do you like my perfume? Does it remind you of anything? I'm wearing it just for you. May I call you Mitch? Come in. Come in."

She kisses his cheek lightly, pulls him into the living room and he trips. She steadies him, takes his face in her hands, holds it tightly and says teasingly, "You didn't forget my face, you charming man."

"You have the face of an angel and the body of a Greek goddess."

Angelica's smile always excites him. She is barefoot, with beautifully painted toes, and wearing her white bath robe. Her hair is done in the manner of the previous evening.

"Your attire surprises me. I thought you said dinner."

"Excuse me while I put these wonderful red roses in some water. You are such a gentleman, Mitch."

"I thought you said dinner."

"I did. Hungry?"

"I was until I saw you."

"Oh, red roses. What a wonderful gift." "Did you rest up on my perfumed pillow?" "It's intoxicating, just like you."

"You say the nicest things."

"I'll go to your kitchen and open the wine," he says rising. "How did you know I'd bring you this bottle of wine?"

"I'm psychic," she says teasingly.

He pours two glasses of wine and heads back into the living room. Angelica has lit gold-colored candles that create a romantic atmosphere. "Here's to our evening, already mem-orable and surprising," says Mitchener, who watches as Angelica undoes the ribbon on the carefully wrapped box, opens it, and holds up a radiant black opal.

"There's a story to go with its beauty, Angelica. The jeweler told me that these are the stones that steal men's souls. Stones that men live for, kill for and die for. The ancient Australia Aboriginals feared and avoided these sparkling stones that flash crimsons, greens and yellows. They believed them to be the eyes of the half-devil, half-serpent, Ooluhru, who lures men with rainbow-colored shafts of light."

A tear slips down Angelica's face. After a long pause, she pulls Mitchener to her warm body, embraces him, parts his lips and her tongue explores his mouth in a deep kiss. Then she turns, drops her white bathrobe to the floor and says softly, "Please put this treasure around my neck."

Mitchener, surprised by her nakedness, touches her soft, warm shoulders and takes the golden clasp and gently fastens it while he looks down on her soft skin, the slope of her shoulders, her legs, the welcoming curves of her back and the curve of her buttocks.

"This loving gift touches my heart. I want to savor every moment tonight."

"You say that as if this is the end, not the beginning."

"Shut your eyes. Envision the stars. My body is a dazzling star, sparkling with light. It's dazzling you with its warm orbs, its secret, welcoming places, its mesmerizing flesh. Feel my love awakening new emotions and unknown passions. Feel the warmth of my presence drawing you into me."

She leads him into her bedroom. His clothes drop slowly to the floor as she throws back her soft sheets. He slides easily into bed beside her, gently takes her in his arms, draws her face to his and kisses her tenderly on her forehead, and closed eyes. He weaves his fingers in her hair and pulls her face closer. He opens his mouth and his lips welcome her warm tongue. His supple fingers knead her back; he cups her breast, sending loving energy through her body, en-flaming her desire. She wishes to excite him and give him pleasure.

Angelica moans softly as he lowers his head to her warm, jutting, pink nipples and her areolas darken. As he suckles one, she pushes it deeper into his warm mouth. He tongues her full, well-shaped breasts and his hands caress her buttocks.

Moments later she whispers, "I can feel you losing yourself in me. You shall have your bliss. Visualize how you wish to experience your every desire. You vibrate such powerful energy. It awoke me last night although you were in the other room. It was your dream."

A throbbing demand overtakes him. His hands caress her perfect body, while his tongue explores her secret places as their passions soar.

She rolls over as he closes his eyes and the scent of her perfume bewitches him. After minutes of silence, Angelica says, "I'll share a secret. It took all my will to keep you from experiencing your blissful release in your dream. Now I know your secret desires. I will fulfill them. Let me adjust my resonance to your vibrations as you unite with me. This time I will grant you release."

Angelica embraces him, pressing her body against his. She kisses him while her hands explore his body and massage the aura surrounding it. Her powerful vibrations thrill him. Even when her hands do not touch his body, he experiences a magical, passionate tingling. His breathing becomes rapid, his heart pumps, each cell thrills, his loins blaze. Angelica, too, is surprised by her powers as she fulfills his desires.

But she, too, is lost in unexpected pleasures as their bodies rise and fall, and move in and out as she amplifies his passions, lovingly, erotically and powerfully. Occasionally, he opens his eyes to thrill to the beauty of her soft, yet powerful, body as it rises and he flows rhythmically, deeper into her. Suddenly, Angelica whispers, "Now is the time for your ecstasy. My amplification is so powerful that it will take you days to recover."

Her flesh becomes warmer; her hips move faster and his welcomed thrusts deepen. Her flesh squeezes tightly and then she moans quietly, then louder as a silver stream fills her while she arches her back and pulls him deeper into her ecstasy.

"Don't stop. More! More!"

Then she soars into an exploding reverie.

Time stops. Both lie quietly. Then Mitchener turns to her and says softly, "You are my magic. You draw me like a spiritual, erotic magnet."

"I was not prepared for this," says Angelica. "You see me through a narrow range of the electromagnetic light spectrum. This is less than 5 percent of the electromagnetic spectrum. You can only see wavelengths from violet to red. But I have focused on this spectrum so you have seen me as you have seen no other woman. I have increased your wavelengths so you can see my beauty gloriously in magnificent colors that you have never experienced. Am I right?"

"You are beautiful beyond words."

In the morning, his nearness consumes Angelica and her kisses cover his body, awakening him. He pulls her atop his chest and playfully kisses her nose. He feels her warm flesh as he holds her tightly. She smiles and says, "Did I fulfill your desires?"

"Words fail me."

"You launched me on a journey into the unknown that I have never experienced," says Angelica as she rolls over on her side and gently runs her fingers along his hip. "I did not want it to end. Your love opened new visions and realities."

"Were we in another dimension, Angelica?"

"Sometime I will attempt to answer all your questions, but now I wish only to feel your body and hold you."

He dozes off again in her arms. Later, he feels her tongue against his ear.

"You rascal."

"Oh, no!" He yells, and then turns quickly toward the clock on a table near the bed.

"Oh, my God, I've got a plane to catch to Mexico in a few hours."

"Why didn't you tell me, Mitch?"

"Near you I'm lost in the moment. I am filled with love for you."

"No man has ever said that to me."

"I have never known any woman like you, Angelica. Did you experience this heavenly trip just as I did? Is resonance love, passion, energy?"

"Yes. All those things. I am more powerful than any

woman you shall ever know. My heart is my focal point for the highest octave of human compassion and love, yes love for you."

"I won't be gone long. Will you wait for me?"

⁓⁓⁓ CHAPTER FOUR ⁓⁓⁓

As night enfolds the Mexican town of Palenque a cab drives down an isolated dirt road and pulls up to the dingy Hotel Las Canadas in the tropical blackness. The flight was delayed, the bus trip bumpy and his seat uncomfortable. A tired, exasperated Mitchener walks to a rickety gate and rings a bell.

A flashlight beam illuminates the ground in the dark as an aged caretaker walks to the gate, greets him with mumbled Spanish and hands him the keys to his reserved room. Mitchener follows the gatekeeper, says under his breath "a great spot to get mugged" and disappears into his damp, cheap room.

In the morning, the phone rings. Groggy and disoriented, Mitchener replies, "Who's this?"

"It's Rothman. Isn't my girlfriend a knockout?"

"So true."

"Good luck with the update on 2012 article. Talk to the shamans, Mayan archaeologists, anyone with new theories concerning the new Mayan age we've entered and are experiencing."

After a forgettable breakfast, Mitchener returns to the misty jungle beneath a mountain backdrop. Mitchener again finds the ruins enchantingly beautiful and serene. Archeologists believe Palenque comes from "Bahlam Kin" or "Jaguar Sun," a place where the sun descends into the Underworld, the realm of the jaguar.

Then memories flood back of a Mayan ruler. In 603 A.D. Lord Pacal grabbed power, stating he was the incarnation of an ancient, powerful god. Pacal ruled for 68 years, pushing the construction of grand buildings, among them the palace, with its walls covered with artistic stucco carvings of rulers, gods and religious ceremonies. Inside the palace, so named by the Spanish, many rooms with interior courts overlooked a four-story, square tower that may have served as an observatory.

Underneath the Palace and through a long, corbel-vaulted tunnel a stream ran through Palenque, carrying a constant supply of fresh, running water, a feat of engineering genius.

Then Michener, still drained of energy, remembers to make a reservation to enter the crypt of Pascal. Thereafter he returns to his hotel, orders a drink, ponders his transformation by Angelica, and sleeps. Later, at loose ends, he decides to have a margarita, a light dinner and turn in early.

~~~ CHAPTER FIVE ~~~

Days later, winded and sweating profusely in the tropical humidity, Mitchener feels Palenque's mysterious ruins weave their misty web around him on this mystical morning. The high rainfall supports the rainforest's lush canopy. Ancient Mayan architects channeled the Otulum River into an aqueduct that divided the city and utilized the tall surrounding hills to place their temples. They flattened these hilltops to support temples, which were surrounded by wide plazas, long ball courts and burial grounds.

The temples contain complex twisting corridors, narrow subterranean stairways and wide galleries. Other buildings served as fortresses in times of war. In its heyday Palenque was spread out over 49 square miles.

Mitchener, glad he awoke early, finds he is the first tourist entering the reconstructed Templo de la Calvara, or Temple of the Skull, reached by a tall staircase. Like most of the temples it is made up of unadorned stone. When it was constructed, it was painted vivid shades of crimson and blue.

As his boots move through the dew-drenched grass, he looks in wonder at the Temple of the Inscriptions, site of a massive temple dedicated to Lord Pacal. Its nine tiers correspond to the nine Lords of the Underworld. Atop this temple and others surrounding it are vestiges of roof combs, delicate extensions of the temple's top, giving them a light, airy crown.

Mitchener's goal is the palace, with its iconic tower that was built in three layers and thought to represent the three levels of the universe and the movement of the stars. Below, thick jungle is buzzing with insects.

After an arduous climb, he rests at the top. Soon the last mists lift, offering him a panoramic view of the verdant jungle.

On clear days, the blue, cool Gulf of Mexico appears in the brilliant sunlight. Lost in thought, Mitchener dreams of Angelica, her loving touch, and heart-stopping beauty that draws him like a magnet and captivates him.

Notes for his article, like his thoughts, are scattered, but slowly he realizes that he's enjoying the silence and serenity. Palenque is like seeing an old friend, full of memories yet ever engaging.

I'm drifting and dreaming in the clouds high atop this tower, he thinks. A tap on his shoulder returns him to reality. Irritated, he turns, expecting a guide to say, "Tourist? Welcome to Mexico. Want a guide?"

Soft, feminine hands with long fingernails slip over his eyes. "Hola, gringo," says a familiar voice as a vision in khaki shorts, a short-sleeved khaki shirt, a wide-brimmed straw sun hat, gray hiking boots and flashing teeth appear.

"Angelica, you sneak, surprising me like this," he says as his irritation fades. "This is a dangerous perch up here."

She throws her arms around him and kisses him lightly on the cheek.

"What are you doing here in the jungle, thousands of miles from civilized New York? That is, if you can call New York civilized." She reaches in her khaki shorts, takes out a tiny perfume bottle and dabs myrrh, one of her favorite perfumes, on her neck. "Now do you know it's really me?"

He pulls her into his arms and kisses her, finds he cannot stop when she responds, pressing her body against his. Then he says, "So surprising, so wonderful, so Angelica."

She opens her khaki shirt, revealing his gift, her black opal, flashing yellows, greens, crimson and violet colors in the tropical sun as it hangs on its golden chain. He lifts it and kisses the cleft between her warm breasts, sending a thrill up his spine.

"I missed you. You've enslaved me. Are you satisfied? Guess who has a room next to you in that miserable hotel, Mr. Journalist."

"You think of everything."

"I've been reading about this magnificent place, Mitch. Its grandeur overpowers me. Kiss me again before I wrestle you to the ground in this precarious perch and take you by force."

Her nearness captivates him as her tongue works its magic, and she pulls him closer. He slips his hands under her belt and runs his fingers over her soft, round buttocks.

"So soft, so welcome to the touch."

"Don't take your hands away. I want your hands on my flesh to assure you that I am not a dream. Oddly, I climbed the tower to see if I could locate you in these vast ruins before the tourists arrive. And here you are, lost in thought overlooking this vast sea of rainforest below us. Don't you feel like a Mayan god up here?"

"I do, now that I have my Mayan goddess."

"No, I'm your bewitching vamp. Let's sit cross-legged for five minutes in silence and appreciate all this beauty."

"Only if you hold my hand."

They sit in silence as every cell of his body comes alive. When the silence ends, Mitchener notices that sweat is pouring off his body while her khaki shirt and shorts are dry. Her energy is surging through me, drawing me to her, he thinks.

"Take a deep breath, my love, and inhale the sacred, cosmic energy of this place," says Angelica. "I'll tell you a tale that wasn't in your earlier article I'm sure. I think that the mysterious Mayans have left traces here in Central America of the highest civilization in the Western Hemisphere, including a calendar more accurate than that known to the Europeans at the time of the Conquest. The Conquistadors wrote that the Mayans were Lemurians of a priestly cast who recorded time in relation to the stars. These exact calculations required hundreds of years.

"They obtained much of their information through meditation and contact with spirit beings. The Mayans believed that as long as their records were kept up to date no wrong could befall their people. The Mayans purified their culture with erudition, sensitivity and recall of past lives. They chose to live apart from other peoples to prevent impurities in their blood and to avoid the pitfalls of earthly desires.

"Then new immigrants came to their lands from Atlantis. These newcomers sought their secrets, lands and grains forcing the Mayans farther back into the rainforests. They had no wish to fight the conquering Atlanteans. They were a flawless race until they mixed with other groups who brought disease and decimated their population. They are now waiting for the next shift of the poles. This will end their record-keeping and free them from what they believe is their responsibility for the world's fate. Their calculations cover hundreds of thousands of years. This next pole shift will not end life on earth, but cleanse it of the impurities of ages present and past. This will mark a turning point in man's evolution. What do you think of my tale?"

"Sounds like something my old girlfriend Sara Santiago might come up with. She often spoke of ancient Lemurians and Atlanteans. They are a bit far out for me. But, I admit, you have opened my mind and body to new thoughts, experiences, enlivened my spirit and thrilled my senses."

Angelica peers off over the rainforests, sighs and says, "I have set in motion those frequencies that drew you to me as your frequencies drew me to you the first time we met. Your energy, your love, draws me to you. I did not expect this. Did you?"

"Never."

"Our sexual energy is the closest energy to spirit, to the divine force, don't you think? That is why when we make love, we experience the divine. Rapture. Ecstasy. Bliss. A cosmic orgasm you might call it. I can't wait to make love to you again, but first you must be my guide."

As the two walk to the Temple of the Inscriptions Mitchener tells the tale of the tomb of Pacal. Soon, they gather with a small group at the appointed time and place and the guide allows them to enter the passageway that descends deep into the Temple of the Inscriptions. The visit is allowed only with reservations, but when Mitchener shows the guide his ticket wrapped in a $20 bill, the guide smiles.

As they wait, Mitchener finds he revels in telling Angelica his tale of the tomb. Normally, he is the talker, but with Angelica he finds he is often the listener

"In 1949 someone, whose name I forget, discovered that this stepped pyramid contained a stairway that led down. Several years of excavation cleared the rubble, soil and debris that filled this inner structure. At the bottom of this twisting stairway a triangular block masked an entry way through a blank wall guarded by the skeletons of Mayan warriors. Behind it was a vaulted crypt."

Later the guide continues, "Within a stone sarcophagus, covered by a five-ton, 12-foot-long stone lab, were the remains of a tall man, bedecked with jade and pearl jewelry. His face was covered with a mosaic jade mask. A small jade pendant, with the image of a Mayan god, was found amid the beads that once made up a jade collar.

"This was the first pyramid in Mexico found to contain a tomb. But the depiction on the carved lid created a sensation. It depicted a barefoot Mayan sitting on what appeared to be a plumed or flaming stone and seemed to be operating devices inside an elaborate chamber. Writer Erich von Daniken surmised that the figure depicted was an extraterrestrial being that was operating a spacecraft driven by flaming jets."

They descend into this dank Mayan Underworld and examine all aspects of the tomb. Mitchener notes that the guide is continually examining Angelica from her top to her bottom. Particularly her bottom. The guide seems in no hurry to let the next small group enter. He goes over every possible detail, reaching across her blouse and brushing her breast to indicate she should look closer at the lid. Angelica winks at Mitchener, who rolls his eyes.

Once back in the sunshine, Mitchener says, "I bet you think Pacal was an alien."

"We're all aliens. We're all from the stars," says Angelica. "Personally, I think you're an alien. Let's return to my room where I can examine your body more closely and run my hands and eyes over you."

"Anything for science," Mitchener says as his heart beats faster.

In the noisy, bouncing Combi bus heading back to the hotel, Mitchener puts his arm around Angelica's shoulders, and works his fingers under her loose khaki blouse and slips his fingers under her bra and delicately rolls her nipple and massages her warm, full breast.

"Now I know why we're seated in the back of the bus," Angelica says. "I'll give you two hours to stop that" she whispers. "Do you love me?" Mitchener says seriously.

"Yes."

⁓⁓ CHAPTER SIX ⁓⁓

As they walk to Hotel Las Canadas Angelica says "Soon you will get another surprise from me, one that you couldn't have imagined in your wildest dreams."

They pick up their room keys at the front desk. Mitchener is energized by what lies ahead while he strides down the musty hallway.

"Give me a moment to freshen up, Mitch. Say 10 minutes." She turns her key quickly, and closes her door.

"Ten minutes, not a second more."

After entering his room, Mitchener sniffs under his arms, makes an ugly sound and realizes he is in need of a shower. After repeated blows to the shower-head, an explosion of cold water drenches his clothes and another gusher soaks his nearby hiking boots.

As his heart pounds, he puts on a clean, short shirt and shorts, splashes on some cheap aftershave lotion, locks his door and knocks on Angelica's warped door.

He hears a voice behind it say quietly; "You're one minute early. Are you anxious for me to enchant you?"

"No, you she devil."

Angelica opens the door quickly. He's shocked. Before him stands the picture of a Mayan maid such as he's seen on murals in earlier visits to the Palenque Museum. She wears a colorful, loose blouse and long skirt, both with intricate Mayan patterns. The fanciful designs in blacks and greens stand out against the pink-orange cloth and are similar to those worn in festivals by modern Mayan women; the dress is called a "huipil."

On her neck hangs her flashing radiant opal and around her ankles dangle jade pectorals. She wears an elaborate headdress of plumed pink, crimson and bright yellow feathers tucked into a jade and turquoise encrusted tiara. Huge golden-colored earrings hang from her ears studded with diorite and turquoise settings.

He gasps at her display of living Mayan beauty, just as it was painted on an ancient Mayan mural. Angelica's curvaceous body and flashing brown eyes bring these garments and headdress to life. She throws open her loose Mayan blouse revealing her full, well-shaped breasts with dark areolas and jutting nipples. He feels his heart pound and his knees feel weak. He smells the feminine essence of her warm skin as he reaches out and massages the fullness of her breasts. She realizes how much she loves the warm touch of his hands on her breasts.

"You have stepped out of a Mayan mural. You're beautiful," says a stunned Mitchener, "but the eerie paint?"

"Mayan priests often covered their bodies with blue body paint," says Angelica in a stern voice. Then she screams "Ereeohkee!" points her right arm forward and points at his waist area.

"Disrobe!"

Mitchener senses he is being drawn into an ancient ritual and she has gained new power over him as he takes off his shirt, shorts and boots.

"I see your sword is erect, warrior. Your homage is welcomed. On your knees, warrior,"

Angelica reaches to a nearby dressing table, grabs a small bottle of myrrh perfume, with a pungent scent, and drenches her body with it. Then she pours a perfumed shower on a kneeling Mitchener. As the droplets stream off Mitchener's flesh and soak Angelica's blouse and skirt, the powerful scent fills the room, causing Mitchener's head to spin dizzily.

Angelica roughly grabs his hair forcing his eyes to look into hers.

"Worship me!"

Then Angelica intones softly, "Enter my magical world, worshiper, uniting us in all ways, in spirit and the flesh."

In a flash, she tosses off her Mayan skirt and other apparel. "Behold my blue-painted body. Soon it will welcome your touch."

Her feathered plumes and flashing tiara accent her dark brown eyes, high cheekbones, wide smile, pouty lips, the soft curve of her neck, her finely slopping shoulders and voluptuous, full bosom. Her shapely arms and delicate hands move gracefully. The curve of her hips, her welcoming mound, thighs and shapely legs stimulate his passion.

Angelica turns away from him and lights candles on her dresser that cast a golden glow. Her body seems to radiate a heavenly blue. Mitchener is mesmerized, energized, and transported. Angelica finds this local blue body paint is increasing her powers. The Mayan priests were right, she thinks. This blue paint is empowering me. I see it in Mitchener's eyes.

"Now you will worshipfully kiss my body from my toes to my forehead. You will do this slowly, gracefully and with love. You will satisfy all my desires."

The sight of her buttocks, her female parts, deep pink and inviting, he finds irresistible. Her pulsating energy overcomes Mitchener, transporting and empowering him, compelling him to kiss her blue toenails, her ankles and calves, and then his lips and tongue circles her thighs and teases her curly mound.

He pulls her soft, welcoming hips closer; his lips and tongue worship her full, warm breasts, suckle her soft, erect nipples and lick her aureoles. He kisses her shoulders and neck as his passion rises and Angelica commands. Again. Slowly."

For the first time, a thought cautions her to go no further as Mitchener, who is lost in this dreamlike state, responds to every command as the minutes' pass.

Angelica bids him to rise and softly kisses his eye lids and says, "Shut your eyes. Feel my love awakening your emotions and desires. Feel the warmth of my presence drawing you into me."

Angelica is overcome as his loving energy sweeps through her body, excites every cell, and en-flames her desire.

"Visualize your every desire."

Angelica awaits as his desires form in her mind and then

she responds, saying, "Now I recall your secret desires. I will fulfill them. Let me adjust my vibrations to yours so we can fulfill each other's desires. I wish to nurture and share your passion."

Mitchener pulls Angelica to him, embraces her and feels her blue body press against his as she kisses him, while her hands explore his body and excite the aura surrounding it. She massages it with her fingers. Its powerful vibrations thrill him, his body experiences an intense, passionate tingling, his breathing becomes more rapid, his heart beats faster and each nerve tingles. His loins blaze.

As Angelica fulfills his desires, she finds he is fulfilling hers.

They swoon into ecstasy.

He opens his eyes to thrill at the rising and falling of her curvaceous body as her back arches and flows.

"Now is the time for your bliss. I fear my vibrations are so strong that they will take you days to recover," Angelica whispers. He hears her voice as if from a distance as her flesh warms, her hips move faster and he is drawn deeper into her warmth. She moans quietly, and then louder, shouting with pleasure as his silver stream erupts while her back pulls him deeper. She cannot stop. Then her body explodes in ecstasy and tears stream down her face.

~~~ CHAPTER SEVEN ~~~

Mitchener and Angelica walk happily through Palenque's ruins at midday. Both are overcome by the previous evening as they gaze at Palenque's palace and its surrounding temples.

"As I slept last night a wonderful Mayan priestess worked her magic on me, so real, so powerful, so full of pleasure and love," says Mitchener.

Later, Angelica pulls him to her and says, "I have another surprise for you tonight. It's my secret."

"I don't know if I have enough energy."

"I'll share mine," says Angelica. "Our time is limited. Soon I must return."

"You keep revealing new emotions, new experiences," he says.

"That's what love does. I could not have shared it with anyone else, Mitch. I fear sometimes you forget this. This is not just me, Mitch. It is us. I will never give myself to another as I have given myself to you."

The day's heat draws streams of perspiration off Mitchener, while Angelica's soft, supple skin remains dry.

"Let's wind our way to the Northern Group, which are often deserted. At the Temple of the Skulls, which sits atop a stone staircase, we'll take a quiet walk past the other nearby ruins to the Rio Atum."

"In ancient times, the river was covered, forming a 9-foot high, vaulted aqueduct," recalls Mitchener.

Soon, they stop and Angelica quickly undoes the laces of her gray hiking boots and splashes her toes in the clear, cool, meandering stream that flows over a limestone bottom.

Mitchener strips off his shirt, takes off his hiking boots, and jumps into the meandering stream. He smirks devilishly, dunks his head under the cool, refreshing water and takes her delicate foot in his hands and gently kisses her toes.

Angelica screams with delight as his air bubbles rise to the surface. Then he grabs her other foot, partially to regain his balance, lifts his head, fills his lungs with air, and dives under again; slowly he kisses her other toes as his bubbles stream to the surface. Then his head surges to the surface, breaking the water and sending wavelets across the placid surface.

She splashes his body, yelling "Lover man, my superman of love."

"It's your fault. You inspire me. These are my first underwater kisses."

"If it was deeper, I'd jump in and join you. Water, the giver of life, has blessed us," says Angelica.

Mitchener's shorts are soaked and water streams off his head and body while he relaxes in the sun next to Angelica.

"Mitch," says Angelica as her deep brown eyes overpower him, "Take my hand. Now close your eyes."

Mitchener closes his eyes and focuses his mind on the murmuring of the stream.

"I am going to focus my energies. Give yourself the suggestion to welcome this loving energy."

Soon he can feel her energies.

"Pull my energy through your system until it is blocked. Now let it return to your pineal gland and this will open you to a creative force that joins us. It helps us both reach our destinies. This divine source can be used to heal or create. Dance with my vibrations, my octaves. When we make love, we must hold that octave while we lose our separateness. Our electric impulse will flow. My body will welcome your entrance and stimulate your manhood. You will pull my fluids and receive them as I send them into you and you send your fluids into me."

"But?"

"Be silent. Visualize them until the pulsing begins." Moments later, he mounts her and the pulsing begins, slowly, powerfully increasing until their bodies unite in a blissful release. "You're a wonder, Mitch, you did it."

~~~ CHAPTER EIGHT ~~~

The two, hand in hand, slowly examine the Temple of the Sun and the Temple of the Cross, the largest of the group that has the faded remains of a sculpted panel. Centuries ago, a wet plaster was applied as a base for the mural and then painted in a bright palette of crimson, blue, green and yellow. Then the mural was set under cornices that helped preserve them.

The temples derive their names from these works of art or shrines. Angelica points out a Tree of Life in the Temple of the Sun and marvels at it, while Mitchener rests in the corner.

As they make their way back through the ruins they imagine the brightly painted buildings whose stone skeletons remain. Always the rainforest presses forward, ready to recapture these architectural treasures.

"As I walk," Mitchener says, "I am forced to think that once this was a city dedicated to the arts, writing and astronomy. On my return, it is easier to see its compelling style. That's what you have, Angelica, a compelling style."

"I have more than that."

They halt at the Temple of the Skull and Mitchener motions Angelica to follow him inside as silence returns to the ancient site "Stingray tails and a rope of thorns," says Mitchener. "These are the keys to understanding the Mayans and their sacred kings. Every portal of every temple is a doorway to the Underworld. Inside these temples it was the duty of the king and queen to reenact the mythical moment of Mayan creation. It was the blood of the gods that gave birth to mankind. On the earth, the king acts as the god and blood is the price of power.

"This debt to the gods must be paid. And royal blood, drawn from the tongue and testicles of the king and the body of the queen forever binds that sacrifice to the life of man. So, if you wish to give a powerful offering, you give blood, because it comes from the king's ancestors. Now it is practiced with the blood of chickens."

After their return, they relax on the patio of their hotel. The waiter asks Mitchener if his novia, or girlfriend, would like a margarita?

"A red and a white wine. I fear for my life if she gets anything more powerful than wine."

He turns to Angelica and continues, "Frankly, Angelica, sometimes your powers are so great that I feel you completely control me. I am so captivated by you that sometimes I feel helpless."

"Have I used my powers against you or for you? With love or with hate?"

"Only love. It is your love that has transformed me. With you, my spirit soars."

As the sun dips below the horizon, Angelica takes his hand and leads him to her room. Earlier, he noticed she had a lot of luggage.

"Last night when I dressed as a Mayan priest and covered myself with blue body paint, my plan was to entice you, not control you. But as I entered your room in my priestly garb I felt an ancient power overtake me. Tonight is your turn to be a priest. I bought you all the male priest's garb and materials. Will you try it, Mitch?"

"Anything to gain power over you," Mitchener says jokingly. "Would you feel more comfortable dressing in your room or mine?" says Angelica.

"Do you want to apply my blue body paint in the tiled bathroom?"

She nods and replies, "Perfect, now strip."

Angelica carefully applies the blue body paint to his forehead, nose, around his eyes, down his neck and arms, over his chest, back and butt, down his thighs and calves to his ankles and over his feet and toes.

"Oh, yes, I missed one area," says Angelica as her heartbeat quickens and she works the paint into the pads of her fingers. Then she pushes his thighs apart and rubs his blue body paint into his genitals and tenderly strokes his erection.

Angelica pulls out a colorful orange-pink hip cloth covered with circles and strange symbols. She fastens it and puts another cloth of the same color over Mitchener's head, revealing the open mouth of a jaguar. The cape-like affair flows down his back to his knees, flaring out in flame-like tongues of cloth. Artistic green pectorals snap on his wrists and ankles.

As Angelica tucks a warrior-like mask over his eyes, he feels a pulsing energy shoot up from between his thighs. He recalls that the most elaborate headdresses were inseparable from the Mayan skull shape with its receding forehead. This deliberate deformation was formed from a young age by wearing two pieces of wood strapped to the Mayan child's head to shape an elongated cranium. With everything in place, Angelica turns a switch, filling the room with haunting Mayan music. Mitchener's blue body paint and elaborate costume empower him and he orders, "Strip."

Angelica slowly, as if in an ancient striptease, unbuttons her khaki shirt, revealing a swanlike neck, soft shoulders, and flat stomach. She slowly drops her shirt to the floor, throws her long hair forward and sweeps the floor with it as she kneels at his feet. Then, with graceful movements she circles his neck and pulls has face lightly against her soft breasts. His lips caress her nipples while his hands massage her breasts.

As Angelica's piercing eyes lock on his eyes, her hips sway, and her shapely arms beckon. Dancing erotic, belly dancer-like movements, she plucks a plume from the priest's headdress and brushes his face, and body. He plucks out one of his plumes and sweeps it across her nude body, exciting her skin with its feathery touch.

As her hips circle in enticing rhythmic patterns, she moves her hands to en-flame his aura until his heart beats faster. Her finger tips work their magic along his thighs while he feels an overpowering desire to throw her to the floor and take her.

While Angelica's nude, unadorned body dances before him; the priest sees the jar of fragrance that Angelica poured over him last night. He uncaps the lid and pours it over her rhythmically writhing body. The powerful scent slips down her shoulders, over her breasts and anoints her arms and swaying hips. Her fingers work the fragrance into her swaying breasts as she circles her nipples and then slides down to her thighs.

Swept away by age-old urges, he realizes he's dancing with her, moving his hips in rhythm with hers while she rubs her breasts against him and then throws him to the floor and rips off his loin cloth. She pulls his lips to hers and kisses him wildly, drawing him into her body while her hips writhe and he rides her to the heavens.

He wishes to lengthen his ecstasy, yet her power over him is so strong, her pumping so intense, that his silver stream shoots into her while she moans softly, soaring rhythmically into her own ecstasy.

As her movements slow, she releases her grip on his shoulders and looks into his closed eyes. He has passed out. His breathing is shallow, his pulse weak.

She races into the bathroom, finds a small bucket, fills it with cold water, and drenches his face and chest. She repeats it until a slight smile slips over Mitchener's face. Water slips off her nude body while Mitchener says softly, "I never knew what a wonderful dancer you are. It was the dance of my life. No one will ever dance with me like this again."

"What a wonderful gift you have given me, my angel."

"No, Mitch, yours was greater. Your love."

He falls into her bed and passes out.

Angelica murmurs to herself that she will never let her lust overpower her love again as she covers Mitch with blankets, turns on a fan and locks this night of love away in her memories.

∼∼∼ CHAPTER NINE ∼∼∼

Angelica rises early, gets a steaming cup of coffee and then brings it into her room. It is a damp mess. She sips her coffee slowly and then opens her purse and checks out her bus and airline tickets.

Knowing Mitchener will sleep for hours, she writes a note, places it on the bed table, showers and smiles as she notes tinges of her priestly blue body paint under her arms and on other parts of her body. The pungent fragrance lingers in her bedroom. Famished, she heads for breakfast.

After two omelets, fruit, coffee and toast, Angelica relaxes in her chair.

When he arrives, she can feel his loving presence as he leans over and kisses her forehead.

"I feel as if a great weight has been lifted. And, my angel, I owe it to you."

"Thanks for the good news. Here's my bad news. I thought I had two days left, but today's my last day," she says, taking his hand across the table.

"What?" A hint of irritation slips into his voice.

"You surprised me and flew away after a last-minute word. As you slept last night, I checked my ticket. Tonight is my last night here. But I've an idea. How long will it take to finish your story?"

"Two, maybe three days."

"Take two, maybe three weeks, vacation here. Get a more comfortable hotel room and I'll return so we can visit other fascinating spots that you've mentioned."

"I confess I've had New York up to here," Mitchener says. "I've turned into a workaholic. Let me check with my boss. "

"When was the last time you took a vacation longer than

a couple of days?"

"I can't recall."

"My love for you has grown each day, sharing myself with you. This truly is the planet of the heart chakra."

"Chakra. There's a word I haven't heard for years." "Do you know its meaning?" asks Angelica.

"The chakra system is composed of the body's seven energy centers, as I recall. I haven't heard the word for years."

"I'll share another of my secrets with you," says Angelica. "I have what is known as an observant eye. I usually can tell which stranger will be helpful or dangerous. I don't want you running around here alone."

"Thanks, mom."

"You never had a mother like me."

"I'll contact my boss Rothman, and stay on for a couple of weeks once I finish my story. You're off to Europe on a business trip, right? From what you've said I know you'll be busy every minute. I'll let you know the results of my efforts, where I am, how to contact me on your answering machine. Focus on your business trip, but remember our times together, remember me in your dreams and come back."

The day passes quickly. Angelica repacks her Mayan costume, tosses her nearly empty blue body paint in the wastebasket and recalls the otherworldly beauty of Palenque and then her taxi arrives late. Mitchener hugs and kisses her, wondering if he will ever see her again. She is so overpowering, so easy to love. When the taxi pulls away, he waves and blows a kiss. As it disappears along the jungle road a great emptiness fills him. He goes to the hotel bar, orders a brandy and lets it warm his throat and body.

He is spent, physically and emotionally as he heads for a pool at a nearby hotel, swims briefly and falls asleep at poolside in a chaise lounge. At dusk a nudge awakens him and he walks back to his hotel and flops into his bed.

Then Michener, drained of energy still from his lovemaking with Angelica, remembers to make a reservation again at the museum for the following morning to get a permit to enter the crypt of Pacal. Thereafter he returns to his hotel, orders a drink, and ponders his attraction to Angelica and the gift of her presence.

At loose ends, he decides to have a margarita, a light dinner and turns in early.

***

Later in the week, Rothman's call surprises Angelica shortly before her trip to Paris, but she agrees to join him in a game of tennis at a nearby court. Rothman finds himself mesmerized by the grace of Angelica's firm, well-shaped, athletic body, her dark wavy hair and her gorgeous features. Her trim white shorts and tight-fitting white blouse conceal little of her figure as she moves back and forth across the court.

Whenever she bends over to retrieve a ball, Rothman finds his eyes glued to her tumbling breasts, fine neck and ever cheerful dark brown eyes.

As the match continues a blouse button comes loose, revealing a full, white breast peeking above her bra, enchanting Rothman. After a few games, Angelica discovers that she is winning by vibrating at a higher level than Rothman. Her serves are faster, her ground strokes more powerful, and she's winning point after point. She finds she can focus on the corners and her balls go there.

She seems to know instinctively where the ball will be hit, which aggravates Rothman, who considers himself a good singles player. He swings harder and places his ball well, but at the last second she blasts the ball across court or down the line. She wins point after point, but is always smiling, which he considers a welcoming look.

Angelica finds her mind is slipping back to her wondrous night of love with Mitchener, his loving, his caring, and his powerful resonance which draws her to him and excites her. And she loves his laughter, which can suddenly captivate her.

Across the court, Rothman's fascination with Angelica grows. Finally, he checks his watch and asks Angelica if she would accompany him to his hypnotist's office where he is making a last attempt to quit smoking. Angelica realizes Rothman is better at commanding than requesting, but she agrees because she has nothing planned after tennis.

In the hypnotist's office, she reads a magazine patiently, preparing for Rothman's hypnosis treatment to end. In the other room, Rothman pulls Dr. Samuel Haymet aside and asks quietly, "Do you have an appointment after mine?"

"You're it for today."

"If I pay for another hour could you attempt to hypnotize this beautiful woman waiting for me?"

"You and I know that I can make suggestions, but I cannot compel anyone to do something against her will. She's your girlfriend, right?"

"I just met here, but I'd like her to be."

"I like your choice in women. She's a knockout."

"Give her the suggestion that if I touch her radiant opal she will wish to go to bed with me."

"No promises. I'll give her the suggestion under hypnosis, but the rest is up to you."

The two men enter the waiting room and the hypnotist is surprised by Angelica's sweat-stained blouse that does little to hide her curvaceous body. His eyes linger as he explains that her tennis partner wishes to pay for a hypnotic session, if she desires it. It will relax and refresh her after a hot day on the court.

While waiting, Angelica has decided to plead exhaustion so she can skip dinner and have Rothman drop her off at her apartment. Perhaps by accepting this offer, she thinks, I can escape a dinner with him.

"I'll give you a relaxing session to make you sleep soon and deeply," suggests the hypnotist after Rothman has left and Angelica has relaxed on his comfortable couch.

"No, let's try a past life session," says Angelica.

"This is difficult in the first session, but we'll try. No guarantee."

Soon Angelica finds she is resting and staring at a black

and white circle that seems to circle inward as it spins. Then the hypnotist starts the beat-beat-beat of his metronome.

"Relax and listen to the beat of the metronome in the background," he says soothingly. "Beat, beat, beat. Deeper, deeper, deeper. Relaxed, relaxed, relaxed. Beat, beat, beat, 20, 19, 18, deeper, deeper, deeper, relaxed, relaxed, relaxed."

He continues this for about eight or nine minutes.

"Now you are in a deep, relaxed level of hypnosis. Now every cell of your body is relaxed, a deep, relaxed level of hypnosis. Now you hear nothing but the relaxing sound of my voice. Deeper, deeper, deeper, down, down, down."

"20, 20, 20," Angelica hears as she sinks into a deep hypnotic state as the numbers go down, beat by beat to 1. "Image a white light flooding your body," says the hypnotist. "It becomes lighter and lighter. You are protected by the white light as a door appears. Where are you?"

Soon Angelica realizes if she focuses her mind, she might be able to receive a past life of Rothman. Why not? The session is not being recorded. The hypnotist will not know she is focusing on his past lives. Rothman's first life is as a knight in the south of France, who sells his sword for money and favors. His life is one of plunder, rape and, if necessary, torture. After his first murder, each killing comes easier.

Then the scene changes. She is in a French palace during the late Middle Ages. Elaborate tapestries with vibrant colors adorn the walls below the frescoed ceiling. An artistically sculptured face, surrounded by intricately floral designs, stands above the door. Four masterly painted scenes bring the walls to life. A wide bed with a high canopy and a mattress draped with rich fabrics makes the bedroom a work of art.

A tall, handsome, 50 year-old, gray-haired noble dressed in rich fabrics, his clothes fastened by ornate metal brooches, asks the dirty, sweating maiden kneeling before him, "Will you yield to me as I enjoy your lovemaking or will your parents be thrown off my estates?"

The maiden is so spellbound by the luxurious bedroom and inexperienced to such riches that she momentarily forgets where she is. The disgruntled noble claps loudly, bringing her back to the moment.

"Well?"

"Your wish is my command, noble sir," says the unsure, trembling girl who has just reached puberty.

"Disrobe and my maid servant will wash, perfume you and comb your snarled hair."

"I will do my best to satisfy your every wish, but I am inexperienced in lovemaking. You have much experience. Forgive me, but you are so handsome and I am but a young serf in your fields. But I will try to learn quickly and pray that I can satisfy you, for you are my master."

The aging noble disrobes, enjoys a glass of red wine, and discovers while his maid servant washes and towels his serf 's young, nubile body that she has a bounteous bosom for one so young, and possesses wide, welcoming hips and dark, penetrating eyes. One could get lost in her dark, penetrating eyes, he thinks. She will bend to my will quickly or be back in my fields.

Yet he finds innocence in her quick smile and would never have guessed this grace and charm hidden under this unwashed garment. His ardor overcomes him and his large manhood stiffens and rises.

"This is my first time, my lord. I have just reached womanhood, but I see that my body excites you."

The aging noble explains his wishes to his maid servant and commands her to undress the youngster. The maid quickly disrobes her and gasps at her young but bountiful breasts, wide hips, hairy mound and shapely legs. She leads the girl to the lord's bedside and soon the lord's lips are suckling at his maid servant's flushed breasts. The girl thinks her breasts are as big as lush melons, but my master is looking adoringly at my body.

Soon, the lord's shaft has disappeared inside the maid's lips while she sucks, licks and demonstrates her abilities to make him moan loudly. Then she stands at his bedside while the young girl works her lips and mouth and the maid servant corrects and instructs her.

Next the maid returns to the lord's bed, mounts him and rides him as her breasts bounce wildly. Then she demonstrates other positions that bring the lord great pleasure, while the excited young maiden watches closely at his bedside and asks questions.

Then the aroused maid, whose face is now flushed, climbs nimbly back into the lord's bed, pushes him back and bends to kiss him, opening her mouth and using her tongue as her Lord's maid servant has demonstrated.

Then she surprises him by licking and kissing his neck. Her tender kisses have more power to arouse him than his experienced maid servant, she realizes. He finds his untried young woman electrifies him as she continues to embraces him and follows his maid's instructions to passionate perfection, while thrills shoot through her shapely body for the first times.

She finds the lord is quivering, closing his eyes and giving himself up to her. Following the maid servant's example, her lips and tongue make wide, wet circles on his flushed body. When she reaches his navel, she cannot stop, while he pulls her head lower and works his shaft in her warm mouth. Soon, she finds unknown thrills electrifying and shooting through her own body, while the lord's maid servant improves her techniques and the lord moans.

As her actions bring more expressions of pleasure by the lord, she becomes more confident and enjoys her explorations as her body throbs. Her nipples swell and her breasts flush as she suckles him and her warm hands squeeze and adore him. With each passing moment, she finds with each new technique her passion grows along with the lord's. She slowly realizes her curvaceous body is transporting her lord.

The lord's maid, who has done this before and finds she looks forward to her lord's request for her command performance, pushes the young maiden aside and pleasures the lord so long that she suddenly screams out in pleasure as her body writhes.

The young maid is shocked and then thrilled by the maid servant's screams.

The lord smiles, embraces the maid servant and commands, "Be gone."

"All praise to my lord," she says satisfied.

"I am no beginner in the arts of love," the lord says to the young maiden. "You will scream louder before you leave this room."

She defiantly throws her leg over his body to straddle and mount him. Her body draws him deeper and deeper as her face flushes, her breasts welcome his fingers and he feels an uncontrollable surge as he cries out and she moans, writhing blissfully.

Exhausted, he later pulls her down again, his mouth worshiping her breasts and nipples. He nuzzles one and then the other, relaxes beside her and cradles her head.

Later, as she prepares to leave, she begins to put on her simple clothing once again. The noble nods, smiles and gives her an elegant pair of pointed leather shoes, a great luxury in her times. Then he circles her neck with an elegant golden brooch.

"Fear not, you and your parents will never suffer under me. And whenever you see me, which will be often, you will be rewarded."

After relaxing for five minutes, during which the powerful remembrance of her lovemaking remains, the hypnotist says, soothingly, "The next person who touches your skin to lift your radiant opal will give you a passionate, driving desire to go to bed with him. It will bring you great pleasure. Do you understand?"

Angelica nods her head and smiles.

Soon the session ends and Angelica returns to her present reality. She rises from the couch, feeling refreshed, but the power of the lovemaking in her vision remains. Was she the maid in the vision? Was the hypnotist the noble, she wonders?

When Angelica returns to the waiting room, Rothman rises to meet her and the young hypnotist, with the excellent physique, smiles at Angelica.

"How did it go?" asks Rothman smiling.

"She's an excellent subject and goes into a deep, somnambulistic state with ease."

The three exchange small talk about hypnosis and related topics for about 15 minutes. As the two go to leave, the hypnotist gently turns Angelica's shoulders toward him and lifts her radiant opal from between her breasts. He examines it closely as though he sees a secret in it.

"What a beautiful stone."

"It's a radiant opal from Australia. I love it when its colors flash."

The hypnotist bends closer to Angelica's face, gently pulling on her golden chain with the radiant opal, which seems to flash in his dark eyes. She feels his warm breath and smells the scent of his pungent cologne. She feels her desire awakening against her will.

"What a magnificent stone. It matches your beauty," says the hypnotist.

As the power of his suggestion sweeps through her body, she feels a tingling and surprises herself when she gives the hypnotist a tender kiss on his lips. Rothman is stunned, but hides his emotions. He grabs Angelica's hand roughly and moves her away from the hypnotist. Only then does Angelica recover from her impulsive gesture.

"Thank you," she says lightly, her desire for him diminishing as her heartbeat slows.

"You are easily hypnotized and go quickly into a deep state. I would like to offer you a free session next week at your convenience."

"It would be an enlightening experience," says Angelica. "Perhaps you'll tape it next time for me."

"I'd love to. I found this session fascinating."

In Rothman's car, she recalls the hypnotic session and realizes that she was not the girl, but that Rothman was the evil lord with the commanding voice. Angelica retains a sense that the future holds only doom for the lovely young girl.

"Where shall we go for dinner?" interrupts Rothman, becoming agitated by Angelica's silence.

At dinner, she adoringly says how wonderful Mitch is and showers Rothman with praise, but leaves no doubt that her feelings are for Mitchener. When he drops her off, she leaves the car quickly and says, "Thanks for the tennis, the dinner and the hypnotic regression. Interesting."

～～ CHAPTER TEN ～～

Later in the day, a light plane flies over the steaming jungle and passes the ruins of Palenque. Science writer Daniel Christopher, 41, blond, lean and Nordic looking, peers down in awe as his cell phone rings and the pilot says, "We'll be landing in a minute." Then his wife, Susan Christopher, shouts into her phone,

"This is a horrible connection."

"Please call later, Susan. We're landing." Christopher clicks off his cell phone.

His wife, Susan Christopher, 42, known for her family fortune, her snobbishness, her pleasing face, and an eye-turning bosom, shouts into her phone, "This is a horrible connection. I should have come along with you."

His wife hangs up and rolls over in bed. Her divorce lawyer cuddles up, kisses her gently, lowers his head to her bosom and buries his head in her breasts.

It all began innocently enough, she recalls. A chat with a recently divorced friend, the exchange of a divorce lawyer's card, her hints that she got a discount after a she bedded him, that he was charming but could not keep it up, that he suggested she get her tiny breasts surgically enlarged, that he got her a lot of alimony and that he wined and dined her, sent red roses after she paid her bill and that he had possible underworld connections.

Armed with the advice of her friend, Susan went to the law office of Jonathan Handcock. She found herself anxious and more concerned about her appearance than she had been for years as she applied her makeup and fixed her hair. She chose a low-cut dress that accented her treasures, looked in the mirror and decided she didn't look that bad for age 42.

Maybe, just maybe, she could get a discount. She adjusted her golden loop earring and put on her golden ankle bracelets.

Handcock's manner was stern, but charming. He was of medium height, well dressed, a bit heavy around the middle and easy to talk with, while she noticed his blue-green eyes were more focused on her cleavage than her case. He asked if she was still living with her husband, listened attentively and realized that she would not have worn this revealing outfit if she did not have the same plan as her friend whom he had bedded for a discount.

After she told her tale at length concerning why she wanted a divorce and he went over his charges, which were higher than she anticipated, he looked at his watch and said, "I have kept my next client waiting. Could we resume our conversation tomorrow over lunch? That is if you have the time."

"Certainly, Mr. Handcock." "Call me John."

She asked if it would create any female problems for him if they went out to lunch. He said no, shook her hand and said he looked forward to their informal lunch. She felt a tingling in her spine as she left his office. When he stood, and walked away, she noticed that he had a limp that he was trying to hide.

The following noon, Hancock arrived early in a well-cut suit, flashy tie and got a quiet table in the rear of a ritzy restaurant. When she arrived, he smiled, complimented her on her dress and they ordered wine and salads. The waiter was kept busy refilling their glasses as she found herself telling her life story.

"All my husband wanted was my money so he could write. Did he work hard to succeed? Yes. Did he neglect me? Yes. Do I feel caged? Yes. I was lost in his quest, forgotten. I withdrew from life. Now I've decided to go after what I want. I feel my husband only wants me for my money."

Then he reached across the table, took her hand, and said that he would like to get a woman's point of view on his new home. Once there he opened another bottle of red wine, took off his coat and tie and gave a tour. As she continued her life story, she realized that she was tense and paid little attention to the tour, although she made complimentary comments. Once in his lavish bedroom, which looked like a Renaissance masterpiece with elaborate tapestries, he sat down on his double bed, patted for her to join him and took her face in his hands.

"May I?"

"Depends."

She smiled, gave him a long, deep kiss as his right hand reached through her loose blouse and slid his fingers under her bra and massaged her full breast. Minutes passed and then she leaned forward, smiled and gently pulled his hand away.

"This is a very comfortable bed, perfect for our playtime," she said as her breath came quicker. "I feel if we came to an arrangement I could please you."

"You're a beautiful woman with a magnificent body," said Handcock.

Although the wine was creating a desire for her to yield, she stood, partially unzipped her dress which slipped easily off her shoulders, and unhooked her black lacy bra. Her heavy breasts fell forward.

"Oh, my God," said Handcock before Susan turned her back to him and asked him to re-snap her bra. Then he reached around her back and cupped one breast in both hands. After some time, he re-snapped her bra and covered her back with kisses. She realized that she had the upper hand, motioned him back into his living room, and patted the couch.

"This is a wonderful place for some playtime together, don't you think?" Susan said with an inviting smile. "I'd like a monetary gift for our playtime. If you're not satisfied after our first playtime, we'll focus our attention on my divorce and forget further playtime. Is it a deal?"

The following week, Susan wore her pearl necklace and long pearl earrings. To avoid any attention, she dressed conservatively, left her hair fall wildly and wore sun glasses.

When he opened his door, Handcock was wearing a blue cotton bath robe and holding a bottle of red wine in his hand. His hand trembled a bit as she smiled confidently and her eyes twinkled.

After she sat on the couch across from Handcock, she unbuttoned her blouse, unsnapped her purple and pink lace bra and said with an enticing smile, "I'll give you something to think about before playtime."

Then her eyes rested on a dozen red roses in a vase sitting atop three splayed one-hundred dollar bills. She slipped a rose between her breasts, walked toward him and kissed his forehead. He pulled her soft, tempting breasts toward his lips and suckled, nibbled and kissed them for what Susan thought was about 10 minutes while her pulse rate increased.

"I can't get enough of you," said Handcock. "I called my secretary this morning and told her to cancel all my appointments. That's how much I've looked forward to our playtime."

Susan thought I'm in control after all these years. He wants me, not my money.

"This red wine is fabulous," Susan said as she emptied her glass.

"An old Spanish Rioja. I hoped you'd like it."

She drank her wine slowly, savoring it while he filled glass after glass. She hadn't consumed this much wine for years.

"You're driving me wild with anticipation," said Hancock. "I can't wait for you any longer."

He stood up and she undid his bathrobe and let it drop to the floor.

"Naughty, naughty," she said with a laugh while she reached down and whisked off his shorts. His manhood was small, but erect for a moment and then became flaccid. She kissed him lightly and then gave him a knowing smile.

"Just the right size."

His eyes smiled brightly while hers twinkled approvingly.

"I brought a gift for you," she said as she took out a clear rubber tube with a black wooden knot so it could be drawn tightly like a lasso.

"Guess where this goes? But first, let me give you a little pleasure before I lasso you," said Susan teasingly.

She dropped to her knees, ran her soft fingers down the back of his legs and then Hancock felt her warm mouth surround his shaft and her tongue explore its smooth round head. He felt suction and moist warmth as her white-blonde curls moved up and down. She drew him farther in as he moaned and then looped the lasso around his shaft and tightened it.

Susan then rose, took his hand, led him into the bedroom, tossed back the bed sheets and said, "Playtime! You'll never fail me with your new lasso tied tightly."

She stripped off her remaining clothes, indicated for him to kneel as she sat on the bed and smothered his face in her milky breasts. His lips suckled them as her nipples stiffened and he felt the texture of her skin change as he pulled her rosy areola deep into his mouth. She moaned while his loins blazed.

Then she pulled him into bed beside her and covered his face with kisses while his hand caressed her leg, and then reached for her inner thigh. She separated her legs and he entered her warmth. His eyes closed as he fiercely thrust deeper as her back arched to meet him. She held nothing back while she arched to meet his final surge and his body collapsed in pleasure. She felt no guilt about her faked moans and screams.

After a long silence, he turned to Susan and said, "Your gift has changed my sex life. This was unlike any other experience I've had with a woman."

"Happy to have satisfied you." "I must satisfy you too, Susan." "Next time."

Two days later he called and said, "I cannot wait another week for playtime. Twice a week. I can afford it."

Soon he wanted three times a week, but she protested. The money flowed in so she joined a gym and found she liked it as her muscles hardened and her stomach flattened. Unfortunately, she also was turning into his father confessor.

One day after playtime Handcock said tenderly, "You're so good about never mentioning my limp. Everyone does. After I finished Law School I defended a young, cocky gang member and got him off on a light sentence. Months went by. He never paid me. Finally, I demanded pay within a week and added or else. Later that week, he jumped me and broke both my legs with a baseball bat.

"As he stood over me, he said `No one threatens me.' My recovery took months. About a year later, I had enough money to approach a rival gang member and paid him to make my assailant disappear. He did, I paid him, and other arrangements followed. Revenge is sweet."

"During one of our chats you mentioned that you have a $350,000 life insurance policy on your husband. With my friend, I could make him disappear in Mexico for $10,000 or so. He's reliable. He has helped my clients when needed. Not often, but …. We could see each other more often and you'd be far richer."

Susan was shocked, but over the next week she found she was considering the offer. After drinking too much red wine after one playtime, she later recalled she had given Hancock the dates of her husband, Christopher's, trip and the place Christopher would stay near Palenque.

He smiled knowingly and did not mention it again. Playtime continued, he continued to pay and his idea was not mentioned again. Later, when she kissed Christopher goodbye at the airport, she felt a great relief. After a couple of weeks or longer, he would return and soon thereafter they would be divorced. This sneaking around could end. It was getting tiring. It would be heavenly to be alone for awhile. One idea puzzled her. Would she ever marry someone who hired a murderer?

After Handcock goes to work, Susan finds she has nothing to do in her temporary life of freedom so she heads for her favorite lingerie shop to spend some of her earnings from Hancock on sexy, expensive lingerie. Why not she thinks? I earned it. I guess that makes me a paramour. While shopping, she feels a tap on the shoulder. She turns, doesn't recognize the face but recalls an incident two weeks earlier in the shop when she bumped into Charlene, her neighbor who recently lost her husband in a three-car crash. She seldom saw her in the yard and aside from a couple of hellos and short conversations, never paid much attention to her.

"I'm Charlene Bartlet, your next-door neighbor. You're Susan, right? Forgive the baggy pants and shirt. I just finished cutting the lawn and I'm too lazy to get dressed up."

"Looks like we have something in common?" says Susan with a smirk as she looks down at the size on the bra that Charlene is holding. "I've got a double G cup and you've got an H. This is one of the few shops that sell bras big enough for our twins."

"I've got the same problem, if you want to call it that," says   Charlene. "It's hard to find a good fit for our sizes."

"I would never have guessed it looking at your loose blouse," says Susan admiringly.

"I got used to hiding them. My husband said they'd draw too much attention. I'm shy anyway, so it was no problem. We never went out much anyway. He was always working so we had little time for a social life."

"I'm thinking of having mine custom made," says Susan, "If you find a place, let me know. I saw a large, attractive red one your size over there."

"I'll have to wait for that, I'm a little short on cash right now."

"Try it on," Susan says, "won't cost you anything."

When she returns, Charlene says, "Great find, but it's a bit snug."

"I have a confession," says Susan. "I told the clerk to put it on my bill. I've been shopping a lot here lately. If you've nothing to do, come over for a drink at 6 p.m. I'm right next door."

Charlene thanks Susan profusely, lowers her eyes and admits, "I'm alone and often lonely. I haven't had a date since my husband died."

"My husband's in Mexico. Bring some of your lingerie and we'll compare notes."

At 5:30 Susan decides to wear her new black and pink lace bra and bikini panties. She'd been thinking of the two bosomy women that Hancock had on a porno video she glimpsed and finds she's nervous. As she pours herself a double Scotch and sips it she thinks I've led such a protected life. Soon her glass is empty, the kitchen and living room are clean, and while she is putting on her blouse she finds her pulse rate rising and decides to change into a titillating see-through nightgown. When she is about to change her mind, the doorbell rings.

Charlene, 29, 6-foot-1, with long, straight blonde hair, a perky nose, bright blue eyes, and a heavy bust above a trim figure has no resemblance to the woman in the shop. Susan finds her heart pounding as Charlene smiles and hands Susan a bottle of red wine.

"You look gorgeous. Thanks for the wine," says Susan. "You're gorgeous in that sexy night gown," says Charlene surprised. "We should be lingerie models. If you'll forgive me I've never seen such large, pink, attractive areolas. I'm not an expert but I'm busty and they're bigger than mine. If I knew this was going to be so informal, I'd wear my new bathrobe."

"Change your beautiful, well-cut cocktail dress and return in your new gift. You don't look shy to me with that cleavage showing in your beautiful cocktail dress," says Susan with a light laugh.

"I'm tired of being a former wallflower before my husband's untimely death. Anyway, I was nervous before coming into this lavish house so I had a few glasses of red wine to relax. Thanks for inviting me. I'll be right back."

"Wear your new, snug bra, maybe we can do something with it."

Ten minutes later as she opens the door, Charlene laughs, throws open her robe, covers up quickly and then laughs and ties her robe.

"Oh, my God, they're beautiful," says Susan. "I can see why your husband wanted to keep you under cover. And your new lacy bra. It's so sexy even if it is tight. You have a beautiful body. I'm glad I made my neighborly gesture."

"Thanks for the compliment. Frankly, I needed that," says Charlene as she plunks down on a couch. More wine is poured as the music of a Latin crooner fills the room. The two find they have much to discuss and they soon are chatting like lifelong friends.

"I'm starting to feel a bit tipsy," says Charlene, "time flies." "It's time for the lingerie show," says Susan, excited by

Charlene's charm, pleasing manner and beautiful face and voluptuous body.

"I've never done this before," says Charlene, while she sways to the music. Soon she cups her tempting breasts in her new lacy red bra, moves sensuously, laughs and sips more wine as her heart pumps faster and her face flushes and her body sways.

"Charlene, you're a great dancer and adorable," says Susan. "You're so kind. I feel like I've known you all my life. And thanks for this sexy bra, although it does feel snug."

"Here, let me adjust it," says Susan as she reaches her hand inside Charlene's bra, still finds it snug and steps behind Charlene and unsnaps her bra. The bra drops to the floor and Charlene's huge breasts fall forward.

"Could I ask a favor, Charlene?" says Susan while her pulse quickens. "I've always wanted to suck another woman's big breasts. Yours are magnificent. Would you mind if I sucked yours?"

"I've always wanted a woman to suck and caress my tits," says Charlene burying Susan's face in her huge beasts. Soon Susan's lips are nursing and her hands are massaging Charlene's cuddly breasts before sucking them, pulling them deeply into her mouth and licking her nipples. At one point, Susan pulls away and says, "What a wonderful way to smother. This is such a thrill. I hope it is for you." "Susan, you're wonderful. How can I pay you back for your kindnesses?"

Out of breath, breathing hard and tipsy, Susan asks cautiously, "Am I giving you pleasure? I get so turned on and hot when I suck and caress them."

Soon, Susan slips out of her sexy lingerie, while her female juices slip down her thighs. Susan rises and gently takes Charlene's face in her hands and says, "No woman has ever worshiped, massaged and sucked my huge breasts. Would you be the first?"

"I'm honored," says Charlene as she kisses Susan deeply and pulls her naked body toward hers. Then her lips take Susan's breasts and circle her pink nipples with her tongue.

She sucks her full, heavy breasts, pulls them deeper into her mouth, and continues suckling as a charge of electricity shoots through Susan's body. Momentarily shocked by her actions, Charlene takes a deep breath, relaxes and lightly kisses Susan's shoulders, neck and Susan's pouty, sensitive lips, first lightly, then harder, then lightly as she pulls Susan into a tight embrace and Susan's tongue explores Charlene's sensitive wet mouth. Soon both women lose themselves in deep kisses. Never did I dream of this, both women think.

Sweat runs down Charlene's shining, perfumed skin. The room feels hotter and hotter. Susan watches, spellbound, lost in the moment. Both women are silent, while the aroma of perfume fills the room.

"You have such a loving touch, Susan. I feel so close to you. It's so wonderful to get to know you and your body. I'm so grateful.

"Would you like to kiss my breasts again?"

Susan thinks that I'm just like Hancock. Now I know how thrilling it is to take Charlene's huge breast in both hands and massage it as I suck and tongue her hot, en-flamed nipple. I can see her aureole darken with desire.

Charges of electricity shoot through Charlene's body as the pads of Susan's fingers caress and then fondle her heavy breasts and her tongue and lips worship her stiff, en-flamed nipples. Susan worships them for what seems like hours.

"I think my bed would be more comfortable," says Susan as she throws back her black satin sheets. Charlene slides easily between them and pulls her warm flesh against Susan's. Then she sobs quietly, her body shaking. Susan holds Charlene tightly and her heart goes out to her. Minutes later, Charlene quiets as Susan kisses her cheeks and forehead.

"I've never felt this way with anyone," says Charlene.

"I know it must be terrible losing your husband, so tragic, so fast, so quickly in an accident."

"It was horrible. But the truth is I was driving and I screwed up. The accident was my fault. I didn't feel terrible when it happened. Did I want it to happen? I'm not sure. I felt caged. I wanted out of my marriage."

Charlene weeps again while Susan embraces her, kisses he cheek and her hand slips down between Charlene's wet thighs.

"I always wanted a child, but I couldn't have one," says Susan. "I've always wanted someone to mother. That's why I bought you the gift. I love mothering you."

Tears run down Susan's face as she pulls Charlene against her hot, full breasts, her nipples stiff with pleasure.

"I desire you, love you near me, too, Susan. I want you to thrill me, with your loving ways and touch."

Charlene spots an artistic bottle of scented oil on Susan's dresser and jumps up easily from the bed. Soon a powerful scent fills the room, rousing both women's passions.

"Sit on the side of your bed," Charlene says sweetly. Carefully and slowly she works the oil over Susan's shoulders and down over her breasts. She looks up and sees the desire in Susan's eyes. She reaches for Susan's hand, holds her fingers to her lips and kisses the palm of her hand and then the pulse in her throat and then slowly, lovingly, her tongue draws Susan's breasts deeply into her mouth and suckles.

Charlene wants Susan to never to forget this night as she worships Susan's breasts, slowly, lovingly, sucking, nibbling lightly with her teeth en-flaming her nipples and massaging her full breasts with her gentle touch. Susan moans softly while Charlene's lips work their magic and her nipples become flushed, thrilling her.

Susan's heart pounds and her face warms as Charlene's nostrils fill with Susan's womanly scent as she brushes aside the blond curls of Susan's mound and slips her tongue inside her while pushing Susan's thighs farther apart. Slowly, softly her tongue sets Susan afire until Susan's hips quiver violently and a shower of feminine fluids cover Charlene's face.

Soon Susan moans and then screams as her body writhes, arches and quivers while Charlene's tongue finds its goal, works feverishly and Susan's body quivers until she finally screams "Stop, please, stop. No more."

In the morning, Susan slips out of bed and makes coffee. Charlene sleeps later while Susan calls her beautician and explains the plan. Then she draws a warm bath and perfumes the water in her expensively decorated tub. She shuts her eyes and imagines herself as beautiful as Charlene. Then she peeks into her bedroom, marvels at Charlene's voluptuous body, awakens Charlene, leads her into the steaming bathroom where she helps her slip into the tub.

Surprised by the oil, Charlene's large pink nipples quickly rise and swell, exciting both women. Then Susan smiles warmly, aware she is exciting Charlene, and pours oil on her breasts and massages them, working the oil lovingly. Charlene feels her womb moisten and droplets of fluid slip down her thigh as waves of passion en-flame her body. Susan smiles and whispers in Charlene's ear, "It gives me pleasure to give you pleasure."

Susan pours more aromatic oil on her palms and fingertips and gently rubs the oil over Charlene's shoulders, arms, breasts and stomach. She looks into Charlene's excited eyes, and drops to her knees as Charlene slides her buttocks over the rim of the tub. She gently parts Charlene's thighs and her three oiled fingers enter Charlene and rhythmically work while Charlene's hips rise and fall.

Susan, lost in her own reverie, feels Charlene's warm, interior muscles are contracting to the rhythms of her fingers. Charlene moans softly "more" and her body quivers while Susan's fingers move faster and deeper sending powerful waves of pleasure with each motion. Charlene arches her back as she moans and her body quivers as she collapses in ecstasy.

"You have the soft finger tips of an angel," says Charlene breathing heavily.

Soon Susan again spreads wide Charlene's soft, wet thighs, and softly licks and sucks her inner layers until she feels her knob stiffen again. She throws her arms around Charlene's buttocks and pulls her thighs softly against her face as her tongue works its magic and Charlene arches her back and moans until she explodes with pleasure, spasm after spasm shaking her body.

Minutes later, breaking the spell she has cast over Charlene, Susan looks at her watch and says, "Oh, oh. We'll be late for your surprise."

In the bright, shiny black Cadillac that smells new, Susan says, "It will take me years to figure out what all these bells and whistles are for."

"What's the surprise?" says Charlene coyly.

At a ritzy shopping center, Susan motions for Charlene to follow her. They walk into a salon, and a spritely young beautician winks and says, "Follow me, Charlene. It's a gift from Susan. Just one rule. Say nothing until I'm finished. Agreed?"

"Agreed. I'm in your hands."

Charlene, weary from her lovemaking and slightly hung over, slips into a chair. The facial, the haircut, the permanent and other surprises relax Charlene and she dozes until at the end of what seems like hours she stands and looks in the mirror.

Her dull blonde hair has been transformed into flaming red curls that fall to her shoulders and surround her fine facial features. Her eyelids and eyebrows are professional done.

"I could fall in love with that image in the mirror. I've always dreamed of having red hair."

"After meeting you, I picked out the color, the long curls and this styling. I think it works perfectly with your complexion," says the beautician.

The beautician points at Susan, who adoringly says, "Put it on my bill. Give yourself a nice tip."

In the car, Susan praises Charlene's new look and Charlene is filled with gratitude.

"How did you know that I've always dreamed of having red hair?"

"I looked into your eyes last night and realized it was the perfect color for your hair. I planned a massage too, but you've had enough for one day."

"Enough what?" says Charlene joking. "Forgive me when I say that you've changed my life."

"It's not over yet," says Susan. "I'll whip up an egg omelet and we'll salute your new look with champagne, get some sun and chat on my patio."

After her second glass of bubbly, Charlene excuses herself, goes home and returns wearing a drab, faded, stretched out bathing suit.

"Don't say it," says Charlene laughing, "but your streamlined red-striped bathing suit fits you perfectly."

Susan blows her a kiss and points to her stomach, saying "My tummy is not flat or muscled as it once was, but it's improving. I'm going to get a personal trainer for you and me. You've inspired me. I want us to look ravishing for the cruise."

"What cruise?" says Charlene as Susan pours two more glasses of champagne. "Thanks for the golden shower. It thrilled me as much as you. It's so easy to speak with you about anything. I love your red stripped swimming suit that highlights your twins."

"Then worship them, my darling," Susan says as she drops her swimsuit straps and her scented breasts fall as she puts her arms over her head and her golden hoop earring sparkle and tinkle. But first, take off that, ugh, bathing suit. You look so beautiful otherwise. No one can see us in here."

Charlene slips out of her suit and says, "We look like a breast lover's dream."

"Wait a minute. I want to remember you as you are now."

Susan skips off and returns with an expensive camera and shoots a series of evocative poses. As she reviews them, Charlene is amazed at her transformation into a voluptuous woman. Soon, they fall into each other's arms and make love yet again, kissing, hugging, sucking and massaging, their tongues and mouths, palms and fingers leading to wildly arching backs, driving hips and spasms of pleasure.

"Each time we make love, I want more," says Susan in the soft light of evening.

"This is a surprise for me too."

"I cannot believe how beautiful I look. I could fall in love with that image in the mirror. I've always dreamed of having red hair."

"I love your red stripped swimming suit that highlights your twins."

"I love you, too.," says Susan. "This is a surprise for me too."

Again, a long silence hangs on the air and Susan says, "I've always wanted to travel, but always with a loving companion such as you. Let's see what happens, when and if my husband gets back from the deep forests of Mexico. Each time we make love, I want more," says Susan seriously as she looks at Charlene in the soft light of evening. You look like a Madonna painted by Da Vinci."

"I'm happy to bewitch you, Susan. You bewitch me too with your loving ways and your voluptuous body. I never thought I'd say it again. I love you."

"This was a surprise for me too,," says Susan. "I love you too." A long silence hangs on the air.

"I've always wanted to travel," says Susan. "Let's see what happens."

~~~ CHAPTER ELEVEN ~~~

Guide Sara Santiago, 32, a strawberry blonde with teasing blue eyes, addresses her group of 20 New Age tourists on a tour bus, and points to the TV behind her. Years ago, an aged gentleman told her she resembled bronzed-haired actress Esther Williams, the swimmer who was a World War II pinup and later talented businesswoman.

Santiago then looked up her pinup photo and thought that her face is a bit more glamorous, she's got fabulous legs, but I'm a bit fuller up to now. I like the idea that she had her ashes scattered at sea. Quite a woman, she thought.

Then Santiago returns to her lecture as a TV screen flickers on behind her.

"Here's what the murals of Bonampak and pottery show us of Mayan appearances and rituals, followed by discussions on the Mayan calendar and its prophecies."

The video showing the murals and pottery from Bonampak and Palenque appear as the narrator says, "On December 21, 2012, a rare alignment of the solstice sun with the black hole in the center of the Milky Way took place. This is the cosmic womb from which stars, and we, came. It is also the entrance to the Mayan underworld.

"The Maya believe the fifth world would finish at the end of the 13-baktun Great Cycle on Dec. 21, 2012, the winter solstice. All previous Mayan epochs ended in cataclysm."

Later, Santiago walks to an empty seat in the rear of the bus and sits next to a woman known by her group as a Chatterbox. Soon, Chatterbox is telling her life story emphasizing her love affairs. Santiago dozes off until the woman says sharply, "Am I boring you?"

"Not at all."

"What's your story?"

Santiago thinks it's none of her business, but finds she's telling her story. "I've been living with a man; let's call him Black, for some time. He's been exceedingly kind to me after a difficult period in my life. A very difficult time.

"I've lived with him for what seems like a long time, but recently I have taken notice of his rages, not at me but at circumstances and events. They are getting worse. I find my affection for him is turning into fear. His latest rage occurred when I got this job, which gives me more time away from him. I find I'm enjoying it. I get the feeling he fears he is losing control of me.

"I feel now is time to move on. I've paid my debt to him. At last I can put my former lover behind me and forget about our child that I put up for adoption. My appearance would be unfair to my daughter. I've let go of her. I always pray for her, but that's it. A great peace has settled over me.

"I've been offered a contract with this company. I'll take it or try something else. The more affectionate I am to him, the more jealous he is if I even speak to other men. He showered me with gifts before I left for this trip. Then one morning a friend and neighbor pulled me aside and warned me of his violent nature. She told me that "his last live-in girlfriend, who was beautiful, told me that she was going to leave him. Some nights later I heard her screams as he beat her. I was going to call the police, but then I heard a loud thud and silence. He was not a man to trifle with. I didn't see him for another week. When I asked him where Linda was? He made a disparaging remark about her and said, good riddance, and smiled knowingly. He lived alone for a year until you moved in. Don't trust him.'

"Since that encounter I've decided to get away from him. I've seen him fight bigger men than him and he's 6-foot-7. I've also noticed his requests sound more like commands. Time to move on."

***

Science writer Daniel Christopher walks up to Mitchener, who sits at a cafe table in the sweaty, humdrum town of Juarez, a base for visiting the ruins of Palenque.

"Remember me? I met you here in 2012. You're Mitchener, right? Like the famous deceased author."

"How'd you know it was me?"

"The note pad gave you away. May I join you? I'm Daniel Christopher, the science writer. I wrote a book on 2012. You may remember me."

"I do. Vaguely. What brings you back?"

"My wife, Susan, urged me to return and update it. Surprised me."

"Summarize your book."

"The start of the fifth Mayan world began with the birth of Venus, the Quetzalcoatl Star, on 12 August 3114 B.C. The last day of this Mayan world was December 21, 2012, when the cosmic connection between Venus, the sun, the Pleiades and the Constellation of Orion occurred. The Mayans thought that Venus would symbolically die and give birth to a new age. We were wrong about the cataclysm."

"Timekeepers?"

"Mayan chilams or visionary shaman receive messages from the gods in a trance state. These timekeepers have charted the transits of the stars and planets for millennium."

"Very esoteric." "No scientific."

"Now, I remember. I checked your work. It has two sides, rational and scientific, intuitive and artistic. Your work mixes psychics and metaphysics."

"For me, the two blend. I'm a bit far out. Some say if it's cataclysmic, Atlantis will rise again."

"You sound like an old girlfriend of mine."

"I didn't say I believed it. Let's try an experiment," says Christopher as he leads Mitchener to a spot where they can easily look up at the tropical sun.

"Look directly at the sun."

"Are you nuts? I'll go blind."

"My studies on the solar cycles taught me how blind we

are to the sun and its properties. The sunspot cycles determine our destiny, weather, everything. I discovered to my amazement that the Mayans believed the same thing," emphasizes Christopher.

"Whoa! Our destiny?"

"If the sun doesn't come up, we're shit out of luck. If the Mayans are right, we'll have to rewrite the history of Central America." "With alleged global warming, the thinning ozone layer, worldwide pollution, overpopulation and the weakening of the earth's magnetic field that could produce a pole shift, our day is coming faster than many think." Christopher signals the waiter, Jose. "Dos brandies, por favor."

They raise their glasses.

"To the sun," says Mitchener.

"To the Mayan and their accurate calendars that they used to forecast the future. The Mayan astronomer-priests used the stars to build their calendar. They used their calendar for everything. The Mayans believed biological evolution is the result of divine creation. Those divine cycles are described by their calendars, the Long Count and the Short Count. Energies defined by the Mayan calendar define the limits of human creativity at any given time."

"Interesting," says Mitchener with a smile, "I have to meet my guide, Pablo. See you around campus."

Mitchener and Pablo tour Palenque's vast ruins; palaces, temples, pyramids, stele, stuccoed murals, glyphs and ball courts. Everywhere the rainforest encroaches. The two walk, climb the ruins and enjoy the panorama of the rainforest.

The guide points at El Palacio, a palace harboring a maze of courtyards, corridors, rooms and stucco murals. An ancient tower looms over it.

"Some believe the tower was used by priests to observe the heavens," says the guide. Mitchener recalls Angelica's surprise meeting there and finds he's longing for her presence, her thoughts, her beauty, her tender nearness.

Pablo points to the nine-stepped pyramid, the Temple of the Inscriptions, and says, "Many inscriptions were found here. Famous Lord Pacal is buried within it."

They descend 90 feet within the pyramid to a funerary crypt. At the far end is a tomb. The guide's flashlight beam traces a stone tube above the stairway and says, "The tube is a channel of communication for the dead man to release his spiritual energy." Mitchener finds all he thinks about is his time with Angelica. Above ground Pablo points out the Temple of the Jaguar, the Tomb of the Red Queen, the Temple of the Sun, The Temple of the Cross, the Temple of the Foliated Cross, the Forgotten Temple, the Temple of the Count.

Mitchener shakes his head and says, "Time for a beer."

They climb to a shady spot and sit while they overlook the ruins of the palace. Sweat pours off their faces as a tour group emerges from the Temple of the Inscriptions and heads toward them and the palace. Mitchener looks down at the advancing tour group, squints, shakes his head, adjusts his sunglasses, stands up and says, "I can't believe it."

"Yes, sir, this is a wonderful site," say Pablo. "No, that woman."

"Which one?"

"The good looking one."

"To me, all women are beautiful, senor."

Mitchener descends hurriedly and enters the palace. His lost love, Sara Santiago, enters a dark room as Mitchener jumps from the darkness, wildly waving his arms and shouting, "Boooooooo!" Santiago jumps back and screams. Her group of women back away from this wild intruder. Then a surprised smile spreads across Santiago's face and she shakes her head in disbelief. "Oh, no!"

"Oh, yes!" replies Mitchener loudly, as the group retreats. "It's you!"

"It's me," Mitchener says laughing as he races up and hugs her. Stunned, she laughs, goes to kiss him, recovers and carefully gives him a peck on the cheek. Mitchener picks her up and swings her in a wild circle, barely missing an older woman.

"Who would have thought it?"

"Who would have planned it? Not me. Your place or mine?" says Mitchener, surprised by his words.

"Hotel Mercedes at 8, if you're interested. That's 8 p.m., not a.m.," says Santiago amused, irritated and taken aback.

He laughs, blows her a kiss and disappears before the women summon guards. A woman grabs Santiago's arm and says, "Who was that horrible man?"

Santiago finds it hard to conceal her smile, but frowns and says, "He is horrible. I could not agree with you more."

The woman pulls her aside and whispers, "My advice is stay away from him. I can tell trouble when I see it."

At 8 p.m. Mitchener walks into the Hotel Mercedes, glances at his watch and enters the bar-dining room where a small band plays, spots Santiago at a table and trips, nearly falling. He laughs as he approaches her table.

"Foot problem?"

"Heart problem," says Mitchener.

"I didn't know you had one."

He reaches down to kiss her cheek and she offers her hand. He smiles, shakes it and says, "Come on, we're old friends. I cannot believe it. After all these years."

"You might be old."

"Sometimes I feel it, but you're looking sensational."

"I know you. You tell all the women that."

They start to speak in unison, but Mitchener wins, saying, "What brings you here?"

"What brings you here? Still a journalist?"

Mitchener sees she's put on a few pounds, but her eyes still sparkle and her wit is sharp as ever. Yet, beneath the humor, he feels a deep sadness. She feels it too, even under these weird circumstances.

"What brings you here? Synchronicity? "Or is it duplicity?" Santiago says.

"Electricity. I feel it. Don't you?" replies Mitchener easily.

"I feel eccentricity. I should. I knew you once, long ago and far away."

An uneasy silence follows their patter. Then they sigh

and reflect on earlier, happier times together, but the sadness lingers beneath the memories.

"Where to begin?" says Santiago, angry with herself for the long time she took to put on her makeup perfectly, to choose her best outfit, to check her suntanned legs. Yes, I've still got great legs, screw the fingernail polish. She tries on a new bra that reveals a hint of her cleavage in her red blouse and checks that her diamond earrings accent her perfect ass; he used to love to tell her how perfect it was before he pulled her to him in an embrace. The hell with it, she thinks, I'll wear my white tennis shoes, that asshole.

"The tour had the money, I had the time," Santiago says, explaining her position as a guide.

"The newspaper had the money, I had the time. And I'd written about Palenque as an advance story in December of 2012. And now I'm back. A follow story. Another end of the world story. Who knows? I bet you do."

"I'm as ready as I'll ever be. I have no last wishes," says Santiago lightly.

He takes her hand and she smiles sadly, then slowly pulls it away.

"You bastard. You disappear from my life for ages and then you scare the hell out of me. It's just like you. You bastard."

"How long are you here?"

"Why? Do you want to scare the pants off me again?" Santiago says smirking.

"Frankly, I'd love too. You are a beautiful, adorable woman," Mitchener says seriously. "I don't want to dwell on it, but you are an enchanting woman. You stole my heart, you know."

"You're right. I don't want to dwell on it. Let's keep the conversation light. Palenque is a wondrous spot, one of my favorite places on the planet."

"How long are you here?" "Depends."

"Where have I heard that before?" says Mitchener with a slight irritation.

"Then what?" says Santiago.

"I forgot how much I love being near you," says Mitchener.

"Tough," she says, a hardness in her voice and eyes.

"It's your golden aura that surrounds you."

"You never noticed it before, Conflicted Mitch."

The waiter approaches and Mitchener orders, "Two margaritas, big enough to swim across."

"I didn't bring my swimming suit,"

"Will you be eating dinner, sir?" "No," says Santiago firmly.

"We have more exciting things to do," says Mitchener.

"Such as?"

"How could I have let you go?" Mitchener says softly.

"I've often wondered that myself," says Santiago, whose memories return, depressing her.

"Together again," says Mitchener, trying to remain happy.

"Temporarily."

The waiter arrives with margaritas in two huge glasses.

"If you think I'm going to drink all that and collapse in your arms, you're wrong."

"What a wonderful idea."

"I'm interviewing a scientist here. He may be as eccentric as you," says Mitchener.

"You know what I believe. Knock it off."

"You're the worldliest, most otherworldly woman I've ever met," says Mitchener immediately thinking of Angelica.

"Great line."

They sit in silence and look at each other. Neither can believe that they are sitting across the table from each other. Santiago doesn't know if she wants to punch him or snuggle up to him. Mitchener smiles, kicks off a loafer under the table and runs his foot up Santiago's thigh. He did it once as a joke to recall his old signal to her that he was bored and it was time for them to make love.

"Have you ever lost any toes doing that?" She says, taking a deep swallow of her drink and putting aside her urge to punch him. She decides to remain horribly sober to control her emotions.

"Long ago we had so much laughter," says Mitchener. "What's on your Mayan calendar, senorita? Or is it senora?"

"I'm not answering any personal questions from you, Don Senor. Maybe the Mayan timekeepers are right, maybe tonight is the end of the world. You tried to end mine once."

"I regret that. Then you disappeared," says Mitchener.

"Kiss me," she says, "for old times' sake."

Mitchener stands up, walks over to her and lifts her up. At the last second she turns away and he gives her a peck on the cheek.

"I changed my mind. A woman's right."

Nearby dinners clap and he bows and says, "Thank you."

"I needed that for some perverse reason," Santiago says.

Mitchener sighs and says, "So did I."

They sit looking at each other in silence. Finally, Mitchener takes a deep breath and says again, "What's your take on the Mayan calendar?"

"The Mayans say that evolution and creation are the same thing. They see today's world as a time of transformation of consciousness."

"I could use a transformation."

"I'll drink to that," says Santiago while she takes two large swallows and wants to throw down her glass of margaritas and order another. Mitchener lifts his glass as Santiago says, "You bastard. To your transformation. And the world's."

Mitchener clinks her glass and swallows.

"Don't bullshit me, Mitch. You don't believe a word of it."

"I'm not as cynical as I once was. Really," says Mitchener.

Many replies cross Santiago's mind, but she's not drunk enough to say them so she smirks and says, "Here's hoping." She raises her glass and clinks his and says, ""Let's do a scientific test. "Tomorrow my group will meet a Mayan visionary shaman."

"A chilam?"

"Chilam or shaman, call them what you will. I could make an appointment for us."

"That would be great for my story," says Mitchener kidding. "Your frigging story. Nothing changes, does it?"

"Leave me a note at my flea bag hotel, Hotel Las Canadas, and pick me up at the appointed time."

"It's been a long day," says Santiago sighing. "One dance before we go, senorita bonita?"

They rise as the band plays a slow number. She takes his hand and they walk slowly to the dance floor. Once there, he bows, takes her hand and pulls her to him so he can feel her body once more beneath her blouse and slacks. He feels her pulse rate increase as he pulls her to him, imagining her flat stomach, but not as trim as it once was, lovely hips, heavier breasts and shapely legs. They dance easily, slowly to a romantic Mexican song. She buries her head in his chest and he kisses her neck lightly.

Remembering what they once shared, he says, "Let's leave after this song ends."

They walk to her hotel room door. She smiles and points to her cheek.

"Kiss it."

"Of course," he says, taking her shoulders in his arms and embracing her. He quickly lowers his head and kisses the soft skin between her breasts.

"Rascal."

~~~~ CHAPTER TWELVE ~~~~

The old jeep bumps its way down a rutted, remote rain-forest trail. Parrots and howler monkeys squeal in the night. The dark forest dims the jeep's lights as it threads its way perilously through the humid air. Scents of flowers overpower them. Mitchener reaches down to take Santiago's hand. She moves it away as the jeep stops at a solitary Mayan hut much like others following the age-old custom of building with natural materials.

The chilam's son, Katu-Quila bows in welcome and takes Santiago's hand.

"It's been so long, Miss Santiago. We are honored to have you come to our home again. My father liked your group, but especially you. You spoke to his heart."

"This is Howard Mitchener. He has no heart," she says more sharply than she planned.

"If he is with you, Miss Santiago, he has a large, warm heart," says the shaman's son.

Mitchener bows politely and says, "You have a greater understanding of my heart than my companion, Senorita, or is it Senora Santiago?"

"Senora to you, gringo," she says, suppressing a smile.

As they enter the simple, stick-walled hut, the aged chilam rises, embraces Santiago and shakes hands with Mitchener.

"No heart?" says the chilam, who bends over, listening intently to Mitchener's chest. "I can hear something beating."

"The only thing beating is lower down," says Mitchener, pointing to his crotch and adding, "No heart."

"I like jokes, Mr. Mitchener. That was a funny joke."

"Men with good hearts like yours understand jokes. Senorita Santiago does not like jokes."

Soon, they are sitting in a circle on the floor, holding hands.

The chilam swings his pungent copal incense, inhales deeply, takes his hallucinogenic mushrooms, chews them and passes them to his son, and Santiago, who chews hers. Mitchener takes a sidelong look at Santiago, hesitates, and then chews his mushrooms. He thinks I was once a sane man before I met Angelica. Now everything out of the ordinary seems ordinary.

All eyes close. A vision forms:

An otherworldly feeling takes command of their minds and bodies. It's Palenque about 15 or 20 centuries ago. A teenaged Mayan brother and sister follow a deer. The brother whispers to his sister, pulls back on his bow string, but the deer bounds away. As they laugh, the brother hugs his sister adoringly.

"My brother is a poor hunter, but a fine timekeeper of our calendar," she says, her long, raven-black hair catching the light. It's tied in loose bun atop her head, revealing her perfect facial structure. She bends to pick a flower, revealing her firm, full breasts. Her soft shoulders and rounded buttocks attract his eyes. She is becoming a woman. He watches her delicate fingers as she lifts the flower for him to smell. Silver bracelets dangle on her forearms and wrists. She wears brilliantly colored woven leggings over her calves.

Her brother is tall, well-muscled and wears a short cotton loin-cloth, its ends decorated with colored objects that he has collected. He shuns his headdress when hunting. He sighs as he says, "Nightly I observe the transits of the stars, record them and dream of hunting."

"Sometimes I feel you are looking at me more than you are searching for deer now that I am becoming a woman," she says, teasingly lifting her breasts in her hands, making her silver bracelets jangle.

"Father told me our fates are entwined." "Your husband will be a lucky man."

"Were you not my sister, I would marry you. You are the fairest of women, the first in my heart. Will I will ever find someone like you. I live for the days that you go hunting with me."

"I hope my husband is like you," she says. His hands softly cup her breasts and feel her nipples swell. She notices his loin cloth has risen and reaches for it and squeezes.

"I will not remove my fingers from your body until I relieve your longing for me."

He kisses her wildly, cups her breasts and tenderly pulls her toward him, his heart pounding. She pulls away his loincloth and they fall to the ground where she pleasures him with her soft hands until he moans and reaches his hand toward her thighs.

"You, too, shall have your pleasure, but I do not wish to embarrass you with child."

Soon, she moans with pleasure as their love is fulfilled for the first time.

As the vision fades, another takes its place:

The Mayan brother and sister reappear. He again fails to kill a deer as they laugh and he hugs his sister as she looks into his eyes adoringly. Both are older.

"You are still a poor hunter, brother," she says smiling.

She pulls him to her and kisses him wildly. Soon, she pulls away his loin-cloth and they fall to the ground where she works her hands until he moans with pleasure. Then he reaches down, puts his hand between her thighs and her back arches to meet his fingers. Soon, she moans with pleasure and collapses to the earth.

Then they race into a lake where they swim naked. On shore a Mayan warrior hides in the rainforest, glares at his wife and reaches for his black obsidian knife before he fills with anger and disappears.

Then the two relax on the bank as she says, "We shared such wonderful times together before you wed. Now it is so difficult to see you."

"How is your husband?"

"He must love someone else. His heart is empty. I, too, feel empty and distant from him."

He pulls her to him and kisses her passionately. "Forgive me," she says.

"For what?" replies her brother.

"Loving you, my brother. What of your marriage?"

"When I make love to her, I think only of you."

"But it's forbidden," she says as tears stream down her cheeks.

Then they kiss hungrily and their naked bodies passionately entwine.

Then the scene shifts again:

A Mayan king wearing his elaborate royal garb confers with the Mayan brother.

"I do not blame you," says the king. "I blame your mother. She should have raised her daughter to be more chaste. Your sister weds and then commits adultery with you. Punishable by death. She was beautiful beyond belief. I understand why you could not refuse her. You are a timekeeper. Your labors help and protect us. You have a difficult life. I have spared you and your family grief. Those who carried out our laws will say nothing. Everyone will think that she ran away to be seen no more."

That night the Mayan brother returns to the cliff where he last embraced his sister with so much love. He looks at the majesty of the sparkling stars and the rising half circle of a brilliant moon. He whispers, "I shall always love you. Tonight, I will join you."

He takes a running leap off the cliff and jumps defiantly to his death.

As the vision fades away, a tear runs down Mitchener's check and Santiago takes his hand as tears stream from her eyes.

The vision ends. Mitchener feels a nudge on his back as his eyelids part and he slowly realizes that he is in a Mayan hut. The chilam's son hands him a cup of steaming hot chocolate and says, "We call it the drink of the gods. Did you experience father's vision?"

They nod. Santiago looks down at the silver amulet on her wrist and recalls the recent scene where she is walking with her group through the ruins when a young Mayan boy hands her an amulet covered with mud.

"Por tu. Poco pesos."

"No, gracias," says Santiago as she wipes away the mud and the silver gleams. When she looks up, the boy has disappeared. Now she closely examines the silver bracelet given her by the boy. It looks exactly like the silver one worn by the young Mayan sister in her vision.

"Can we find a quiet place in your hotel where we can talk?"

At a table in a quiet corner, Mitchener sighs and says, "I found these visions very moving. I believe that young Mayan brother was me in a former incarnation, or former life, and the sister was you."

"I can't believe this is the cynical, rational Mitch that I once knew and loved," says a serious Santiago shaking her head.

"It's not. I've changed recently. My closed mind has been opened, I guess. As I recall you once believed in reincarnation, Sara. Do you believe that was us in that former life, in that former love, in that vision?"

"I could tell you did. Tears streamed down your face. I felt a closeness to you I never thought I could feel again," says Santiago.

"I felt a great sadness, a great sadness that I felt when you disappeared from my life," says Mitchener as a tear slips down his cheek.

"You know, Mitch, that I have studied reincarnation, believe in it and after we parted had past-life visions under hypnosis. Do I believe it? Yes. Can I prove it? No. And you?"

"Experiencing it made me realize why I feared love, feared togetherness, feared marriage, feared family, feared your love for me. When I realized this, I felt a huge burden was lifted. I felt an emotional release. I understood a part of me that I could not face before. I felt I was experiencing those painful visions for a reason. To understand my inner myself. To understand myself better, who I am and why I have reacted as I did. It is not an excuse for my past mistakes. I feel a great relief. I loved you, but not as I should have. I did not want to repeat the visions that we experienced tonight. I cannot relive my past mistakes, but I can better understand them."

"I can't believe you said this, Mitch. This is the man who I loved and left, who did not understand me and made me feel cast off. I am shocked, stunned."

Mitchener takes her and says, "I could not confess this if I had not experienced a great weight lifted from my heart. I feel better about myself. I feel I can be better."

Mitchener motions over a waiter and soon two brandy snifters appear.

"This will help us sleep," says Mitchener. "Let's recall the good times and end our conversations with a couple of laughs. "Let's go to bed on a positive note, otherwise we won't sleep.

They click classes. Hours later Mitchener walks Santiago to her door. He kisses her on her cheek and tears stream down her face.

In the morning after Mitchener and Santiago share breakfast they decide to head for a local lake and Misol-Ha, a thundering, dazzling, cascade of white water. At Misol-Ha the two find a marvelous place for a dip in the turquoise waters after following a path through the verdant jungle that leads behind the waterfall. Here, the power of the waterfall sends powerful echoes off the cave walls as water drips from the ceiling and boughs crash down into a pool far below.

They thread their way to a secluded, inviting pool of placid, aquamarine waters. The two strip off their clothes revealing their tight bathing suits. Santiago's tight blue suit flattens her stomach, accents her lovely hips, shapely legs and full breasts.

Mitchener recalls entering her living room once when she was resting nude on her crimson couch, her strawberry-blonde hair in bangs, a phone in her left hand and her right hand with its delicate fingers supported her weight. Light from her window accented her full left breast, highlighting her pink nipple and two faint blue veins, making it appear whiter. Her other breast, pushed up by the couch, appeared larger; her left thigh was pulled up in a coquettish angle. She smiles gently at his approach and reaches up and pulls him atop her.

Suddenly, a splash of water ends his vision, delivered by a laughing Santiago. He dives, grabs her ankles and pulls her under water. She surfaces, screams wildly, gasps for air, gulps, regains her footing and whacks the water again and again, showering Mitchener.

Just as he turns away, she grabs his trunks, pulls them to his ankles and pushes him backward. Just before his head hits the bottom, she pulls his trunks free, revealing his erect manhood, the result of his vision.

"Show off!" she yells as she tosses his trunks away from him. He turns, splashes waves of water over her. Swiftly, his hands pull off her bathing suit to her waist.

"Show off! Showing off your beautiful breasts," he says laughing. She lunges at him, cups her breasts in her hands, and says, "Not bad for an older mermaid, you monster."

Mitchener trips her and pulls her legs up to his shoulders, and her air bubbles rise, she fights free and gives him a kick in the crotch.

"Monster."

"Vixen."

"Masher," she says as she pulls up her suit and Mitchener struggles to get into his bathing trunks that float nearby. "Never trifle with a mermaid."

Regaining his composure, Mitchener reties the strings of his bathing suit and says, "What did you tell your group?"

"Migraine. Same thing I'll tell you if you try anything."

They swim toward shore, walk up the beach and Mitchener spins her to attempt to kiss her. She struggles, tries to trip him and laughs. He trips her, but catches her in his arms before she hits the ground. Their lips nearly touch, but she pushes him away. They separate, look at each other for a long moment, and she pulls his body to her wet flesh and kisses him deeply, her wet body against his. Then she looks into his eyes and pulls him wildly against her body, pressing her breasts against his chest and her thighs against his loins.

Then a Mexican couple passes and they break their embrace.

Mitchener smiles and says, "I've waited a long time for this."

"In other women's arms."

"It didn't help."

"I bet."

"I did love you, you know."

"I know."

Mitchener feels her mood change while a cloud passes over the sun.

"I've never experienced anything like my visions last night," says Mitchener. "Oh, I had one. After you disappeared from my life, I felt my heart would break. Then I had a dream. You were wearing a glistening white robe, your face and body glowed brilliantly against a galaxy of stars that exploded in violets, blues, reds and brilliant yellows. I was filled with love."

"I know when it happened," says Santiago, "When I had our child."

"What?"

"You heard me. When I had our child."

"When you ... Why didn't you tell me?"

"What was to tell? You told me that you were not ready to marry me. I was not going to beg you. I was not going to raise our child alone."

"Your rejection was so painful, I left. I never wanted to see you again."

Mitchener shakes his head in unbelief as a repressed rage surfaces in Santiago and she nearly screams, "I told myself, if I ever tell him, I'll do it with love. But I can't. I felt like I wanted to die. Do you hear me, die? I never wanted to see you again."

He reaches for her, but she backs away. "Don't touch me."

Stunned, Mitchener sits on a rock.

"Without you, it was not our child. I put our little girl

up for adoption. I know, yes, know that God has put her in a family that cherishes her."

She puts her head in her hands and weeps. Then she collects herself, takes a deep breath and says, "Why wouldn't you marry me?

"I felt I wasn't good enough for you. I felt all was going well with our love. I felt marriage would ruin it. I could not risk our love."

"Didn't feel right? You loved me," she screams. "I loved you from the first time I saw you."

In the morning, Mitchener wonders if Sara will ever speak to him again. He doubts it. Later the phone rings in his room and a happy voice says, "Greetings from Paris, my love. All goes well. Might have to stay longer. Can't wait to see you."

"Angelica! I can't tell you how happy I am to hear your voice."

"Love you. There's a knock at my door."

~~~ CHAPTER THIRTEEN ~~~

Santiago's hand reaches for the phone as it rings in her bedroom. She had a long chat at the bar the previous evening with hotel guests she can't recall. One handsome, blonde-haired gentleman kept refilling her wine glass and walked with her to her door when she left. While she slipped her key in the lock he embraced her and attempted to kiss her. She thanked him for a nice evening, slipped from his arms, opened her door and collapsed in bed thinking I still attract men, even when I'm drunk.

She picks up the phone.

"Sara, it's Byron Black," the voice roars. "I'm down here at the local Mexican airport. I'll see you soon, honey. I know this whole New Age trip is a bunch of crap, but I came anyway. I missed you and your warm body."

"What's your hotel again, the Mercedes?"

"It's the Hotel Las Canadas, Byron, the Hotel Las Canadas."

The phone clicks off as Black hangs up. She sighs and thinks here comes trouble.

Soon, Sara gets a call in her room from 6-foot-7, burly Byron Black, with a receding hairline and a don't-screw-with-me look having his third beer in the bar. Two empties sit in front of him on the table. Black, known as a straight talking, nononsense construction entrepreneur who has worked his way to the top, smiles and motions Santiago over.

Sara wears sexy tropical shorts that show off her shapely tanned legs and a tropical tank top that leaves little to the imagination. She waits patiently for a cool margarita as Black says, "Hi, great to see you. Let's go to my bedroom. I've missed you."

She orders a double margarita and heads for his room with him. In his room, he says, "You look great, lover. Work your magic," as he sets his beer on his desk and she throws down her margarita.

She knows what Byron wants, but it's the last thing she feels like right now. She thinks I've forgotten how damn big he is, but I haven't forgotten his impatience. She knows two words set him off after a request, "no" and "later."

Black disrobes easily, smoothers her with beery kisses and carefully lifts her naked body that he adores on his bed and climbs in beside her. The bed sags under his weight.

"You know what I like, my love."

Sara tosses back her hair, mounts him smilingly and forces herself to make love in the many ways that satisfy him. Often he is insatiable, but she wants to milk every ounce of sexual energy from his body because she experiences a tinge of fear. Sara tries to think of all the loving things he has done for her as her back arches and he drives himself into her, pulling her hips toward as he drives his huge shaft deeper.

When she excuses herself from his room, she is exhausted and her body feels as though it has been in a wrestling match. Her jaws hurt and her body aches all over. She feels sex is how he vents his inner rage.

Dinner starts well in the dining room as he tells her of his latest business ventures, compliments her on her lovemaking and informs her that he just got a business call and will have to return tomorrow to a construction site where he's been awarded another job.

"That's wonderful, not that you're leaving, but that you've got that contract."

She decides to tell him that she's leaving before he goes to the airport in the morning. Just as Sara thinks things cannot get worse, Mitchener enters the room. Quickly Santiago motions him away. Black glimpses her action out of the side of his eye.

"Who's that?"

Mitchener wonders why she is motioning him over after recent events. He comes over to her table anyway and says, "Hi Sara, who's your friend?"

Black stands up, gives Mitchener a get-lost look, and

says, "I'm Byron Black. Who are you?"

"I'm Howard Mitchener. Just leaving."

He turns to leave as Sara rolls her eyes. Black's pulse races as he shouts, "Howard Mitchener, the scum bag who abandoned my soon-to-be wife."

Sara thinks that's news to me.

Black stands, pushes back the table, advances on Mitchener, and says, "I've got a present for you, scum bag."

His powerful punch to the head lifts Mitchener off his feet and throws his body to the floor, where he briefly passes out. Santiago screams, "Stop! Stop!"

Slowly, Mitchener regains conscious, but keeps his eyes closed, deciding the floor is the safest place with this gorilla around. Black shouts, "Let's get out of this dung heap before I tear him limb from limb"

The dining room has cleared after the assault as an infuriated Black turns Sara and leads her to his bedroom.

"With a group, heh?"

"It's true. I'm here as a guide to a New Age group of women. I bumped into him in the ruins of Palenque. Not planned. Just an accident. He just turned up in the ruins."

"That's a likely story. Well, I don't believe it. I fly to this God-forsaken place to be with you and here's this scum bag out of your past, Mitchener."

"I didn't plan this. You must believe me. I've tried with all my heart to repay your many kindnesses."

"No more talk. We're in Mexico. Hell, marry me here. Probably wouldn't stand up in a civilized country anyway. This place pisses me off. They live like jungle animals and presume to tell the world what the hell is going to happen."

"Byron, please."

"I come here to surprise you and what do I find? That rotten bastard. Nobody cheats on me. Nobody. You bitch. When I return, I'm burning your clothes and every item of yours in my house. No bitch gets away with this. That's a promise. You used me. I helped you. Bitch. I've had better in the sack. You're not an original or the best."

Suddenly, Sara feels another tinge of fear. He grabs her by the arm in his vise-like grip and says, "I'll see you in your room in the morning. Better be there, bitch."

~~~~ CHAPTER FOURTEEN ~~~~

Sara returns to her room and fears the worst from Black. She decides to lock her door and dials Mitch's room number. He's resting in bed with a bag of ice on his swollen black eye and a bruised cheekbone caused by his fall. He lifts the phone wondering who even knows he's in this room.

"Mitch, this is Sara. Listen closely. My life is in danger. Get one of the hotel employees to drive you to my hotel. I'll meet you on the road where the hotel sign is. I'll stand out of the light with my suitcase. I'll run out when you call "Sara. OK?"

Click.

Mitch finds a hotel employee who's getting off work and wants to make some extra money. They jump in his rusty, old Chevy and Mitchener explains the plan. Some 20 minutes later as they pull up by the sign, Mitch says, "Blink the lights."

When they get no response, Mitch eases his way out the door as his eye and cheek ache. He starts to shout "Sara" when she appears, races to the car, jumps in and slams the door. She gives him a peck on the cheek and says, "My hero. I'm so sorry. Thank you. Thank you. Does the driver know of another out-of-the-way hotel not too far from here?"

"Where's your suitcase?"

"In my hotel room. I have my money, my passport and my lipstick."

"Good, we're ready for anything," says Mitch.

"Black threatened me. He's a violent man, a man of his word. He told me he's flying out tomorrow. Business he said. Who knows? I'll call the hotel, tell them to save my room and ask them to call me when he checks out. Word of the fight has spread, I'm sure."

"Some fight. I hit him with my face. Remind me not to use that tactic again."

Mitchener looks at a rundown, large family dwelling on a remote, dumpy back road. A sign in Spanish indicates rooms.

"Momentito," Mitch says to the driver, gets out of the car, finally finds someone to show him a room, has him turn on the air conditioner, and decides to take it after finding out it's the last room. He pays for two nights, says he'll sign in the following morning and gives the young Mexican a big tip.

He returns to the car, helps out Sara and gives the driver a big tip. Then he asks him to tell no one of this night's drive.

"Seguro, amigo," the driver replies with a smile.

"I got us a room. It's not the Hilton" Mitchener says as the two walk stealthily down the dingy hall. He plays with the lock and the key finally opens the door.

"This key was last used in 20 B.C.," she says, examining it. "Nice," Mitch says as Sara looks at the room with two chairs, a double bed, and a door that she hopes leads to a toilet.

"This looks right out of a 1920 movie set with little light, a loud air conditioner, and a D- for housekeeping."

Sara laughs, bounces on the moist sheet and the spring dips. She throws one of the flat pillows at Mitch and says, "Perfect. Is this the honeymoon suite?"

"It looks as if it was used as a hospital recovery room 20 years ago."

Mitch excuses himself and walks down the hall looking for anyone from whom he can purchase a bottle of liquor to ease his pain. He fails.

"I got it for two nights. We can decide later a course of action."

"Are you looking for some action, Big Boy?"

"Yes. Some sleep action."

"You're to romantic."

"You're not getting out of my sight tonight," he says as he pushes back the deadbolt on the door.

"What if I hide under the sheets?"

"I'll find you."

"Want to bet?"

"No. You'll go to any length to get me in bed with you again."

"It worked," Sara says, patting the place next to her on the sinking bed.

"Do you still sleep nude?" "Yes, do you?"

"Yes."

"Well, we got that out of the way. God, I'm so tired, so fearful and at a turning point in my life. I need someone to hold me and comfort me," Sara says as the takes off her shorts, bikini underwear, bra, revealing top and slides into bed. She pulls up the sheet and then tosses it off.

"Too hot. What are you starring at, you voyeur?"

"You, beautiful one. I can see why that King Kong is attracted to you."

"Don't go there," Sara says sternly, shaking her head.

Mitch strips, slips into bed and holds her gently in his arms. "I'd forgotten the smell of your skin."

"Like it?"

"I love it. I always have. I've tried to forget it," Mitchener says seriously as the events of the day pass through his mind.

Sara snuggles up to his warm body and smiles, pushing her butt against his warm skin.

"Is that a warm pistol against my butt?"

"I apologize. You've always had that effect on me. My body and mind respond to you automatically. I cannot control it."

"I'll forgive this once, my hero. It thrills me. Truly it does. It's so loving."

Mitchener switches off the lights, but leaves a small toilet light on so he doesn't trip over something. When he returns to bed, Sara is already asleep and soon he joins her, forgetting his pain.

In the morning Mitch returns to the room bearing two cups of steam coffee, places his on a small table and passes Sara's under her nose. With her eyes still closed, she moves her nose toward the coffee cup. Mitch moves it away.

"Mitch!"

"Say Captain may I?"

"Captain may I?"

"Make it more pleading, like you'd do anything for a cup of coffee."

"Captain, may I?" asks Sara in a sexy voice as her hand pulls her cup of coffee toward her lips.

"So seductive. Nothing ever changes," says Mitch as his light-hearted voice becomes serious. "God, what a gorilla. I can see why you're afraid of him."

Sara repeats her story concerning Black's helping hand and how as she came to know his quirks, his ways and how she came to fear him and seek her freedom. She winds up saying, "I'll never go back. I've saved enough money to start over. I planned to quit this job after this trip. But now?"

"I feel I must go somewhere Byron Black cannot find me. Did I hurt your eye when I rolled over?" Sara says kissing his cheek. "Are you on deadline for a story?"

"No, finished it and I have a bunch of vacation time."

"You always were a workaholic."

***

Meanwhile, Black knocks on the door of Sara's old hotel room, pounds when he gets no answer and goes to the hotel desk where he discovers she has her room reserved for three more days. Still angry, he decides to go forward with his plan after drinking and angrily fuming the night way.

On his way to breakfast, he stops to chat with the young Mexican desk clerk. He smiles, hands him $50 in tens and says, "Here's what I want you to do while I'm having breakfast – cancel my flight number 347 on Mexicana, find me another hotel nearby and someone who can solve a problem for me. Bang, bang. Intiendo? Call me a cab. We'll talk later, amigo."

Just before Black's cab arrives, he says, "I'll call you from my new hotel room. How late do you work?"

"Until midnight, Senor Black. Many thanks."

Once in his new Hotel Durado room, he can feel his anger slipping away as a weariness overtakes his body after a sleepless night. Then he makes his long-distance calls to reschedule his appointments, heads for the pool and swims laps until he's ready to collapse. Soon, he's fast asleep under a blazing sun and a light breeze.

After a steak, rice and beans dinner, he heads for the bar. He notices the bartender, whose name tag states Domingito, and has scars on his arm and one on his check.

"Do you like dollars?" Black asks and smiles knowingly, while he flashes a couple hundred dollar bills. He takes a photo of Sara from his wallet and says, "Bad woman. She stole money from me. Do you know someone with a pistol? I want her to disappear."

"I do not shoot women, but my friends might. How much would you pay, amigo?"

Black returns to his room, calls his friend, the deskman at his former hotel, and finds his brother wants "$20,000 for the hit. Cheap for a Yankee."

He gives him his room number at the Durado and his phone number, saying, "Call me if you see Santiago returning to her hotel room. I'll pay you another $100."

Within 30 minutes, two of Domingito's friends appear and he introduces them. They settle on a price.

"I'll pay $5,000 for the hit, $5,000 after the hit when I identify the body," says Black. He tells them how he'll help them to make it quick and easy and buys a couple of rounds of drinks.

In his room, he muses, I would like to do it my own way, but why not take advantage of this cheap labor. I'll get my satisfaction either way. No one cheats on me."

***

Over a light breakfast at a nearby café Mitch and Sara learn that the nearby little pueblo of Juarez, not far from the

Palenque ruins, celebrates Mexico's Independence Day with a parade on the main street where they can watch the Dia de Revolucion parade as costumed Mayan school children march, sing and play their instruments.

A short, humid walk takes them to a small café with an excellent view of the parade as the anxious young students form up. Boys in freshly pressed white shirts and blue trunks link arms and form a human pyramid to start of the parade. The top boy waves a Mexican flag as young drum majorettes, in crisp white blouses and socks, blue shirts and neckties, march proudly. Other costumed young girls hold up a "revolucionarios" sign while a boy wearing a sombrero whips his papier-mâché horse and a drum corps beats its white-fringed drums.

Soon, high-stepping marchers wave feathery pompons. A Mayan float with a pyramid, flanked by costumed guards and featuring a princess wearing peacock feathers for a crown, is pulled by an aging car. Marching girls place green masks over their faces and remove them in varying rhythms. Other girls dressed as nurses, wearing starched white uniforms and caps, carry white boxes with Red Cross symbols. Smiling young girls dressed as senoritas and boys dressed in white with painted mustaches and ammunition belts, search the crowd along the route for their parents.

Mitchener turns to Santiago and says, "These kids are wonderful."

"Fantastic! Just fantastic," Sara says and turns away just as Mitchener waves across the parade route to Christopher, who waves. He's with the shaman's son, Katu-Quila.

"Joyous music, talented children. Isn't it wonderful? says Katu-Quila. "Mayans are like happy children, co-creators with our creator. Oh, I meant to tell you when I last saw you that human attitudes have more to do with sunspots than anything in the sun. We are co-creators with our creator. Together, with God and one another, we will overcome evil and darkness as these children have."

A little Mayan girl looks up at Santiago, smiles, jumps up

in the air and takes her hand and gives it a soft kiss. Smiling, Santiago bends down, brushes back the girl's hair and gives her a kiss on her forehead.

"The joy of the children is contagious," Sara says and turns to Mitchener, "They're like little stars. Sometimes I think this is outer space and we're the aliens."

"In your case, I agree," says Mitch, "I'm coming around to your point of view."

Sara laughs and says, "As a child, I was always a dreamer. I collected chunks of quartzite from the hills behind my house. I put them carefully in my room that was overflowing with rocks, fossils and arrowheads. I begged mother to take me to a crystal shop. Once there I picked up a perfect pointed crystal, held it up and watched the prism of colors change as I turned it. Other kids went to movies. I dreamed of crystal pyramids.

"Years later, I had a mystic time in the Great Pyramid and then a mind-bending time in the center of a great Crop Circle near Stonehenge. I have channeled voices from the sixth dimension. Much happened after you left me. My heart ached but I wondered if I was meant to be alone. Why is it so hard to believe we can pick up and record thought waves? Transistor radios pick up and broadcast radio waves. We're much more fine-tuned."

"Will this new Mayan age mark the end of us all?"

"To the Mayans it's the beginning of the fourth dimension. To astrophysicists the collapse of a star system a million light years away appears catastrophic, but in the eye of the cataclysm, it's natural, exhilarating."

"And sunlight?"

"The physical manifestation of pure cosmic light. It passes through your body and illuminates your soul."

"And the Mayans?"

"The Mayans were aware of the eight-minute journey of the sun's light to the earth. They interacted with multi-dimensional beings that brought them knowledge of the universe's workings. And they used crystal skulls. The crystal skulls al-

lowed the Mayans to read the conditions of the sun and other heavenly bodies instantaneously."

"I could have used this in my article," says Mitchener. "If you're not in a hurry, let's buy some bottled water and walk back to the ruins."

Walking down a supposed short cut they pass spongy carpets of leaves out of which sprout vines and broad-leafed plants that compete for the little light that filters down through the towering trees above. Small birds tweet as they make their way back to the ruins and the Tomb of the Red Queen. A sweating Mitchener wipes his brow with a handkerchief as Santiago enters the hot, humid, moldy tomb.

"It's like a tomb in here," jokes Mitchener.

"The jungle leader's humor has returned," says Santiago. "It's hotter than hell in here. I thought it might be cooler than outside." Mitchener takes her by the hand, which she considers a warm invitation, and leads her around a narrow ledge to the back of the pyramid. The steamy, lush jungle is only yards away. Birds chirp and call and swarms of insects' hum.

To her surprise, Sara says, "I forgive you. We were young, stupid. In love. You're such a sweet man. No wonder I'm hopelessly in love with you when I'm around you."

"And I forgive you," says Mitchener. "It was as much my fault as yours, but because of recent events here I can understand my motives and it's always a great joy to be with you and to help you, anytime, anywhere."

She gives him a hug and says, "We've at last made peace. I'm so thankful."

"Me, too."

Tired, sweaty and dirty, Sara and then Mitch shower and nap. While Mitchener sleeps, Sara applies her lipstick carefully, combs her long, burnished copper hair, and takes her clean, now dried low-cut white halter off the air conditioner that accents her sun-tanned shoulders and cleavage, slips into her white shorts, readjusts her bra and puts on her new earrings.

Mitchener wakes, looks up, raises an eyebrow and says, "You look wondrous."

"I remembered how I used to love to have you undress me."

She lifts her arms high and arches her back as he stands and slips off her white halter. She turns around as he unfastens her lacy bra and pulls down her white shorts and then slowly turns toward him in her nakedness. She fondles her nipples, while he bends forward and then cradles her warm breasts in his palms, slowly massaging them. She grabs his hair and pulls him closer while he suckles and licks them. Then he stumbles forward, saying, "Trying to trip me up so you can capture me?"

"I'll do that over there," she says pointing to their sagging bed.

She relaxes briefly in Mitch's arms as her hair falls over her face as she laughs and kisses him softly on his eyes, his nose, his lips and then down his neck and wide shoulders. He looks adoringly at her red-gold hair, lightly curled and falling on her breasts, her tanned shoulders and breasts and her shapely, athletic legs.

"Isn't it wonderful?" she says as she kisses him deeply, probing his mouth with her tongue, her body pressing against his. He admires her fine, rouged facial bones, the soft curve of her neck, her flashing eyes, the curve of her hips, the glistening hair of her mound, her shapely thighs and perfect legs. Her breasts swoop forward and her nipples are hard, flushed with excitement.

Santiago feels Mitchener's powerful energy as his heart pounds and his breathing rate increases. Mitch kisses her forehead, behind her ears, on her closed eyes and softly licks her neck as her pulse rate increases. He weaves his fingers in her hair and pulls her face even closer. Her lips welcome his warm tongue that sets her afire. Her supple fingers knead his back softly as he cups her full, warm breast in his hand, sending a tingling feeling throughout her body.

His loving energy sweeps through her body, excites every cell, and enflames her desire. Santiago just wants to give him pleasure. Waves of pleasure sweep through her body.

Mitchener rolls slowly away as a vision of Angelica fills his mind.

"I can't hurt you again, my love. I've found another love. I'll always love you and have a special place in my heart for you, but I can't make love to you again. It's too painful for me."

Stunned, Sara rolls away and tears stream down her cheeks as she sobs quietly.

"I don't know what to say," she says. "It's all so fast, so unexpected, but we've made our peace with each other; we've acknowledged our love. We've told our stories and been honest. We've both changed so much in the intervening years. I've paid my debt and you've found a new love. We're parting as friends. We've shared our love in this life. Will we love again in our next lives? Who can say?"

Sara kisses him lightly and he holds her while tears stream down his cheeks.

Hours later, Sara smiles and admits, "I knew you were holding back. I was selfish. I wanted to make love to you once more. You were honest. It's better this way. We'll always be there for each other."

Sara dials her tour's second in command, tells her that she will be unable to continue and asks her to take over, to which she gladly agrees. Sara feels a great burden has been lifted because she is no longer under Black's control.

They spend a lazy day at the hotel pool, retelling stories of their happy times together, touch on their misunderstandings and Sara bounces ideas off Mitch about how he feels concerning the various paths her new life might take.

A finality hangs over their dinner conversation until Sara says, "I cannot spend another night in bed with you. It is easier for us both if I return to my hotel room. Anyway, this is a saggy, lousy bed even with you in it. Will you return me and my lipstick to my hotel room tonight? I found out that Black has checked out. I'll feel safer if you'll accompany me to my room."

"Of course. I'm good at lying on the floor after he hits me." "You're exactly right," Sara says smiling. "You're my guardian angel."

~~~ CHAPTER FIFTEEN ~~~

The key slides easily into the lock of Room 21 in Las Canadas Hotel. It should. A mold was made earlier in the day. Yesterday one of the assassins entered and sketched the room's layout after telling the maid he had an upcoming reservation and just wanted a quick peek. Later, the trio rehearsed their plans using the sketch.

That night the three men, their faces covered with black stocking caps, with holes cut for their eyes, slip noiselessly into the room. Lightning streaks across the night sky and thunder crashes as a powerful storm hits the Yucatan. The leader checks his watch. It's 3 a.m. The trio moves silently toward the head of the bed. Lightning illuminates the room for a nanosecond and he easily identifies Santiago's face from the photo.

The leader tiptoes forward, motions the other two to the head of the bed, and removes a diaper drenched in chloroform from a plastic bag. Instantly, a man on either side of the bed pins Santiago's shoulders, while the leader covers Santiago's mouth and nose with the diaper. Santiago kicks for a second and then goes limp, no longer conscious. A hypodermic needle is shot into Santiago's buttocks. One removes a body bag from his backpack, nods and the other two unzip the body bag.

Within minutes, the body bag is zipped shut and thunder booms again and again. One man checks the hall, tiptoes down it and holds open the far door. A blast of wind hits it, but at the last second the assailant grabs it. The other two men carry the body bag down the hall and lift it into a waiting pickup.

The pickup slowly pulls away from the hotel and disappears in the darkness. Then a second car, a rusty Chevrolet, pulls up and one of the trio re-enters the hallway and walks silently to Room 21. Inside, he opens the closet, grabs the clothes, toiletries and cosmetics and tosses them into a gunny sack and then drops to his knees, looks under the bed and pulls out a pair of hiking boots and tosses them into a sack. He relocks the door and quietly slips away.

Later the three rendezvous at a remote shack, toss the gunny sack in a hole and shovel dirt over it in the rain. When Black comes out, the body bag is unzipped and he identifies Santiago's unconscious body and murmurs, "Good riddance."

The pickup follows a dirt road to a large, normally unvisited pond and parks in a secluded spot along its shore where their boat is anchored in the tossing waves and tied to a palm tree. After a brief look at the rolling waves and driving rain, the leader agrees to wait for 30 minutes for the storm to abate.

Soon the rain ends and the three muscle the body bag into the boat next to five oversized cement blocks. After a 15-minte run, the body bag is shoved to one side of the boat. Two ropes tie it to the cement blocks. Then the body bag is lowered carefully into the water and the roped cement blocks moved to the edge of the hull. As the body bag sinks, the cement bags are tossed overboard. The boat nearly capsizes, but then rights itself as bubbles rise to the surface. When the bubbles cease the leader nods and the trio returns to shore.

~~~ CHAPTER SIXTEEN ~~~

In the morning, a refreshed Mitchener heads back to this hotel and heads to the dining room and a steaming cup of coffee. He feels a great sense of contentment in the fresh air of dawn and a great loss after his time spent with Santiago. But he cannot forget his new-found love for Angelica. Yet, he feels a bit uneasy. As the song says, breaking up is hard to do.

Christopher pulls up a chair and interrupts his musings.

"Morning, early riser."

The waiter Manuel pours the two men coffee, bends over the table and whispers, "I've got a secret. I discovered a Mayan tomb in the jungle. Meet me in an hour and I'll take you there. Forget breakfast. Soon, it will be steaming hot. Dress for the heat, I'll bring water. Meet me down the little path near the parking lot."

Perplexed, but ready for a diversion, they dress for hiking and meet Manuel at the small, not easily discovered path where Manuel pointed. Manuel arrives and Manuel leads, whacking brush and branches along the overgrown path. Christopher and Mitchener follow beneath kapok trees through some of the largest uninterrupted rainforest in Central America. Jaguars, scarlet macaws, howler monkeys and leaf-cutter ants are just a few of the astounding varieties of flora and fauna.

Not far away in Guatemala stand the glorious Mayan ruins of Tikal in an area of hundreds of lost and discovered Mayan tombs and relics. In this giant rainforest are found strange turkeys, the blue morpho butterfly, and the capuchin monkey. The jaguar and other species still roam during the days and nights.

After an arduous hike, Manuel spots an old tennis shoe he left as a marker, and then the trio veers off on an overgrown trail into dense rainforest where he earlier hacked a rough trail.

Mosquitoes buzz, land and bite. The three pass small, half buried ruins entangled in roots and vegetation. The going is slow as Manuel's machete hacks away. Sweaty, tired and bitten after passing through clouds of insets, Mitchener and Christopher stop while the waiter climbs a half buried, hardly visible, ruined pyramid overgrown with trees, roots, branches and brush.

Half way up the ruin, the waiter, slips, falls and curses. Unhurt, he gets up and continues climbing carefully. The two carefully follow Manuel, and then halt again and again as he pulls aside vines, grasses and branches that at last reveal a descending tunnel that Manuel has arduously cleared. He pulls out a flashlight and motions them to follow.

They slowly and carefully descend a narrow, decrepit staircase to a humid room where the walls are covered with black mold and peeling stucco murals. To the right another narrow limestone stairway descends farther, passing under a corbel arch just bigger than a man, and find themselves in what looks like a burial chamber.

The waiter motions them over to an opened catafalque and shines his flashlight on the boney remains of a skeleton surrounded by gold jewelry, jade necklace and other burial goods. Four skeletons lay scattered around the catafalque in the small burial chamber. Their long hair hints these are the remains of women. Other artifacts, wrapped in moldy textiles, stand upright. Twenty-six clay vessels line one wall.

"You like?" says Manuel, sweat running down his face. His long-sleeved shirt and pants are covered with sweat.

"Incredible!" says Mitchener, nodding his head. "Unbelievable!" adds Christopher.

"I took a necklace from the king," says Manuel pointing to the skeleton in the catafalque and the leading them to a golden necklace wrapped in his handkerchief and hidden in a crack.

Christopher whistles and asks, "Does the government know about this?"

Manuel shakes his head. "Who knows about this?" "Me and my amigo."

"Oh God, an amigo," says Mitchener after a long pause.

"Let me have your flashlight." He shines the flashlight beam inside a partially sealed clay vessel, where he can barely make out Mayan glyphs on an ancient, long, rolled deerskin codex.

"God, a codex! There are only four in the world," says Christopher as he goes from one vessel to vessel, shining a beam into the other partially opened clay vessels, each containing a codex. "Good God, twenty-six codexes.

"In the mid-sixteenth century, Spanish inquisitors tried to rid Mayan pagan influences in massive bonfires where thousands of sacred Mayan books, artworks and descriptions went up in flames, lost to the world. The Grolie Fragment marked the cycles of Venus; the Madrid Codex referred to the omens about crops; the Paris Codex concerned rituals and New Year ceremonies. Lastly, the oldest, dated to about 1200 A.D., contained astrology, the history of Mayan kings and predictions of the harvest. None survived from the Classic Mayan Era."

Manuel says, "Si, but what about the gold and jewels?" "Momentito, amigo. Are you planning to become a tomb raider, Dan?" Mitchener says as he turns to Christopher.

"Well, his amigo could return, take the gold, burn the codices and ..."

"Oh, God! Howard Mitchener, journalist, tomb raider, prison inmate."

On the arduous, exhausting hike back, Manuel continually swings his machete yet vines entangle their hiking boots and branches swat their bodies and faces as they move through clouds of insects. Before they reach the hotel, they are forced to stop at small clearing and rest, their energies sapped. The three agree to meet the following day and discuss a plan.

Upon their return Mitchener and Christopher shower, take a catnap and later head for the bar. Mitchener finds he cannot quench his thirst as he throws down beer after beer while munching on a fried egg sandwich. Christopher excuses himself and Mitchener signals to the bartender for two more beers.

Later, when he stands up his head spins. He walks slowly down the hall but bounces off the walls a couple of times. At his room, he fumbles with his key, at last opening the lock and the door swings open. He turns up the air conditioning. A great sense of relief hits him as the cool air hits his body. Within minutes he's deep asleep, and snoring. He's fully clothed.

Mitchener awakens later, flicks on a light, heads for the bathroom and returns to his bed. Before he falls asleep he looks at his watch. It indicates 3 a.m.

CHAPTER SEVENTEEN

When the strong light of the sun hits his room at midday, Mitchener wakes up. His head throbs. He takes a cold shower, towels down and puts on fresh clothes. He walks uncertainly down the hall to the dining room, where a waiter greets him and brings him a cup of steaming coffee. Mitchener's head begins to clear after the third cup as he ponders yesterday's discovery. He hasn't had a hangover like this for years.

Later, he orders lunch, picks at the unappetizing mashed potatoes, vegetables and meat, tips the new waiter, and walks down to the hotel's desk.

"Did Miss Santiago leave a note in my box? I'm in room 32, Howard Mitchener."

"No, sir."

"Is the large American group still here?"

"No, sir, they all left this morning."

"Has Sara Santiago checked out?"

"Her room was paid for. The maid has cleaned her room and we're expecting another guest for her room this afternoon. I saw a note that she forgot to leave her room key."

"Didn't she tell you she was leaving?"

"Not a word."

~~~ CHAPTER EIGHTEEN ~~~

That evening Christopher surveys the Las Canadas Hotel bar and sees an attractive brunette with long, dark, straight hair. At a quick glance, he sees that she has wide hips and shapely legs, a fine figure. Her narrow shoulders accent her breasts in a revealing magenta halter. She has soft cheeks, a mystical smile and is cross-eyed.

Marsha Bushnel, an alluring 25-year-old, locks her eyes on Christopher, waves and says, "Over here."

Christopher smiles and ambles over. His eyes flow down her tanned narrow shoulders and examine the cleft between her tempting breasts. She darkens her eyebrows and has false eye lashes that give her a direct, seductive look above her pink lipstick.

"Care for a drink? I'm buying." "Forgive me, you're ...?"

"Marsha Bushnel. You never invited me for a drink, so I'm inviting you."

"Thanks. Why me?" he says, noting there is no one else in the bar.

"You have no competition."

"What's the occasion?"

"My settlement with a large alimony."

"Lucky you."

"If I die, it ends. Might as well enjoy myself now."

He pulls up a chair, smells her pungent perfume, and says "I'm Daniel Christopher," and motions over a waiter.

"Bring the lady another drink and two beers for me."

"Why two?"

"You might change your mind. Women have that option."

The waiter Manuel brings the drinks. Christopher raises his glass and Bushnel clinks it.

"Salud dinero y amor! To love and money."

"I like that," she says and sips her margarita slowly.

"How old are you?" Christopher asks, smiling as he enjoys looking at her beautiful face. He finds her crossed eyes strangely enticing.

"About half your age."

"How big was the settlement?"

"Very beeeeeeeeeeg," she says, spreading her arms. "What did you have in mind when you called me over?"

"What did you have in mind when you came over?"

"I'm a gentleman so I won't tell you. Actually, I think I'm ending a chapter in my life."

"I'm beginning one." "How does it begin?" "That's up to you."

The waiter, Manuel, comes over to the table holding a phone, and nods at Christopher.

He looks at it. She looks at it. Bushnel says politely, "It's for you."

"It's for you," says Christopher politely. Christopher's wife, Susan, screams, "Hello! Hello!"

Bushnel picks up the phone and says in the sexiest voice she can muster, "Hola! Hello! Darling?"

"Who's this? Who are you? Where are you?"

"In the Las Canadas Hotel."

"Where are you?" Brunel says sweetly, "and who are you with?"

"What's your name?" asks Susan.

"Daniel Christopher," replies Brunel in her sexiest voice. "Put him on."

"It's your lucky day, Mr. Christopher," says Brunel as she hands him the phone and smiles.

"I'm worried to death about you," says his wife, Susan.

"Having a beer," says Christopher, enjoying Brunel's changes of expression.

"In your bedroom?" asks Susan.

He looks around the bar carefully, pauses for a long minute sips his beer and replies, "There's no bed in this room."

"It's not funny!' Susan says and hangs up the phone.

"Anyone I know?" says Brunnel. "Oh don't tell me. It will spoil all the fun."

"We may have more in common than you might think," says Christopher, laughing. "At last, a woman who understands and has a sense of humor. Bravo! You're very attractive. And you've got wonderfully crossed eyes. The Mayans considered them a mark of beauty."

"I thought you'd never notice."

"It's a compliment," says Christopher, reaching across the table and taking her warm hand.

"When I was young, I thought I'd attempt to have them fixed. But I don't like the idea of doctors screwing around with my eyes. I enjoy seeing."

After three hours of convivial conversation, three empty beer glasses stand on the table beside three empty margarita glasses.

"These slippery beers slide down so easily in this heat."

"So do Margaritas. What do you do when you're not drinking beer?"

"I'm a science writer."

"You don't look like one."

"I agree. I'm too good lucking. What brings you here?"

"I closed my eyes, put a pin on the map, found this spot in Mexico, got on a plane and a bus and here I am. You?"

"I wrote a book on the Mayan calendar."

Christopher motions over the waiter and says, "Bring us two surprises."

After a long wait, the waiter Manuel brings over two sizzling, thick steaks, browned potatoes, big green salads and napkins, bows and returns with another beer and another Margarita.

"Now that's a surprise," says Mitchener as Brunel cuts anxiously into her steak. They find their humorous conversation flows easily, and the food goes down quickly. After the hearty meal, Brunel asks, "What's on your Mayan calendar?"

"You," says Christopher as a guitar player comes over to

their table and serenades them. Christopher invites Brunel to dance, pulls back her chair, takes her hand and leads her to the dance floor. The music is slow and their movements rhythmic as Christopher pulls her tightly, feeling her breasts against his chest.

"I never had a real adventure. Mind if I share yours?"

Christopher is enchanted by the pungent scent of her cologne and finds he's breathing harder and his pulse is quickening. As he sways, Brunnel comes closer and finds that something in his khaki shorts is pressing against her body.

"You're excited, aren't you? I can feel it. Thanks for the compliment" she says looking into his eyes as they become lost in the music. After many numbers, Christopher gives her a spin and she passes out in his arms.

Although a bit dizzy himself, Christopher motions over Manuel and asks him to open her room for him as he carries her limp body in his arms. Fortunately, it is not far from the dining room. Manuel opens her door, pulls back the covers and leaves, while Christopher gently lays Brunel in her bed.

Christopher unbuttons Bushnel's blue blouse, notices her magnificent breasts in her lacey bra, and then slips off her skirt, is tempted to lift her bikini underwear, kisses her forehead and leaves, shutting her door quietly.

The following morning, Christopher sits by the pool reflecting on the previous evening after breakfast and a lazy morning swim. No one else is in the pool, but an older couple relaxes under a cabana. He decides to read a book, but just as he opens it, two hands cover his eyes and a voice says, "Remember, me?"

"Vaguely. You were my dinner companion, Marsha Brunel.

How did you find me?"

"Manuel, the waiter said you were probably here."

"I met this nice man at bar last night who bought me dinner and we danced. I had too many Margaritas. As I remember he was a good dancer. This morning I awoke in bed and found my blouse unbuttoned and my shoes off. Did you like what you saw?"

"It felt hot in your room so I unbuttoned your blouse, took off your shoes, gave you a kiss on the forehead and turned up your air conditioner. I was tempted to join you."

"Did you like what you saw?" she teases.

"You were a vision of loveliness. You don't look bad in that bathing suit either."

Her straight, long, dark hair flows down over her shoulders and covers the front of her swimming suit. Her darkened eyebrows and false eye lashes give her a direct alluring look. She wears pink lipstick, has soft cheeks, a mystical smile and crossed-eyes in her heart-shaped face. She has an enticing figure.

"I owe you one," she says while she bends over and kisses his forehead. The touch of her breasts, the scent of her perfume and the warmth of her flesh enchant him.

"Lower," he says, pointing to his lips. "Later," she says laughing.

"You asked about my Mayan calendar last night. Tonight, I'm going to a local Mayan festival. Care to join me?'

"Love to. Will it be an adventure?"

"I hope so."

That night fireworks explode in the darkness, showering the Mayan crowd with sparks. Christopher and Bushnel look up from their blanket as Christopher explains the science of the sun.

"The sun's core is a thermo-nuclear reactor, fusing hydrogen into helium. Because of the intense heat, these gases exist in a plasma state. It takes hundreds of thousands of years for light to cross to the convection zone where plasma bubbles to the surface."

"I'm bubbling. Can you feel me bubbling?" says Brunel suggestively. He slides his fingers down her shoulders and slips them inside her bra, massaging her full breast. She unbuttons her blouse, reaches behind her back and undoes her lacy bra.

"There, is that better?"

He kisses her and cups her breast while his fingers twirl her nipple which stiffens. A colorful fireworks cluster explodes above them, and streams earthward, filling the sky with brilliant, luminous streamers of flaming crimsons, radiant greens, azure blues, sparkling violets, oranges, silvers and golden cascades. Then a pyrotechnic display booms noisily, filling the sky with smoke and floating clouds that dissipate quickly.

Some fireworks explode into flames, others appear as giant, sparkling, circles of lights, streaming brilliant cascades of blues and reds; some descend in long tails and stream earthward like flower stems. Others appear like huge blossoms of interwoven light. Then earth-shattering booms erupt in a heavenly aerial show.

Skyrockets shoot heavenward, stream across the darkness and disappear; pyrotechnic wonders of rotating circles, stars, festival balls and 3D globes, light up the darkness, and disappear in a flash.

Christopher and Brunel relax on their blanket surrounded by enchanted locals looking skyward. For Christopher, the fireworks bring to mind the science of our sun as Brunel moves closer and her fingers run up his thigh, massaging his skin and enticingly playing with his hair.

"Magnetism is the key to solar behavior," he says.

"My plasma is getting boiling," says Bushnel while her hand slips under his khaki shorts and pumps gently. Christopher instinctively pushes his hips forward and sighs softly.

"Naughty. You're not wearing underwear."

Bushel's fingers move a bit faster as she looks up at Christopher, who finds his heartbeat and pulse are becoming more rapid. "The halo-like corona is the sun's outer atmosphere," continues Christopher. The sun's shifting magnetic field opens areas where the solar winds escape at high speeds. When those winds hit the earth, radio transmissions falter."

Christopher rolls his eyes and says, ""I feel my magnetic field is becoming overloaded."

"Good," says Brunel as her soft fingers work their magic.

"A solar flare explodes when a magnetic field is overloaded," says Christopher smiling and looks down at his shorts. Bushnel's fingers give Christopher a squeeze and she says, "Do

I have your attention now?"

"Undivided attention."

"Aren't you glad I took my hand away. I saved your fireworks to share with mine."

Christopher continues, "A coronal mass ejection lets off millions of tons of plasma. This moves into space at 5 million miles per hour and can expand to millions of miles."

"I'm beginning to understand how the sun works," says Brunel as her thighs become moist.

Remind me to give this lecture again," says Christopher, smiling. "We see the sun in the sky every day, but we don't pay attention. The Mayans did."

"When we get back to my room, I'm going to focus all my attention on your magnetic field," Brunel says, rising to her feet as Christopher readjusts his shorts and picks up the blanket.

Back in Bushnel's room, she throws off her bed covers, locks her cross-eyed gaze on Christopher and says, "I've decided to brush my teeth and dab on some perfume."

Soon Christopher hears water running, then the shower splashing. "When I return I want to see you naked in my bed," Brunel orders.

Within short minutes, Brunel returns, the pungent smell of her perfume following her entrance. Her dark brown, long, lightly curled hair frames her heart-shaped face and flows down over her shoulders. He cannot take his eyes away from her bewitching face, her darkened eyebrows and false eyelashes. She has such an alluring look.

"Like my color scheme?" she says pointing to her pink nipples that match the color of her lipstick. "I like everything about you." Their hips undulate slowly. She draws him deeply into her body and savors every second. Soon her moans come faster and louder as her body writhes in powerful convulsions and she slips into ecstasy.

After a long silence, Brunel presses her breasts together, pours perfume on them, holds them together, and Christopher slides his member between them. Much later, her back arches as her interior muscles milk him.

She tells him what a great a lover he is, while driving him deeper into her warmth. She shifts her hips and tries different positions while moaning and urging him on until powerful spasms take over his body, and he explodes in waves of pleasure.

"That's what I call real fireworks," says Brunel. Then she kisses and embraces him.

Brunel has always liked tall, lean Nordic-looking men. Christopher has always kept himself in good shape. His long fingers indicate another long, stiff part of his body, she thinks as she pulls his warm body to hers, and feels his heart pumping, while she kisses him deeply.

She can feel his power when he takes her in his muscular arms and then gently covers her eyes and face in kisses and weaves his fingers in her hair as he kisses her neck. Brunel opens her lips and his warm tongue sets her afire as her supple fingers knead his back.

His loving energy sweeps through her body, excites every cell, and enflames her desire. He moans softly and lowers his head to suckle her hard, warm nipple. She pushes her full breast deeper into his mouth.

Her hand guides him into her body as he caresses her hair. Her body welcomes his entry and her moans excite him while her hips undulate slowly. She draws him deeply into her body and savors every second. Soon her moans come faster and louder as her body writhes in powerful convulsions and she slips into ecstasy.

After a long silence, Brunel presses her breasts together, pours perfume on them, holds them together, and Christopher slides his member between them. Much later, her back arches as her interior muscles milk him.

She tells him what a great a lover he is, while driving him deeper into her warmth. She shifts her hips and tries different positions while moaning and urging him on until powerful spasms take over his body, and he explodes in waves of pleasure.

"That's what I call real fireworks," says Brunel again. Then she kisses and embraces him.

CHAPTER NINETEEN

After a long day at his office, lawyer Handcock picks up his phone as his secretary says, "Long distance."

A gravelly voice with a Mexican accent says, "I'm your friend in Palenque. You wanted a hit the last time we talked. You sounded unsure about hiring us. We're a group of three as I said. If you want a reference I can give you the name of a Senor Byron Black."

"Not necessary," replies Handcock, not wanting to involve others in his scheme.

"We want $30,000 now. We upped our price. Who's your target?"

"His name is Daniel Christopher, an American. I'll fax you a photo. He's staying at the Hotel Mercedes in Palenque. I've just learned that he's extending his stay."

"Do you want his body to disappear?"

"Yes, I don't care how you kill him. I'll send $15,000 to the bank account that you mentioned and another $15,000 when I can confirm that he's dead."

"Done my friend, done."

Handcock hangs up and calls Susan, Christopher's wife and his client.

"When can we meet?"

"How about playtime?"

"I'll be there at noon, darling," Susan says using the word darling for the first time.

At noon Handcock opens his door and blows a kiss. He wears his blue bathrobe and holds a glass of Rioja, Susan's favorite wine. She throws off her white blouse and expensive gray skirt. Handcock's passion rises as he feels her power overtake him.

"Keep stripping, beautiful one, including that magnificent black and pink lace bra and pink bikini. I've got important news.

"While we chat, it thrills me to look at your magnificent body."

Susan finds life without her husband is great. Her freedom is enthralling her and her new low-cut tops are attracting attention. She's lost weight, gained muscle and is more careful of her diet. Slowly her old desires are returning as she works out in the gym and even Handcock, wearing his new lasso she gave him, is improving as a lover. And she continues to get paid for her playtime. She decides to cultivate him with adoration, which he always seems to seek. She's even enjoying her treachery and intrigue as Handcock works to finalize the divorce. She wonders if she is becoming ruthless as she develops a phenomenal appetite for portraying love and passion. With each playtime, she discovers more of his weaknesses, while her power over him increases and more of his secrets are revealed to her. She even finds herself witty as her self-confidence grows.

"When we last discussed your divorce, your husband's possible disappearance and his life insurance policy for $350,000. I made some calls. Today I got a call from a trio in Palenque who can make him disappear. You left this possibility unanswered. Their first cost was $20,000 but they've upped it to $30,000. What do you think? We could get married or continue our present arrangement twice a week. It's no secret I'm infatuated with you."

Susan is stunned, surprised and strangely excited. Her marriage seems years ago.

"Your time at the gym, Susan, has transformed you into my secret Greek goddess."

"I'm not the woman who went to you to get a divorce. I've adored making love to you since my gift. Your lasso has turned you into an incredible lover. You reawakened passions in me that were dead. Forgive me if I've been demanding or cross at times."

"Thank you, Susan, for your praise. You've changed my

life. I've joined a gym because of your example; you've improved my sex life wondrously, and strengthened my muscles and self-image."

He walks over to his couch, kisses her deeply and buries his face in her breasts and worships them until she lifts his face and whispers," How much was that again?'

"$30,000 for a professional job."

"Let me think about it and I'll let you know at our next play-time. Today's session is on me, pardon the pun, my lover man." With each adoring look, she feels her power grow.

At the close of their playtime, Handcock asks, "Did you send me the two cases of Rioja that were delivered yesterday?"

"Yes, and I've got another surprise. I bought a porno flick to get you even more excited before our next playtime."

"I don't need wine or a porno flick, only you," he says as they adjourn to his lavish bedroom and he hands her a glass of Rioja. She bends forward, pushes his thighs apart, adjusts his lasso and kisses, and sucks his erection. Then she turns his body, mounts him and buries his face in her breasts as she looks out the corner of her eye at the TV where bosomy women are engaged in sexual acts she had never considered.

As their lovemaking nears its end Susan finds herself moaning as she drives herself into Hancock and her writhing body implodes again and again and they collapse in bed. Later, she treats Hancock to an expensive dinner. When they return to his home, she strips and says, "I'm yours. Work your wonders on me as long as you want. I'm sleeping over. And the answer is yes.

"Yes, what?"

"Go ahead with your plan to make my husband disappear. We'll discuss terms in the morning. My lips and body will work their wonders on you tonight until you beg for mercy."

~~~ CHAPTER TWENTY ~~~

When Mitchener returns to his room, his phone rings. His heart races and he thinks it must be Sara, but realizes she has moved on with her life.

"Despite your reporting, the two-part series is generating interest, Mitch," says Rothman. "That should excite you, but you sound distracted."

"I guess I'm a worn-out workaholic."

"Well, I'm not surprised, but you're covered. Are you sure you're not in some kind of trouble down here?"

"Nope. Tell Angelica when she returns that I hope she had a successful trip."

Mitchener decides to walk through the ruins silently, soaking up the majesty and the mystery of this first explored Mayan site. Still dwarfed by the towering rainforest, he knows that it still holds many secrets. But its sense of serenity remains. It's not as expansive and spread out as Chichen Itza, but its intimacy captivates him as the days' pass.

Then, after writing the last segment of his series, he puts on his trunks and goes to the nearby pool. For Mitchener water always soothes his body and comforts his spirit. He recalls Angelica once said that water washes my aura and resets my electric field.

He remains lost in his watery world and sun for an hour before returning to his room where he winds up writing his series, after deciding to highlight the mysteries of Palenque.

Mitchener writes the site's original name was "Nachan" and although the subject of archaeological research since the 1920s when the temples and palaces were given their current names, yet its fame took off in 1949 with the discovery that the Temple of Inscriptions contained an internal stairway. Here, a triangular stone block and skeletons of Mayan warriors blocked the entrance to a vaulted crypt that held a stone sarcophagus covered by a large, rectangular stone slab weighing about five tons.

Opening it revealed the skeletal remains of a tall man, still bedecked with jewelry and pearls. His face was covered with a jade mask, nearby the jade pendant bearing the image of a god lay amid scattered beads that once made up a jade collar. With one exception at the ruins of Tikal, no Mayan edifice has been found that served as a tomb. The depiction on the lid of a barefoot man sitting on a flaming throne and seeming operating mechanical devices inside an elaborate chamber caused a sensation.

Only after he finished more reading at the library did he adjourn to the bar for a beer and he found himself thinking of Sara, recalling a scene:

"Did anyone ever tell you you're the most beautiful woman in the world?"

"Make it the most beautiful woman who ever lived."

"You are the most beautiful woman who ever lived."

"You say the sweetest things."

That night Michener decides to return to the hut of shaman Zak-kuk and his son Katu-Quila, who are joined in the circle by another shaman from a nearby Mayan community. As a young man, he was trained by his community's shaman to use the power of his Third Eye. In an attempt to accelerate his perceptions, the elder chiseled a shallow hole in the center of his forehead. Since that time, few could match his power to visualize the past, present and future.

The three sit in a circle and hold hands in the candle-lit hut. Copal incense burns. They chew the hallucinogenic mushroom Tenonanactl and close their eyes. The visiting shaman says quietly, "I feel as though this is Palenque around 2080 B.C."

As the vision unfolds one Mayan priest says, "You wish to know the story of our ancestors. Some 48 millenniums ago, the people we call Lemurians, the wise ones from Mu, a continent in the South Pacific, came here. Later, their home in that far-off place sank in a cataclysm. They recorded time in relation to the firmament. Unearthly beings gave them charts and crystal instruments and instructed them in their use.

"Their exact calculations required hundreds of years of work and study. As long as the record was maintained nightly no wrong could befall their people. That explains why these records are so important. Now, after the end of the fifth Mayan world, we time-keepers are free from this responsibility.

"Now we know the fourth dimension is opening humanity to new ways of living. A new race is destined to help us."

"Do you think our people understand this? Wise One," asks Mitchener.

"I do, but not as our ancestors did, who gave us the calendar."

"And sunlight?"

"The physical manifestation of pure cosmic light. It passes through your body and illuminates your soul."

~~~~ CHAPTER TWENTYONE ~~~~

The next evening Mitchener joins his shaman friends at a gathering:

A long bed of magenta-colored, red-hot coals glows. The short, old shaman, Zack-Kuku, stares resolutely into the darkness, his eyes focused on an unseen object. The firelight highlights his gray-streaked long hair that hangs loosely down his back. He wears his traditional white smock that reaches nearly to his feet. Watching him intently nearby is his young son, Katu-Quila, who sits cross-legged.

The chillum walks resolutely and slowly over the glowing, sparking coals. He has done this many times before. The ritual appears as if it could have taken place millenniums ago. Finally, the cool, damp earth meets his warm feet and he walks over to his son. "Only this way could I offset the calendar's bad omens for tomorrow."

Later, Mitchener, his pad on the table, sits down with Christopher who says, "Here's the science in a nutshell. When the sun's magnetic field shifts, it twists the earth off its axis, bringing earthquakes, floods and volcanic eruptions. The sun's magnetic field shifts five times every cosmic cycle. The Mayans believed the earth was destroyed four times."

Mitchener asks, "Why didn't you bring your wife?"

"First, she wanted to come. Then she didn't. Opposites attract, briefly. We're drifting farther and farther apart. If it wasn't for her personality, I would think she had a lover."

~~~~ CHAPTER TWENTYTWO ~~~~

As his secretary is dealing with a client, lawyer Jonathan Handcock answers the phone.

"We have him under surveillance. It's just a matter of time. Get the money ready," the Mexican gang leader says, "The men are in place. You know how to get the money to me." Click! What he fails to say is that if this ancient Mayan tomb is undisturbed, this venture could yield him a fortune.

Susan wishes this would end. The crazy dreams are beginning. I never knew I had a conscience, she thinks. Soon the divorce will go through, but Christopher's death must be confirmed first. Now I wonder if I my scheme to marry Handcock was a good one? I can't break off my affair with Charlene.

One day Handcock's bedroom is being painted and playtime is transferred to Susan's home. After she exhausts Handcock, he walks into the kitchen to refill his glass of wine. Humming and brimming with sexual satisfaction, he walks around the kitchen until he spots a basket of clothes. Atop it is a very large, elegant pink bra. It has large holes allowing nipples to protrude.

"Is this your bra, darling?" he asks, holding it up and examining it. "I don't recall this one. Is it a surprise?" Hancock says as he puts it around Susan's blouse for a joke. She pokes her finger through a hole in one cup and says, "No, it belongs to my neighbor, Charlene. Her washing machine is broken and I volunteered to do her washing until it's repaired. As you notice, we share one physical trait."

"They're not as wonderful as yours," says Handcock, returning the bra to the clothes basket.

"She's a wonderful next door neighbor. Her husband was killed recently in an automobile accident and I've tried to help her out. She's a 29-year-old, 6-foot-1, and I occasionally have her over for a drink. She's quite attractive. A red-head."

"Tell me when you have her over for a drink and I'll join you."

"I'll ask her if she can come at 6 p.m. on Thursday."

Susan finds she's enjoying more sexual pleasures recently than she's had in her whole life. She increases her verbal admiration of Handcock, but does not drop her charge for playtime. However, she purchases him fine wines, ties, shirts, a painting and other gifts. She even practices her looks of admiration in the mirror. I'm getting better at it, she thinks. She also tries to use his sexual fantasies in their playtimes and introduce new ideas, new themes, and finds that everything thrills him. He's spellbound. While he cannot get enough of her, she cannot get enough of Charlene. Her whole thought patterns are changing.

After she leaves Handcock's one day, she ponders her secret wedding plans with him. She decides to assume her husband will not return and to put aside his disappearance, which Handcock keeps hinting at, and concentrate on her new life, new possibilities and new passions.

That night she invites Charlene over for drinks and a romp. After a few glasses of wine, Charlene, wearing revealing shorts and a daring T-shirt, looks at the floor and says, "Could you do me a favor? I hired a private detective to look into my deceased husband's affairs. It turns out he was not only supporting the two of us, but a girlfriend. He even set up a secret bank account for her. While I tried to make ends meet, she was living high off him. She still had a substantial amount in her secret account. I feel less guilty about his accidental death in the car crash after that discovery, but the detective cost me a small fortune. Now everything costs me more than I anticipate.

"I'd be happy to give you a loan, Charlene. You know how I feel about you."

"I get a small pension from my deceased husband's employer, and fortunately my home is paid off. No mortgage payments."

"I guess it's secrets time," says Susan as she refills Charlene's glass of wine and looks down on her lover's full breasts bulging from her T-shirt. "Before I went to my present lawyer, Mr. Handcock, a girlfriend told me that her divorce charges were reduced for sexual favors and that he loved big breasted women. His fees were more than I expected, but when I met him I wore an expensive low-cut grown. I kept leaning forward as I spoke.

"As I left, he invited me out to dinner that night where, after a great meal, I discussed lowering his charges if we had playtime once a week. He agreed on my $300 charge and now we celebrate playtime twice a week. He wanted to increase it to three times, but I demurred. He adores me, but I have lost much of my interest in him since I met you."

Charlene laughs, throws her head back, and says, "I never would have guessed. Was it exciting? You're so beautiful I can see why he agreed to your arrangement. If I had any money, I'd pay to just be near you."

Susan rises and pulls Charlene's face to hers, kisses her passionately and says, "You say the sweetest things."

"It saved me thousands. He loves large breasts and cannot get enough of mine. And he no longer charges me for his work, which in my case is nearly finished as my divorce nears. He wants to marry me, but I want to leave things as they are. My loving feelings are for you, Charlene, not him.

"You have such a wonderful body," says Charlene, "such loving ways and you're such a giving person. You know how I feel about you. And I can't wait to get in bed with you tonight, Susan. You are so kind and passionate. You have given me undreamed of pleasures and have a special place in my heart. I was naughty tonight. No bra or panties."

"I thought I noticed some hairs winking at me when you put your knees up."

"Want to undress me?" asks Charlene.

After an hour of lovemaking, chatting and laughter, all their desires are fulfilled, and their bodies are exhausted. When Susan rises from the bed, she nearly falls. Charlene jumps up, catches her and they fall back in bed laughing and lose themselves in each other's arms as they satisfy each other's desires again.

On Thursday night at Susan's place, she opens the door and Handcock enters, wearing the tie she gave him and his new pin-striped suit. Susan wears her pressed new dress with a deep décolletage and pulls him to her and presses her breasts against him as she kisses him. Handcock looks over her shoulder while she makes small talk and 6-foot-1 Charlene stands to greet him. He's shocked by her beauty, her flaming red hair, and magnificent bust above a trim, voluptuous body. Her full, milky breasts bulge over the top of a low cut, fashionable cocktail dress. Her innocent smile is radiant. He feels weak in the knees as her height dominates him and her beauty overcomes him.

Susan winks secretly at Charlene and leaves to get three glasses of red wine. Within minutes the three are deep in conversation, laughing and exchanging tales like old friends, Handcock recalling divorce and legal cases, while Susan contents herself refilling wine glasses and serving snacks.

Handcock's face becomes flushed after this third glass of wine and then Susan appears with a brandy snifter of expensive cognac and asks his opinion.

"Excellent. Absolutely superb."

"It should be for what I paid for it," says Susan with a smile. "You've been so kind to Susan," Charlene says. "She's such a wonderful person and so loving. I could not have a more wonderful or beautiful next-door neighbor."

"I was just about to complement your beauty and say the same thing about you," says Handcock while he takes her hand in his. "You are a delight to my eyes."

"Susan told me about your playtimes together and the discount that you've kindly given her and how she's enhanced your sexual prowess with her gift lasso. You've been so generous in this difficult time for her."

Handcock is shocked, amused and then strangely aroused she knows all this. Charlene smiles so innocently as she retells Susan's tale that Handcock finds it impossible to take offense.

"She's a beautiful friend who has graciously shared herself with me and I'm honored," says Handcock as Susan refills his cognac and kisses him on the forehead.

"He's the most wonderful man I've ever met," says Susan with a practiced adoring look. "I cannot express what his kindness has been to me."

Handcock swirls his cognac and looks at Charlene.

"I guess we don't have any secrets, do we? It's such a pleasure to chat with you both and share our secrets."

Charlene takes his hand, looks him sweetly in the eyes, and says, "You've made such a success of your life."

"Well, thank you. Now could I ask you a question, Charlene? After Susan's and my last playtime here, I noticed a bra with elegant holes for nipples in her clothes basket. She said it was yours."

"Oh, yes," says Charlene excitedly, "It is so kind of Susan to wash my clothes while my washing machine is being repaired. She is such a giving woman. She has been so good to me since my husband died in a horrible automobile accident. I was driving, but it was not my fault."

She lifts her dress over a left, san-tanned thigh revealing a light scar and fancy bikini underwear.

"It was difficult for me, the recovery that is, and then discovering he was supporting his mistress in high style. But enough about me. Susan says you questioned her about my bra."

Handcock, breathing heavily and his pulse racing, is speechless.

"Frankly, I was amazed by the size of your bra. You must be very proud of your bounteous breasts."

"Now that my husband's dead, I am. Excuse me for a moment. Susan, can I use your bedroom for a moment?"

"Sure, Charlene. You know where it is."

When she stands up, she towers over Handcock, sitting on the couch.

Susan returns, takes his brandy snifter, refills it and kisses his lips lightly with a knowing smile.

"Isn't she wonderful?"

"She's a busty goddess, just like you."

Charlene returns to the room, kicks off her heels and stands close to Handcock in her red bra and matching bikini underwear.

"It's my surprise. Susan said you'd like it."

"I do. Oh, God, yes, I do. You are the most voluptuous creature I've ever seen … beside my wonderful Susan."

"I'll make you a deal, a Susan deal," she says as she unfastens her lacy bra that accentuates her already full breasts. Her magnificent breasts with long, tempting nibbles fall forward.

"If you'll forgive me I've never seen such large, dark pink, and I must say attractive areolas, and such full, milky white breasts. Magnificent!"

Charlene comes, pushes Handcock down on the couch, smiles and gives him her warm bra.

"A gift to remember me by."

As Handcock holds up her bra to kiss it, a cloud of her perfume overcomes him and Charlene gently pulls his head forward, burying his face in her huge, warm breasts for about ten seconds and then pulls them away.

"I never expected this," says Handcock.

"Neither did I. Susan is a woman of the world. She has taught me so much about living and loving. Because of recent tragedies, death and financial difficulties, I'll make you a deal. I'll have a play-time with you for $500, but only once. You can worship my breasts as long as you like. But that's it. Everything but the sexual act. I know that you and Susan are close and I've never done this before. I don't know if you're a weirdo. I don't think you're one, but I feel I can trust you because of Susan. Am I right?"

"Of course, my dear. I know I'm older and certainly not handsome, have a limp and one who you might not chose to share yourself with if you didn't trust me. Ask Susan, if I'm trustworthy. Next Tuesday? Susan can drop you off. I want to show her my new painted bedroom."

"I don't want to come between you and Susan."

As Charlene leaves, Susan enters and says, "I'll call a cab. You're in no shape to drive. I thought you'd enjoy meeting her and I'll be happy to drop her off next Tuesday.

"Make it the morning. I could not concentrate at work. Say 10 a.m."

"We're still on for Thursday and Saturday?" asks Susan and unzips his fly.

"Come in the kitchen for a moment," she says. When they reach the kitchen, she kneels and slips her fingers and lips around his tumescent member, and works it until a silver stream hits her dress.

"There, feel better?" She kisses him and says, "Wait until our next playtime. It will be memorable. I don't know how to thank you, darling. Remember, adorable one, you're all mine."

After Handcock leaves, Susan yells, "Are you still in the bedroom."

"Come in and find out."

When Susan enters, Charlene jumps from behind the door and throws her to bed and pins her arms. Then she kisses her passionately and says, "Now we'll share our bodies and our love. And I have a new toy to surprise you with once I rip your clothes off your loving, wonderful body."

In the morning, Susan awakes first, brews coffee and makes a cheese omelet before awaking slumbering Charlene with a kiss on the forehead. Over breakfast, Charlene says, "Your gift was fun, a great idea. So was the $500 tag for playtime. He's such a nice man. If I had not met you, Susan, this would never have happened. You've given me confidence, a new outlook on life, a stronger body with your gift of a gym membership, flaming red hair and, most important, love."

"Now let's plan your playtime," says Susan.

Later, as scheduled, Susan pulls the car up to the curb in front of Handcock's lavish home, pats Charlene on the shoulder and smiles.

"Good luck, darling, you know the plan. Take it slow and easy. Don't be nervous."

"I am nervous. But I'll do my best. I'll call you when I

want to be picked up."

Susan gives Charlene a peek on the cheek. As she drives away she reflects on her new-found powers and passions. Her life is so different, so full of surprises, and love.

Charlene rings the bell, waits and then Handcock opens the door and puts his hands on her shoulders.

"All dressed up for me. You look gorgeous. I could not sleep last night. You're a dream come true. Come in. Would you like a glass of wine to relax? With heels on, you have a commanding presence over me."

"Soon we'll be on the same level," says Charlene, smiling. "Don't feel nervous at all. I hope that we don't rush things, that we get to know each other slowly."

"Of course, my darling," says Handcock, his pulse racing, his heart beat soaring and his loins on fire. "Excuse me for a moment." Handcock returns with a dozen red roses wrapped with a white bow. Five one-hundred dollar bills are attached. He hands them to her and kisses her for the first time. She slips slowly into this new, unfamiliar role and finds it's thrilling her. Her perfume overpowers them both.

"Oh, thank you. What a wonderful welcome."

"I want you to feel at home in my house … and my bed."

"Do you have to be back at the office at any special time?"

"My time is your time," says Handcock as he passes her a glass of wine and puts on romantic music.

"I hope to please you," says Charlene innocently.

After they chat and finish their wine, Charlene cackles sweetly, "I'd like to have you undress me slowly and cover my nude body with kisses."

His fingers tremble as he unzips her tight dress, unsnaps her bra, and lets her dress fall to the floor. Then he puts his hands inside her bikini underwear and it drops. He trembles as he kisses her back and then his fingers explore her breasts. It takes both hands to encircle her one breast as he suckles it.

"Let's move to your lovely bed. I know you love my breasts, but I want you to start your kissing, licking and caressing with my toes and work up my body until I tell you to stop. I want you to know and worship all my curves."

Handcock's passion for her body amazes her. This older gentleman is tireless as his lips and hands caress and kiss every inch of her body. At last, she says, smiling, "Now, adorable man, my breasts are yours to fondle and enjoy."

Three hours later, Charlene phones Susan to pick her up. In the car, Charlene says, "I hope he got his money's worth."

Later, relaxing on Susan's patio in the nude and chatting, Charlene says, "I got a return engagement."

"Engagement?"

"Yes, we made an engagement to meet again for playtime. I didn't fall in love," she says laughing. "I'm with the one I love now. I followed your plan to a T with one exception. I felt guilty just before I left and pumped him into quick ecstasy. My nipples hurt after all that massaging, nibbling, suckling and you name it. But I'm saving myself to share my bliss with you.

"Without his lasso, his release came quickly. It surprised me. We talked during much of our playtime and at times it seemed like he just enjoyed looking at my body before rolling over and again worshipping my breasts.

"What's the plan for our next playtime?"

"I've got some ideas, but first perhaps you'd like to show me your soft bed."

"I had three hours of foreplay. I'm ready," says Charlene as she pulls Susan to her and kisses her longingly and deeply as her tongue explores her mouth. After intense lovemaking, the lovers relax, their passion spent, their writhing bodies in a state of serenity.

"I've got a confession to make," says Susan. "My original plan was to divorce my husband; our marriage had died. Then I met Handcock, we became intimate, and I got a discount on my fees. He's a great talker, and as I've come to know him, a lonesome man. I wonder if anyone has really listened to him before. My body satisfies him as does my listening to his tales. He told me about his limp and then went on to explain in detail how he got even with the gang member who attacked him. He had him murdered. As he said that the scales of justice balanced even again. It was my gift to society.

"Then he noted that I had a $350,000 life insurance policy on my husband and he knew a man who could make him disappear. He asked where he was staying in some little Mexican village and for how long.

"That was some time ago. The plan had two options. We could wed secretly and split the $350,000 or wed and remain friends and lovers. Our arrangement continues to our satisfaction. Handcock is rich, although I don't know how rich he is."

"He sounds like a man to be reckoned with," says Charlene as she massages Susan's thigh lovingly.

"True in a way, but I feel much more in control now. I know I can fulfill our desires and his. One idea was to wed him and we'd each live separately. Another idea was I'd keep my house; you'd sell yours for its income and you could live with me. We could fulfill Handcock's desires and that $175,000 would set us up well financially."

Susan lets her words hang on the air as Charlene says, "Either way, we cannot lose. If his plan succeeds, you'll get $175,000. If it fails, you'll be divorced soon and we'll live together. I'll sell my house if I can live with you."

Susan runs her hands through Charlene's flaming red hair and looks lovingly at her voluptuous body.

"I can see how Handcock loves just looking at your curvaceous body. It thrills me. Truly it does. I cannot look at you without wanting to touch you," Susan says as she runs her fingers lightly over Charlene's breast and sees her nipple stiffen.

"I owe it all to you, Susan. All of it."

Susan's heart opens and she pulls Charlene to her body and she suckles her breast. Charlene says, "Let me fulfill all your wishes" as her tongue enters Susan again.

～～ CHAPTER TWENTYTHREE ～～

Meanwhile, one night in the Mayan shaman's hut, the elderly chillum, Zak-kuk, his son, Katu-Quila, are joined in the circle by Christopher and Brunel. Both Mayans welcome the couple warmly. Brunel is amazed how warm their welcoming hands are, but feels a tinge of fear after the long ride through the dark rainforest As they chat easily, Brunel slowly feels more comfortable in this simple hut. Then the two invite Christopher and Brunel to sit cross-legged. Earlier, Christopher explained in great detail how the ceremony would unfold, assured her she was in no danger and kidded her that this is just the beginning of their adventures.

The elderly shaman lights copal incense in a pipe. It flames and gives off a pungent smell. He chews the hallucinogenic Tenonanactl mushrooms, hands some to his son and his eyelids close. The ceremony is repeated as Christopher and Brunel take part. The elder shaman allows extra time for Brunel's fears to evaporate.

The vision unfolds:

They feel a white light flooding their bodies as a mystical door opens. The elderly chilam says, "It feels like it's the Yucatan town of Mani. A voice is telling me the year is about 1660 and the priest is well known to all Mayans. He is Fray Diego de Landa, who has done us much evil."

Before their eyes stands Fray Diego de Landa, a Spanish priest, dressed in black friar's robes. He holds a silver cross above his head that flashes as he waves it wildly. A brilliant fire blazes in the night behind him, illuminating Spanish nobles, soldiers, and behind them Mayans who push forward at a square's edge.

De Landa's eyes shine with fanaticism as he shouts, "Idolaters! Only an Inquisition can cleanse your sinful souls" and crimson flames leap skyward.

The priest's black robes flow upward in the heat as he walks to the pile of 5,000 idols and hurls them viciously into the fire. The Mayans cry out in disbelief as De Landa turns, grabs a soldier and shouts, "Help me, you fool."

Sweat pours off De Landa's face as he grabs a pile of deer skins covered with Mayan glyphs. The Mayans gasp and surge forward. A tall, muscular Mayan priest lunges at De Landa, his eyes blazing with hate. Beside him stands his wife, who is holding their child. She screams and falls, landing hard trying to protect her child while the crowd presses forward.

As De Landa feeds the leaping flames with precious Mayan codices, the Mayan priest grabs a handful of the sacred deer skins from De Landa and throws the precious Mayan writings over his head to Mayans behind him. De Landa pulls a knife and slashes the Mayan priest's leg. As he falls, a soldier grabs his long hair, and De Landa slashes his throat.

The Mayan's wife, her eyes filled with horror, races forward, hands her baby to a Mayan woman, and cradles the head of her dead husband, sobbing and screaming, lost in rage and horror.

The scene shifts. Flames illuminate a purple birthmark on the left arm of the murdered Mayan's wife. The scene fades slowly while Brunel feels her heart beating wildly, filled with a lost love. Tears stream down her face and she sobs. Christopher holds her close to comfort her.

Other visions unfold and dissolve. After long minutes, the elderly chilam touches their foreheads and their eyes open.

"Where do these visions come from?" asks Brunel.

"The spirits of our ancestors open the windows of our souls." Later, the four enjoy hot chocolate and discuss the visions before the old jeep's journey back to the hotel. At Brunel's room, Christopher hesitates and asks, "Shall I come in? I know it's been a difficult night for you. I had hoped tonight might give you pleasure or answer questions."

"It's been emotional, but I wanted to talk to you about the Mayan vision."

Christopher sits on her bed as they review the visions. Then Brunel says, "I felt it was us in the vision. I felt my heart breaking."

"Do you believe in reincarnation?"

"I never gave it a thought," says Brunel. "But I felt that was us in that vision. I felt my heart breaking. And there is something else."

Brunel unbuttons her blouse and throws it on the bed. She points to her right arm.

"See."

"See what?" says Christopher. Brunel leaves the room, wets a cloth and returns. She wipes off the makeup on her right arm, revealing a birthmark.

Christopher examines it closely and says, "It's just like the one I saw in the vision."

"I've wondered about it since I was a young girl. I felt it held a message for me, but I did not know what that message was. Now I do. It was a reminder of a long-lost love, you."

She buries her head in his chest, lies back on the bed and pulls him to her.

"This wasn't the adventure I expected. Sleep beside me. I'm exhausted."

Before the dawn, Brunel rolls over, kisses Christopher on the cheek, and then pulls his face to hers as she kisses him softly and then more passionately.

"If you think I was a romantic tiger after the fireworks display, when I'm finished with you, you won't be able to stand up."

"Promise?"

Brunel sweeps her long hair down his body, pausing briefly to lick, kiss and suck as his body comes alive. As the minutes' pass, she slowly, gently excites him while her juices slip down her thighs. He moans and lovingly plays with her hair, keeping her lips on his flesh and running his fingers over her soft skin and her smooth curves. His emotional energy surges through him as she arches her back while he rides her into ecstasy again and again.

~~~CHAPTER TWENTYFOUR~~~

Mitchener checks out of Las Canadas Hotel and feels like a great weight has been lifted. He realizes that he could not bear another day there with its painful memories. After taking two sleeping pills, he sleeps through the night and a sense of peace greets him when he awakes.

He downs a steamy cup of coffee, enjoys a light breakfast and picks up his light suitcase and even lighter computer and heads for a nearby hotel with the cool, usually empty pool.

After signing in at the desk, he tosses his suitcase on the bed, puts his computer on a desk and slips into his swimming trunks. On the way to the pool he picks up a paperback novel. He's the sole guest at the pool as he throws his towel over a plastic chaise lounge and plunges into the pool. He swims laps for awhile and then floats lazily, feeling the silky water caress his body. He shuts his eyes and enjoys the heat of the sun.

When he opens them, a voluptuous vision in a perfectly cut dark blue swimming suit appears.

"Mitch!" the vision shouts. "Mitch. Hey, gingo! It's Angelica."

She reaches down and her full breasts struggle to remain in her dark blue suit with slim blue straps. The suit accents her shapely hips and legs as she pulls up a chaise lounge next to his. He swims over and walks quickly toward Angelica. Just as he reaches out to embrace her, she sidesteps his outstretched arms and effortlessly tosses him into the pool.

"Whee!" she shouts as she jumps high into the air and performs a perfect cannon ball next to him. He inhales a mouthful of water, gasps and grabs the side of the pool.

"How do you like my new swimming suit? I paid a fortune for it in Paris."

"I like what's in it more."

She pulls his body against hers, takes his face in her hands and kisses his forehead, and his lips.

"What a wonderful surprise!"

"I felt you needed me. I know I need you."

Her auburn hair is tired up in her pink bows, with a big curl sweeping over one eye. She reaches up and undoes a bow. Her hair falls enticingly over her throat and bosom.

"I need your love. It fills my body with a new electro-magnetic compulsion," says Angelica teasingly.

"Your presence fills me with hope and love." "Good," says Angelica as her heart beats faster.

He laughs and goes to dunk her, wrestling with her shoulders as he kicks hard and presses down with his full force. She escapes his grip, thrusts his arms upward and pushes down on his shoulders, sending his body to the bottom of the pool. Her vise-like grip holds his more powerfully muscled body under water. For a mini-second, he fears she's drowning him. Then panic seizes him, he kicks hard and struggles wildly. He realizes he cannot escape. Then, in a second, Angelica releases her vice-like grip and pushes him to the surface, where she laughs as his lungs gasp for air.

"See how strong my love is for you."

"I never realized your strength. You could have drowned me if you wished."

"It was showing the strength of my love for you."

"I need to be reminded. Forgive me."

"If you do forget it, I will overpower you again," she says smiling, her eyes sparkling.

When they leave the pool, a tired Mitchener swims to the far end of the pool, climbs the ladder and walks back to his chaise lounge. Angelica springs from the pool and lands standing next to her chaise lounge.

"How did you get your strength? Your body is lithe, slender and graceful."

"I'm glad that you think so. Don't waste your energy trying to resist me."

They sit under a sun umbrella and Mitch marvels that they're back together. He fills her in on his adventure with Christopher and Manuel at the unlooted Mayan ruins. When a waiter arrives, they order Tequila Sunrises and enjoy each other's presence. Soon their drinks arrive.

"To all love, but especially our love," says Angelica, her eyes twinkling approvingly.

"I am full of joy to be with you again," says Mitchener with a smile.

She kisses his hand softly.

"When I come to your room after I shower, I'll slip into something that I hope you'll like. I bought it in Paris. Then I'll give you an aural bath. An aura is the electromagnetic field that radiates from your physical body. I can see your aura now. It displays your emotional, mental and physical states. Yours is blue indicating peace, serenity and calmness, susceptibility to spiritual development.

"When I first saw you, Mitch, I felt this magnetic attraction. Some think this attraction is in the genitals, but it's in the heart. My heart opened to you and I hoped yours would open to me. Later, I felt our hearts merging when we made love.

"In your auric bath my hands will circle your flesh without touching it, filling you with peace and love. The bath will energize and empower you. I promise. But it comes with a price. We are both tired. After your aura bath, we will sleep. Later, you will take me to a wonderful spot near water where we will make love under the sun and later under the moon. Do you know of some falls around here?"

"I know of a wondrous spot."

"An aura bath will be my first gift to you on this trip. I wish to never again to leave you. No matter what happens. I want you to love me as I love you. Say it."

Mitchener looks in Angelica's bottomless brown eyes and is filled with love. Yet he cannot deny a tinge of fear, thinking she could have drowned me.

"I love you, Angelica," he says as their first meeting, first day, the dream of the Egyptian goddess and her childlike innocence captives him in his thoughts. Other memories flood his mind: her response when he gives her the radiant opal and says, "This loving gift touches my heart. I want to savor every moment with you tonight." Or her words: "Now I know your secret desires. I will fulfill them. As you unite with me I will fulfill and share your passion." As the visions fade, he realizes her power was always expressed in love.

"I do love you," says Mitchener snapping out of his dreamlike trance.

Her piercing brown eyes seem to look into his heart as a playful smile spreads easily across her lips. She tells stories of her time in Paris, indicates she is tiring after long travels and says, "Let's return to our rooms. Let me show you my Paris outfit and then I'll gave your aura a bath."

Later, she knocks and stands before him in a crimson satin gown that caresses her shoulders in flowing lines, falls in a V-shape to her rounded, full breasts, tucks in at her waist and flows gracefully over her hips, legs and falls to her white sandals. She puts her hands on her hips and says, "How do you like it?"

"Ravishing. Right out of Vogue magazine. It's perfect with your flashing radiant opal."

Her unyielding gaze holds him as bliss fills him "I feel your bliss too," she says. "Undress me."

"Yes, My Lady. It is my pleasure to undress you with these humble hands. Forgive me if the sight of your beauty arouses my desire and my body responds."

"I did not say embrace me. I said undress me."

Why does she always surprise me? he wonders. He moves closer and the pungent smell of her perfume overcomes him and his breathing becomes more rapid. Mitchener moves closer, drops to his knees and growls.

"Careful, my little lion cub," she says as her crimson dress falls to the floor. "Please remove my expensive, Parisian black lace panties with your hands, not your teeth."

As it hits the floor, he pulls her against his body. "Later."

Then his eyes explore her soft shoulders, perfect shoulder bones, unblemished skin on her chest and the high cleft of her bosom, her white breasts pushed up by her black lacy bra that barely hides her pink nipples and aureole. Her radiant opal flashes its rainbow colors into his eyes as he watches her nipples stiffen, and her aureoles darken. He takes her gently, puts her on his wide bed and pins her arms above her head.

"You wonderful animal. My little lion cub. You want to devour me, don't you?" says Angelica.

"You are driving me wild with desire."

"Yes, I enjoy driving you mad, but, no," she pauses for emphasis, "I don't want to tease you. Take off your smelly socks, your khaki shorts and your T-shirt."

He follows her orders, adjourns to his bathroom, and splashes his face with aftershave.

"Good," she says smiling, "I love to see your body respond to my love. It makes my radiant opal shine brighter. Forgive me for putting off our pleasure. It's been weeks since we made love. I wanted to wait until tomorrow. That was wrong. Neither of us would have slept tonight.

"Shut your eyes. Envision my body as a dazzling light, with its warm orbs, its secret, welcoming places and its soft flesh. Feel my love awakening new emotions and unknown passions. Feel the warmth of my presence drawing you into me."

After their lovemaking, Mitchener relaxes in a state of ecstasy he can achieve only with Angelica.

In the morning Mitchener decides to take Angelica to the cascades of Misol-Ha, cascades of thundering white water and turquoise pools surrounded by lush tropical rainforest. Manuel drops them off, and promises to return later.

They stop for photos at one waterfall and then 20-foot white-water cataracts. Where the cascades fall on rocks or fallen trees, the blue water coats them with white, sparkling limestone.

Mitchener leads Angelica down a winding path through the lush jungle to a spot where a 20-foot waterfall descends into a wide pool with overhanging trees. On one side the falls plunges thunderously against a clam-shaped rock sending spray over an aqua-marine pool. He leads Angelica to a cave behind the waterfall, where the waterfall sends powerful echoes, water drips from the ceiling and small branches fall into a pool far below.

At one point the dirt trail curves to a secluded pool of placid water. The two strip off their khaki clothes. Mitchener watches lovingly as Angelica's curvaceous body emerges from her blue bathing suit and slips easily into the cool waters, shouting "This is heaven." They swim lazily in the pool, while a brilliant sun shines down, until Angelica finds a wide limestone rock and motions for Mitchener to sit beside her. He kisses her as she leans back and supports herself with her arms. Mitchener gently slips her bathing suit off her shoulders, massages her breasts and sucks her nipples. "Never stop. I never get enough of you. You'll do anything to get an aural bath. Well, you've earned it."

She motions to a shaded rock. They swim over to it and Angelica assures herself that they are alone. She tugs at his swimsuit and he slips out of it and lies back in the sun.

"Water is a wonderful element to clear emotional energies," says Angelica. "It soothes the body and comforts the spirit. Water washes your aura and refreshes your spirit. Water helps you clear away emotional debris and reset your electromagnetic field. Water is one of the planet's most sacred elements. From it flows the river of all life. I am here to heal you from a past love, but you must do your part. I can do much to end this heartbreak for you."

Her hands move slowly above his body. He feels an energy field warm his body and his nerve endings. Angelica continues moving her hands without touching his body, only his aura, as the minutes' pass and a great sense of peace fills him. Above his solar plexus, Angelica feels a block. She knows this is the center of his emotions, concentrates the energy flowing from her hands, quickens its frequencies to decrystalize its blockages and allow the emotional body to release its blockages.

A mystical vision of Sara floods Mitchener's mind as she pleads, "Release my spirit, Mitch. Remember our love and release all doubts concerning it. Feel my love flow into you. Move on with your life with my blessings and love."

Tears stream down Mitchener's face.

"Every tear you shed adds time to your life," says Angelica. "Release your feelings. To cry is to have a liberating tonic."

He lies on the rock in silence while tears continue streaming down his face.

"Now I know why you brought me here," she says. "This is our spot. This is your gift to me, my lion cub, and my gift to you."

Mitchener slips on his swimsuit, Angelica pulls up hers and they walk to a shaded spot. Mitchener takes a blanket from his backpack, spreads it and they relax silently until Manuel returns with the car.

That night after dinner Angelica takes Mitchener by the hand and leads him to a remote small patio on the hotel's roof. They talk about the wonders of this place and their good fortune to be near Palenque. Angelica tells new stories of Paris, her sales, the food and how she missed him. Only then does he mention his aura bath.

"Thanks for my aura bath. I think you realize how much it meant to me. You know I love you."

"Say it."

"I love you, Angelica."

The moon rises slowly and full over the silhouetted rainforest. The light fragrance of the lush rainforest rides the breeze. They lie back in each other's arms on a chaise lounge and look at the cratered moon.

"The air is so clear here," says Mitchener. Are we in a sacred area?"

"Yes, it's a sacred area. Are you ready to take me under the stars, Mitch?"

"The breeze has kept the stinging little monsters away so far," admits Mitchener.

"First, I want you to see me in these magical moonbeams."

Mitchener gets up as she moves his chaise lounge. She puts

hers in the perfect spot for him to see her in the moon beams. Then she slips off her clothes and relaxes, peering into his eyes as the moon illuminates her dark eyes, pinned up auburn hair, her soft, feminine shoulders, her swooping, milky breasts, her stomach, curly mound, shapely thighs and legs and magenta painted toe nails.

Minutes pass in silence. Mitchener's breathing increases as his chest rises and falls. She smiles.

"Now envision how I can arouse your passions. Do you have new desires? Envision them. Do you want me to create new sensations, new experiences? Say nothing. I'm receiving your visions now. Yes, yes, you do have some new wishes. What an active mind. I will transform your body into a higher octave of energy that nourishes your whole multidimensional being. We'll begin here and then go to your room. First, stand and let me undress you."

He stands, his clothes fall to the floor, and her warm body is pressed against his as Angelica whispers in her ear, "May my love bring you great joy. May my passion fulfill you."

Soon they are forced to adjourn to her bedroom, where she keeps her focus on his eyes as she slips into bed and embraces him. Her loving energy overpowers him as their bodies rhythmically rise and fall and Angelica whispers, "Slowly, my love. We have all night. It fills me with love to have found you. When I first created electromagnetic responses to fulfill your wishes, I did this with my mind. Now I use my heart."

CHAPTER TWENTYFIVE

The hotel clerk at the Las Canadas Hotel answers the phone and says, "Momentito, por favor" and transfers the call to Christopher's room.

"Hola."

"Who's this?' Brunel asks sweetly, recognizing the voice of Christopher's wife.

"Who's this?"

"His wife. Is Mr. Christopher there?"

"Honey, it's for you."

"Hello, he says while a wave of disbelief shoots through Susan's nervous system, shocking her into silence.

"Surprised it's me?"

"What's your address and mother's first name?" He answers correctly and wonders what's up?

"The hotel clerk told me yesterday you weren't there."

"I had checked out, but changed my mind and checked back in at a lower rate."

"I've filed for a divorce. If uncontested, it should be finalized by your return."

"Our marriage died some years ago. You have my blessing if that's what you want."

Christopher feels shocked and then relieved. Her nagging has killed his feelings of love even if she paid most of the bills.

"When are you returning?"

"I'm staying on for awhile."

"Thanks for the call. Stay in touch," says Christopher.

Susan remains stunned. She thought everything had gone so smoothly. Handcock had talked her into her husband's murder and arranged it, not me, she thought. She decided not to think about it. She takes a warm bath and relaxes. Then she calls Handcock.

"I just called my husband's hotel again to ensure that he was missing. He answered the phone. I couldn't believe it. I was shocked into silence."

"You're shocked? What about me? Give me time to check this out. If our target is still alive, he won't be for long."

CHAPTER TWENTYSIX

Christopher decides he needs a change of scene as he converses with Brunel at breakfast in the hotel. As he drinks his coffee he smiles and says "What do you think?"

"After last night, I'm ready to go wherever you wish."

"Good. I've made arrangements at a hotel and I've rented a car which should be here in about an hour. It's a beautiful day for a drive. Up to it?"

"Aren't you going to tell me where we're going?"

"I can't pronounce it."

During a bumpy ride, down dirt roads, Christopher learns why Brunel left her husband, who enjoyed beating her. Marriage reveals many secrets, Christopher thinks as small pueblos and the verdant rainforests pass.

"Have you ever considered that he might try to have you killed to stop his payments to you?"

"I've just started to enjoy my new-found wealth. Don't spoi it."

Christopher has made arrangements at a hotel a short drive from the Mayan ruins of Dzibilchaltun, meaning "the place of stone writing." It's considered by some to be the mother of the Mayan civilization because of its long history. Mayans lived here from at least 300 B.C. up to the time of the Spanish Conquest. More than 8,000 buildings reputedly once stood in its 10 square miles. Its relics mirror its long history.

One Mayan structure is unique in that its top platform offers a perfect view of all points east and west. Twice annually on the equinox the rising sun shines through the portal of the Temple of the Dolls, named for relics found there. People from around the world come to witness this event, says Christopher, as they stand in the portal and he kisses Brunel. The two look down on the ancient scabe, a Mayan dirt road lined with tropical forest that stretches to the horizon.

Then they walk the trails amid a profusion of flora and fauna before going to the Cenote Xlacah that holds in its waters a fish found nowhere else. Locals and tourists often sit above its rim and peer far down into its mysterious waters, pondering the enigmas of this ancient empire.

Along the trail, Christopher attempts to kiss Brunel's cheek, but she laughs and pushes him away as a boy rushes up to them, grabs Brunel's hand and says, "Momentito."

The young Mexican, with wide brown eyes, reaches in his pocket and withdraws a small, carved object. He spits on it, pulls a cloth from his pocket, and wipes it, revealing what appears to be a crystal skull. It gleams when a beam of sunlight falls on it.

"Feels warm," says Brunel as she hands it to Christopher, who examines it and recalls that these crystal skulls are reputed channels for spiritual energy and healing. Recently, ancient and modern skulls have generated interest because of their connection to the Mayan people.

"It looks spooky to me," says Brunel, "real spooky."

"Imagine that you could look into its visions and see the past and the future. The Mayans believe that the past and future exist all around us. At the Mexican Day of the Dead skulls represent death, regeneration and ancestral energy called astral-life energy."

"It's beautifully carved," Brunel admits, confused by Christopher's words.

"Quanto es, muchacho?" asks Christopher.

Christopher, confused by his Spanish reply, turns to Brunel and says, "Give him forty bucks."

Brunel hands him a wad of bills and Christopher counts out $40 as the young boy's eyes gleam.

"Donde descubrise eso, chico?" says Christopher, making up his Spanish.

"Deseo poco mas," says the young bargainer.

Christopher gives him three more dollars and the excited

youth runs off.

After getting lost in the ruins, with the skull safely tucked away in Brunel's pack, they ask directions from a man reading a book entitled "Secrets of the Maya Chakra Temples." He explains that during the equinoxes the temple activates all chakra centers, adding this temple is a major crystal skull channeling site in the Americas. It's supposedly the anchoring site for the Pleiades star cluster.

~~~ CHAPTER TWENTYSEVEN ~~~

After their return Christopher introduces Brunel to Mitchener and Angelica. Later, they set off one night with Manuel along the dirt road that winds through the rainforest. At the hut Angelica meets the Mayan visionary shaman, Zak-kuk, 62, short, with gray-streaked long hair, piercing eyes and wearing a white smock. Next to him stands his son, 30, Katu-Quila, resembling a younger version of his father.

Mitchener explains to Angelica the ritual and then the elderly shaman lights copal incense that flames. The four chew the hallucinogenic Tenonanactl mushrooms, and all eyelids grow heavy and then close.

"Let me tell you of how we look at Palenque," says young Katu-Quila as the group sits on the ground in a circle. "Palenque, or Nah Chan as we call it, is revered by our elders as an ancient university. This is shown by spherical and jade objects held in the skeletal hands of Lord Pacal and on his sarcophagus. He died here in the year 683 A.D. They indicate that he had mastered the cosmic implications of movement and measure to transcend Time. These objects symbolize the inner and outer balancing of the cosmic or sacred mind.

"In his tomb are portrayed the Nine Lords of Time, connected with vast periods of time. They are there to assist him in his journey to the Underworld and rebirth."

How could I overlook these views of my chilam friends for my articles? Mitchener wonders.

Katu-Quila continues, "Yesterday we met with a group of Solar Initiates who were here to initiate their crystal skulls to Great Father Sun, just as the ancient Mayan priests did on a special Mayan day, the Day of the Spiritual Mayan Warrior. They were here fulfilling a prophecy about ancient Mayan skulls.

"In our ceremony at dawn yesterday the sun rose and a deafening roar or chorus seemed to signal us to begin. The group chanted powerful mantras before the skulls standing in a row on an altar illuminated by the Sun that blessed us with pink light.

It was a wonderful moment. Our Mayan name for crystal skulls means light or brightness. We said a Mayan prayer to the Sun at dawn:

Father Sun give me strength. Father Sun make me wise, Father Sun make me into a seed, Father Sun make me eternal.

"You call our sacred sites archaeological zones. We think energy impulses still beat at their hearts. The trees whisper and their energy lives on. The Conquistadors brought only chaos and death. "We Mayans know we are in crucial transitional times. The fate of the world is precariously balanced. We give dire warnings of what could happen if the people of the world are complacent. We must rise up and become guardians of our planet. As our shaman say, we must become Warriors of Light. As we enter the age of knowledge and peace we begin to understand the ancient knowledge of the cosmos. We know that intuition is inner teaching. We can interpret the coming earth changes. We are helping activate the world's ancient temples. We are using crystal skull cellular memory."

He looks at the group. "As you know we can bring back past life memories. It is even better with a crystal skull. We, the Mayans, are called the Masters of Time."

After a long silence, Katu-Quila, his long black hair shining in the candlelight, asks, "Father may I add some thoughts?"

"Of course, my son, speak freely."

"Crystal skulls from the Himalayas and Tibet have different historic fates than those skulls from the Americas. In Asia, they were lost for eons in caves or kept hidden in monasteries recently destroyed by the invading Chinese. Ours passed into Mayan folklore in Central America.

"Today, the modern world uses crystals in their computers and sensitive equipment. The crystal skulls were our ancestors' computers and portals into space and time. We used them as oracles, and in ceremony and prayer.

"While medieval Europe struggled with feudal lords, wars, diseases, and famines, Mayan astronomers were consulting the stars and calculating complex calendars. Then Christian conquerors forced us to hide those crystal skulls. They called them the devil's work.

"We are a people who used the beauty of nature that surrounded us to evolve our consciousness, minds and encourage a loving nature. Only with love can we begin a shift in consciousness. We must combine the marvels of nature with the technology of science.

"We have three Mayan worlds, the Upper World, the Middle Word and the Underworld. We know the foundation of spirituality is found in our hearts. When we meet another Mayan, our greeting means I am you and you are me.

"Crystal skulls have been on Earth since the beginning of time. They were the original star seeds from distant galaxies. In the early days of Lemuria many stellar consciousness's came here to play in crystal skulls. Atlanteans, too, stored information in crystal skulls. Shaman accessed this information by using their third eye chakras. Crystal skulls became our containers for living wisdom. They hold information in a cohesive way in their unchanging crystal matrix.

"We shaman attune to various bodies of energy, auras and chakras, to bring them into alignment."

Brunel slips a glance at the crystal skull in her pocket and decides to put it under her pillow at night.

"In the past crystal skulls were libraries of our histories of our extraterrestrial homes," says Katu-Quila. "They can become beacons for beings in other dimensions. Science is only now beginning to understand cosmic influences that cause Earth to integrate many energy fields. We knew about this power millennia ago. Humanity has a choice between two timelines: One, have powerful governments and ruling elites trap the people in a cataclysmic timeline or, two, humanity will find a way to achieve a positive, self-governing timeline. It is the cosmic plan for humanity to evolve at this time."

Brunel rubs her crystal skull secretly and decides to say nothing. Angelica finds the auras of these men so in tune with her thoughts that she takes Mitchener's hand and squeezes it lovingly.

CHAPTER TWENTYEIGHT

No one wants the evening to end so they adjourn to the bar at the Hotel Mercedes. The group of four picks out a table and Manuel joins them. Angelica is thrilled to meet the Mayan shaman and soak up their knowledge and warmth.

"It was an unforgettable night, one unlike any other I have experienced," says Angelica as the bartender brings over a beer for Manuel and four rum and cokes. It's a quiet night in the bar. Small tables of older foreign tourists chat amiably, but quietly. The few locals drink Corona beers and laugh and taunt each other in good spirits.

"These visionary shamans are holy men. All they say is true. It touches my heart," says Angelica.

"All of it?" challenges Mitchener.

"All of it."

"Do you?" Christopher asks Michener.

"I wish I had spoken to them of Mayan history and its mysteries before sending off my article. In my previous sessions with them, everything was personal."

"And you, Mr. Big Writer?" Brunel asks, taking Christopher's hand in hers and smiling, "Do you believe it?'

"When I write about it, I'll quote them, let them tell their own story. Their history is long and our knowledge is short. However, its wisdom could play a positive role in our present world. We all sense an alarm bell has been sounded.

"But there's more," says Christopher. "I've written about Star Gates. These are the two points in the sky where the ecliptic crosses the median plane of our galaxy, the Milky Way. In ancient Europe and in Africa, there was a widely-held belief that these points were portals through which souls entered or left our world.

"We also have discovered that the sun is less predictable than we thought. The sun is prone to huge storms that affect the Earth's weather. And the sun's magnetic field is going through major changes. Even the world of Mayanology is in ferment as more glyphs are deciphered.

"It is now known that for much of the Mayan civilization, its mini-states were at war. In this sense, they were not unlike the city-states of classical Greece. Greek cities' unending squabbles led to their conquest by the semi-barbarian Macedonians. However, like the Greeks, the Mayans left behind them a legacy of majestic buildings, a written script and an enigma concerning how these things were achieved.

"Archeo-biological evidence now indicates that South America was settled prior to North America. Recent work at Pedra Furada in Brazil has revealed human occupation there at least 56,000 years ago. I could go on but …"

The waiter appears with another round of rum and cokes. He points to a Mexican across the bar, who smiles and waves. The waiter returns to the buyer of the drinks.

"I placed the microphone under their table. You'll be able to hear their conversation. That's the man, right?"

"That's him. When you bring him another round from me, use his last name and see if he responds."

Minutes later Mitchener motions over the waiter and says, "Bring the gentleman over there who purchased our drinks one from us. Put it on Mr. Christopher's bill," he says, pointing at Christopher, who rolls his eyes.

"Just kidding, put it on Mr. Mitchener's bill," says Mitchener, who looks up, waves and yells, "Gracias, amigo, muchas gracias."

When the bartender leaves, Brunel says, "I'm so excited."

Manuel, will you lead us to the lost Mayan tomb?" "Soon, senorita?"

"Meantime, you must swear to remain silent."

"My lips are sealed. I will remain silent," she says anxiously. Manuel looks at Angelica and wonders how Mitchener attracts these beautiful women. He thinks, maybe he's rich.

Mitchener remains silent but thinks this is madness, knowing that Christopher never says no to Brunel. Manuel discusses his family, his pride in his young sons and his love for his little daughter.

"We're off," says Brunel, giving Christopher a come-hither glance and pulling him to his feet.

"See you at our clearing," says Mitchener. Angelica takes his hand and leads him to her room.

"You're such a loving man. I love to touch you," Angelica says once they're inside her room. "But you don't want women going to the tomb's ruins, do you?"

She unbuttons her blouse and tosses it on the floor.

"Even with my air conditioning on full, you make me hot." "Good," says Mitchener, dropping his pants after pulling off his shirt. He sits on her bed as he takes off his socks and shoes. Angelica leans forward and pushes his shoulders flat against her sheets. She brushes her breasts tenderly up his naked body and pulls the hair around his nipple in her teeth, shaking her head wildly and growling.

"Ouch, you vixen. I've worked years to grow those hairs."

"Easy. Now you must do all your Mayan priestess says. Remember? This is such a special place. I can't wait to share myself with you."

"When making love to you, my emotions ..."

Angelica interrupts, "Go to the higher energy of the emotional body. Ride your bliss to ecstasy, your higher self."

"I prefer to experience it rather than define it," says Mitchener laughing. "For me it only happens with you. You open the door of my heart and my love flows into you."

She rolls her voluptuous body atop his, looks into his eyes and says, "My darling, now I know you are mine. Deep inside you there always was a block. I could feel it. When tears ran down your cheeks at the falls, I knew you were all mine."

Mitchener kisses her softly and says, "I've been called a wordsmith, but with you, words leave me speechless as I experience your love."

"First, I want to enjoy you for a few moments," Angelica

says as her hand slips beneath the covers and she pumps and cradles him. Then her curls slip below the covers and her fingers and lips work their magic until Mitchener is lost in his passion and she presses her breasts together, perfumes them, and he slides between them. Then she welcomes him into her warm body and uses her muscles to milk him. Angelica enjoys the passion in his eyes, the smell of his excitement as she moans and rides him wildly until powerful spasms shake their bodies.

~~~ CHAPTER TWENTYNINE ~~~

Brunel closes her door and stands in front of it as she reaches up and takes off her khaki blouse, drops her khaki shorts and steps out of her boots.

"Oh, no, no panties," she says mischievously. "I knew I forgot something."

Brunel always darkens her eyebrows and wears false eye lashes that give her a direct alluring look when she wants to look sexy. Her narrow shoulders accent her full, tempting melons.

"I feel like a new woman," she says after her shower. "Soon this naked body will be in your arms."

She swings her long, dark curly hair and milky white orbs wildly as she puts her arms behind her head.

"Undress, while I belly dance," she says as her hips sway sensually before she sits on the bed and forms a V with her thighs.

"Kneel. You've become such a wonderful lover under my tutelage that it's time for another lesson," she says as she spreads her thighs, pulls his face against her warm mound and encourages his tongue and lips to enter her warmth.

"There," she says softly, encouraging and teaching him until he understands what she enjoys and how to excite her as she reveals her secrets. As her pleasure increases, her flesh warms, her moans grow louder, encouraging Christopher's tongue and fingers to move more rapidly. Soon, she throws back her curls and her arched body quakes with pleasure as sweat runs off her face as spasm after spasm shakes her hips and she whispers more, more, more and she pulls his face tighter between her thighs.

"I hope my love thrills you as much as your love thrills me," says Brunel softly as tears stream down her cheeks and she collapses on the bed.

"In the morning, your time is coming. Let's savor the moment."

⁓ CHAPTER THIRTY ⁓

At noon Angelica and Brunel walk down a rainforest trail as Angelica describes her intriguing trip to Paris and Brunel decides to reveal her new treasure, a crystal skull, which resides under her pillow.

"Where's Christopher?"

"He's exhausted and wished to rest," she says, recalling their morning lovemaking. "Christopher told me more tales about crystal skulls. It might be my imagination, but I thought it heightened our lovemaking. I didn't tell him it was under my pillow."

As they walk, she says, ""I did not tell Christopher, but that man who bought us the drinks reminded me of a man in a vision. That man was a Spaniard, who killed a Mayan priest who I thought was Christopher in a former life. Strange. I never even thought about reincarnation before. Now I feel like I've found a long-lost love, Christopher.

"Christopher said that these mystifying skulls carved from crystal have been appearing worldwide in recent decades. Some are ancient, made by unknown hands in Central America and Tibet. Others are more recent. Mayans include them in their ceremonies. They believe them to have the ability to transform human consciousness.

"The skulls can be used to gain insights, heal, and can transfer information to other crystal skulls. Networking, I guess. They are also involved in a new super consciousness, the key to our future. "I found a book in the hotel library that stated the skulls can project holographic images. Remember, magicians' crystal balls were once supposedly able to produce pictures. As we grow in knowledge of a limitless universe, we should be open to the meta-physics of paranormal and mystical experiences, don't you think?"

"We can talk about concepts, but we must experience them," says Angelica. "We have innate abilities to tune in like a radio to interpenetrating energy fields that account for changes in time when we move from one frequency or dimension to another. Examples are ghosts, dreams, hypnosis, dowsing, drug-induced encounters and every day dreaming."

That night, the foursome meet, discuss plans and Manuel leans forward and says, "Meet me on the path that leads south from here, the place where I left Mitchener and Christopher before in a jungle clearing. Meet me there at 9 in the morning, after the jungle mists have cleared."

The four shake Manuel's hand as he stands and leaves.

The following morning the five meet at the appointed spot. All wear long sleeved khaki shirts and pants, hiking boots, sun-glasses and sun hats and have sprayed each other repeatedly with mosquito lotion.

Soon, Brunel's excitement is gone as she slogs behind the waiter Manuel, who goes ahead, whacking brush and branches along the overgrown trail. Christopher feels much improved, but tires more easily than normal. Mitchener is refreshed and happy to be sharing this adventure with Angelica. The group follows beneath towering kapok trees through an area of the largest uninterrupted rainforest in Central America. Jaguars, scarlet macaws, howler monkeys and a huge variety of insects and flora await them.

Not too many miles away in Guatemala stand the glorious Mayan ruins of Tikal, surrounded by hundreds of lost and discovered Mayan tombs and relics. In this giant rainforest, oscillated turkey, the blue morpho butterfly, the capuchin monkey, the jaguar and other species still roam.

Manuel stops, points down at an old tennis shoe in the brush, and then veers off the trail into dense rainforest where he earlier hacked a rough trail. Mosquitoes buzz, land and bite. The hikers pass hanging vines and then small, half-buried ruins entangled in roots and vegetation. The going is slow as Manuel hacks away with his machete. Sweaty, tired and bitten after passing through clouds of insets, Mitchener and Christopher look back as the women trudge behind them. They watch as the waiter climbs a half-buried, hardly visible, ruined pyramid overgrown with trees, roots, branches and brush.

Halfway up the ruin, the waiter looks down and then back across their hacked trail surrounded by dense jungle, but sees no one. When he reaches a small platform at the top, he lies down motionless for minutes. The barely discernible path seems swallowed up by the all-encircling jungle.

"I'll go ahead and signal for all to follow," Manuel calls down, wishing he had brought along his hunting rifle. He retraces his climb, slips, swears, but doesn't fall. When he reaches the opening, the two men carefully follow him, and then halt as Manuel pulls aside, vines, grasses and branches that reveal a descending tunnel that he has previously cleared. He pulls out a flashlight and motions them to follow. The women start uncertainly, but soon are climbing the ruin with care.

The men descend a narrow, crumpling, stone staircase to a musty, humid room where the walls are covered with peeling stucco murals. Nothing appears changed or unusual as the men carefully look for telltale indications that others recently followed them. To the right another narrow, blackened limestone stairway descends farther, passing under a corbel arch just bigger than a man, and the two find themselves in a burial chamber.

Manuel yells up for the women to follow. After they arduously descend, they press together in the steamy, humid air of the burial chamber. The waiter motions to an opened catafalque where he shines his flashlight on a boney skeleton surrounded by gold jewelry, a scattered jade necklace, jade beads, ear spools, and more necklaces, rings and other burial goods. Four skeletons lay scattered around the catafalque. Their hair hints they are women's remains. Other artifacts, wrapped in moldy textiles, stand upright. Twenty-six clay vessels line one wall.

"You like?" says Manuel to the women, sweat streaming down his face; his long-sleeved shirt and pants are covered with dirt and sweat.

"Incredible!" says Brunel. "It's like something out of a movie." Angelica shakes her head in disbelief.

Manuel whispers, "The government has no knowledge of this tomb."

"There's more," says Mitchener after a long pause. He takes Manuel's flashlight and shines it inside a partially sealed pottery vessel. The women look at the Mayan glyphs on an ancient, rolled deerskin codex.

"They are invaluable. There are only four other codices in the world," says Christopher as Mitchener goes from vessel to vessel, shining a beam on each one.

There are twenty-six, unbelievably twenty-six," says Christopher with finality.

"Everything has changed," says Christopher. "Somehow we must protect Manuel's priceless discovery. Our adventure could easily turn dangerous. This is a priceless find."

"Now that we have cleared a path here, others could follow. We must cover the entrance to this pyramidal burial ruin and the spot where Manuel's rugged trail splits off from the other trail," says Christopher. Soon, all the adventurers can think of is getting back to the hotel and a cold shower.

On the arduous, exhausting hike back, Manuel continually swings his machete yet vines still entangle their hiking boots and branches swat their bodies and heads while they move through clouds of insects. Just before they reach the hotel, they stop at small clearing and rest, their energies sapped. The three agree to meet soon to decide on their plan of attack.

That evening in the hotel bar a Mexican television station broadcasts the news of violent eruptions inside a caldera where American volcanologists are working. Shortly thereafter huge dark clouds climb into the atmosphere, the scientists escape in small boats and the volcano collapses in a chain of explosions, destroying much of the South Pacific island. No deaths are reported so far on this uninhabited island.

Mitchener checks with the bartender who gives him the information. His English is fairly good. Then more images are shown of steam venting from another volcano on a nearby uninhabited island. Ash of these eruptions reached about 25,000 feet and the scientists report hearing massive earlier explosions.

Tides in the vicinity remain extremely high and smaller fishing boats are moving out of the area.

Mitchener pays little attention to the broadcast, but notices Angelica is unusually pensive and quiet.

~~~ CHAPTER THIRTYONE ~~~

"I wish to learn more from the shamans," says Angelica when they're alone. "These are men of wisdom. I would know more. This time is one of great change. This is turning into more of an adventure than I anticipated."

"As I have said, everything is an adventure with you, Angelica." Mists shroud the mysterious jungle at night as Mitchener rents a jeep from the hotel and the two make their way through the dark, foreboding rainforest. Soon, they receive a warm welcome from their Mayan shamans, the short, elderly Zak-kuk, whose hair that hangs loosely down his back, and his son, who is also in his traditional white smock, 30-year-old Katu-Quila. A lantern lights the simple hut.

"I respect your wisdom," says Angelica, smiling. "I would know more of your Mayan history."

"Let my son tell it. My mind is not as sharp as it once was," Zak-kuk says bowing to his son.

"Thank, you father. We Mayans believed that our gods were avatars of certain stars, notably Orion and the planets Venus, Mars, Jupiter and Saturn. Our religion was like that of the ancient Egyptians. That is, it was extra-terrestrial. We believe that the First Father of the human race, the Maize god, came from and eventually returned to Orion.

"We viewed the end of the Great Cycle, or December of 2012, as a time for humanity's enlightenment, rather than the end of existence. Other civilizations have held the same belief – Egyptians, Babylonians, Hopi, Aztecs and Eastern Indians. The years leading up to 2012 had compelling astrological significance for change.

"It's true that Dec. 21, 2012 was the end of the Long Count Calendar. But it was also when the Earth lined up with the Solstice Sun and the center of the Milky Way Galaxy. This connection is called the Galactic Alignment by science. The Galactic Center includes a massive Black Hole of incredibly high energy said to hold the light of several million stars captured by its huge gravitational pull. Our solar system is located in an outlying area of the Milky Way Galaxy.

"This is bringing about gradual changes. Our Mayan elders say that the veil separating us, the living from the dead, is disappearing. Father and I experience this. Communication with the other side will become unremarkable. We will all experience heightened physic sensitivity. We are told our new alignment of the Earth is bringing climate change and alterations in the Earth's magnetic field. Sunspot cycles are increasing in intensity. Solar storms and solar flares are affecting the weather and may have a potential health impact. There is a huge hole in the magnetosphere.

"Father and I agree on aspects of the future. I am unsure concerning the possibility of a cataclysm, but recently the magnitude of disasters such as earthquakes, hurricanes, floods, tornadoes and droughts has skyrocketed. The Asian tsunami took nearly 275,000 lives. Hurricane Katrina destroyed a major section of New Orleans. Earthquakes in Haiti and China. Volcanoes erupt in Iceland. And there are polarizing political debates, gay marriage, abortion, government corruption, religious disputes, and wars causing millions of refugees. We must raise the global vibration. We are still creating the future."

"You speak the truth," says Angelica and a long silence follows. "We have another matter that we would like to discuss."

After detailing, with the help of Mitchener, Manuel's discovery of the Mayan tomb and its riches in history, jewelry and other treasure, Mitchener says, "What is the right thing to do?"

"The tomb and its contents are the property of the Mayans," says Zak-Kuk. "They will end up in the hands of thieves and dishonest officials if we do not move them. Bring the codices in the pottery here. You and Angelica and Brunel and Christopher. I do not have a good feeling about Manuel. He is a good man, but poor and will do anything to ensure the health and wellbeing of his family. My son and I will do what we can and what is best for the Mayans."

"Tomorrow I will show you a spot for you and Angelica to bring the pottery containing the codices. The codices are most important. Take backpacks so as not to arouse suspicion. Make four trips each way. Then have Christopher and Brunel make four trips each way. Say nothing to Manuel. In three days or so we will have removed all the codices to safety. Then we will send Mayans with pistols and rifles to get the jewels."

CHAPTER THIRTYTWO

The following morning Mitchener, Christopher, Angelica and Brunel meet with young Katu-Quila at a prearranged spot in the jungle not far from the tomb. It is an exhausting hike from the tomb, but young Katu-Quila, who continually swings his machete tirelessly, has cleared a spot and an easy-to-follow trail if one is careful of the entangling vines and branches.

"I'm glad you are wearing protective clothing in the jungle as our friends in the insect world provide many opportunities to swat your bodies and heads," says Katu-Quila, laughing. Then at a turn in the trail a small ravine opens and off to one side a small opening to a cave appears.

"I never would have spotted it," says Christopher. "Our ancestors found it," says Katu-Quila.

As they descend, they pass a small altar with offerings. Deeper into the cave, they veer off into a small cavern.

"This is where you will place the pottery vessels with the Mayan codices. Earthquakes seldom reach below 60 feet underground so it is a safe hiding place. The pottery and its precious texts will be safe here," says Katu-Quila.

"We will now retrace the trail to the tomb until all four of you can find it easily."

They find the ravine makes the trail easier to follow as they are walking downhill from the tomb and uphill from the cave to the ruins of the tomb.

"As we are all here, the five of us will make the first trip. Then I will leave. The four of you can make a second trip and then, after waiting some time, Brunel and Christopher will return to the hotel. May Father Sun bless our efforts."

Soon their water jugs are emptying and their khaki shirts and long khaki pants, tied at their hiking boots, are soaked with sweat The loads are not heavy, but sweat pours off their backs and soaks their knapsacks. The men slowly and carefully descend the narrow, crumbling, stone staircase to a musty, humid room.

Nothing appears changed or unusual as the men carefully look for telltale indications that others recently followed them. None are found. To the right another narrow, blackened limestone stairway descends farther, passing under a corbel arch just bigger than a man, and the two find themselves in what looks like a burial chamber.

After they arduously descend, Katu-Quila, the Mayan chilam, shines his flashlight on the boney remains of a bejeweled skeleton and then finds twenty-six clay vessels along one wall. He carefully lifts one pottery vessel and hands it up to Mitchener, who in turn, hands it to Angelica and she hands it to Christopher who hands it carefully to Brunel.

"You're a man after my heart, Christopher, you keep your word," says Brunel setting down the pottery vessel on the damp, lush earth. "This is truly an adventure that will last a lifetime, especially every time I take a shower. I'm exhausted and we've just started."

They return once again to the cave with their precious cargo in their knapsacks and hand the pottery and its contents to Katu-Quila, who takes it deep into the cave. When he returns, he says, "I'll leave you now. The sooner the precious codices are in the cave, the better. Bless you, my good friends."

Brunel and Christopher set off first and the four decide that Angelica and Mitchener will return to the tomb the following day and Brunel and Christopher the next day. Until their mission is complete, they decide not to meet for dinner or drinks as this may arouse interest.

Angelica examines the glyphs on one codex and wonders at its meaning. Then she replaces it in its pottery vessel as if a sacred object. Then it's back in the heat, the humidity, the mosquitoes and the entangling branches and vines along the trail. At last they are back at the hotel and in Angelica's room. The cool air blasts their bodies like a blessing of a Mayan god.

Angelica takes off her boots, rushes into the bathroom, throws the shower curtains aside and within seconds the water splashes down, soaking her hair, face, shoulders and khaki outfit. For minutes, she just stands under the cool, splashing water.

"Come in here this instant and share this blissful shower," commands Angelica.

Mitchener's clothes and boots are on the floor in seconds as he says, "I'm on my way. Reach out with your hand and tell me if you are grasping my shirt or trousers. No fair looking."

The cool, delicate fingers of Angelica's right hand reach out from behind the wet shower curtain, but catch only the air.

"Nice try. Try again."

This time her fingers grasp erect flesh. She holds it in her grasp and pulls the naked body of Mitchener into the shower, shouting, "Trickster. I thought you were dressed. But look what my fingers found. I'm not going to release you, until ..."

Her fingers grasp the fleshy object between his thighs in a vise-like grip. Recalling her strength in the pool, he says, "Careful, I know your strength. If you let go, I'll take off your dirty clothes and bury the object in your flesh. You'll enjoy it."

"Promise! But I won't let go until you undress me."

"OK. Easy, you don't realize the strength in your fingers."

He runs his fingers through her dark, wet curls and kisses her forehead, nose and mouth.

"Ouch! God, you've got strong fingers."

God, she's strong, Mitchener thinks, as he undoes the buttons on her long-shelved khaki shirt and it drops to the wet floor of the shower. He looks at her bountiful breasts, pushed up by her white, lacy bra, pauses to enjoy their beauty and unsnaps her bra as her white orbs with their large aureole and enticing nipples fall forward, inviting his touch. He unbuttons her long khakis, and lets them drop.

"I cannot take off your socks. You'll have to release your grip," says Mitchener smiling impishly.

She releases her grip, bends forward, kisses his magic wand and pulls him against her wet body and kisses him, her lips and tongue further exciting him. She dabs some aromatic oil on him and guides him lovingly into her curvaceous body as the shower splashes water over the lovers.

"At last. Welcome home," she says as she grabs his thighs and he carefully walks her to her bed and gently lays her body down under him. He admires the curve of her neck, her dark, loving eyes, the curve of her hips, shapely thighs and legs. Her breasts press against his chest and her nipples are flushed with excitement. As his heart pumps faster and his breathing rate increases, she weaves her fingers in his hair, pulls his face closer, opens her mouth and welcomes his tongue. Her supple fingers knead his back softly as he cups her warm breasts, sending tingling feelings through her body. She feels his loving energy sweep through her body, enflaming her desire.

Angelica moans softly as he lowers his head to her warm, erect nipples, suckles one and pushes her flushed breast deeper into his mouth. He trusts deeper as her strong muscles milk him. She drives her hips into him again and again. He moans as he explodes, throwing his silver stream into her warmth. Then spasms grip her body as she writhes in passion, sending her into ecstasy.

They relax for a long time. Then Angelica smiles and covers his face with kisses and places his hand on her breast. He cups it again and her nipples stiffen to his touch as he twirls them in his hand. Her hand replies, twirling and then pumping below his navel.

Soon, she rolls atop him and he slides easily back into her warm flesh. She sees the adoration in his eyes, smells his excitement, and says, "I am slowly going to drive you wild as I milk you and pull you deeper onto me."

~~~ CHAPTER THIRTYTHREE ~~~

Early the next morning, Angelica and Mitchener pick up sandwiches from the hotel cook, put on their khaki outfits, hiking boots, spray each other with mosquito bombs and head down the jungle trail. Fortunately, the mists are rising from the jungle canopy as they begin their hike to the ruins of the tomb. Parrots squeal in the morning light. Howler monkeys roar as the two thread their way through the lush, humid rainforest. Scents of flowers over-power them in one low area.

Mitchener stops as the sweat runs off his brow and takes Angelica's hand.

"I see you've recovered," says Angelica smiling. "We're making good progress along this vine-entangled trail. After you went to sleep, I lay beside you, watched you sleep and thought how lucky I was to love you."

She smiles and takes Mitchener's hand. Mitchener presses on in the lead, but is unable to find the tennis shoe.

"It's a good thing, I'm along," Angelica says as she leads Mitchener back to the tennis shoe and leads the way down the thin path to the ruins of the tomb. With no hesitation, she pushes the brush and vines aside that conceals the entrance, pulls out her flashlight, shines it down into the tomb and slowly and carefully descends a narrow, crumpling, stone staircase to a musty, humid room where the walls are covered with peeling stucco murals.

Nothing appears unusual after a careful examination. To the right another narrow, blackened limestone stairway descends farther, passing under a corbel arch just bigger than a man. Angelica motions for Mitchener to wait here as she descends into the burial chamber.

She hands up pottery vessel after pottery vessel, which

Mitchener arduously and carefully takes up to the entrance without tripping or banging his backpack against the humid stone walls. They decide to leave the four pottery vessels near the entrance to the ruins and replace the camouflage, branches, vines and fronds disguising the opening.

"You were born for the jungle," says Mitchener with a look of admiration.

"I was born for you," she says.

"I might as well let you take the lead. You appear to have a better memory and keener ability to spot details in this tropical wilderness than me."

Angelica takes her time as she examines everything along the trail. Then at a turn in the trail a small ravine opens and off to one side a small cave opening appears.

"I never would have spotted it," says Mitchener.

As they descend into the cave, they pass the now familiar small altar with offerings. Deeper into the cave, they veer off into a small cavern. Here they place their two pottery vessels alongside the others.

Again, they find the ravine makes the trail easier to follow as they walk downhill to the cave and uphill from the cave to the trail that leads to the turnoff trail to the tomb. Although it's late morning, their water jugs are emptying and their khaki shirts and long khaki pants, tied at their hiking boots, are soaked with sweat. Sweat pours off their backs and soaks their knapsacks.

Mitchener leads back to the larger trail as they again leave it and return to the ruins of the tomb and Angelica quickly finds the other two pottery vessels under camouflaged vines. Mitchener wishes he had brought a machete to make the trails easier to follow, but admits that Angelica is his personal GPS.

After they drop off their last two pottery vessels with the codices in the cave, Mitchener says, "Amen. I'm glad our partners will make the trips tomorrow. I wasn't born for this life in the jungle. I cannot wait to hit the pool."

With their journeys for the day nearing an end, Mitchener and Angelica feel a sense of relief.

"It's a pleasure to help these Mayan chilams," says Angelic as she stops abruptly, bends down and picks up a long, black snake that struggles to escape. Immediately, Mitchener jumps back and nearly falls.

"Be careful, for God's sakes," he yells as Angelica holds the head between her thumb and forefinger and it warps itself around her arm. She moves the creature toward Mitchener, who takes another step backward, and warns, "The damned creature might be poisonous."

"I saw it in a book on snakes in the hotel library. If I remember right, it's not poisonous."

"Well, Jungle Jane put it down and we'll be happily on our way. I'll be ecstatic."

Mitchener and Angelica discuss snakes as they walk the final distance to the clearing before the hotel.

"No more snakes, OK?"

"As you wish, my darling."

Soon the maid has their dirty, sweaty outfits in the wash, and the two duck in and out of the shower in Mitchener's room. Angelica throws a towel around her shoulders, goes to her room and reappears in her dark blue swimsuit with straps around the neck which accents her voluptuous figure.

"A vision of loveliness," says Mitchener.

"I like it when you compliment me."

Again, at the pool she shouts "Whee!" jumps high into the air and does a perfect cannon ball that splashes Mitchener's towel, soaking it.

"How do you like my new swimming suit? I paid a fortune for it in Paris."

"I know, you told me."

Angelica swims laps, Mitchener floats lazily and then they sit under a sun umbrella at a remote end of the pool, discuss New York, her job and the wonder that they're back together. Mitchener takes a catnap. Angelica relaxes for an hour while Mitchener sleeps and then looks at a hammock chair across the pool and goes to find out how you use it.

When he awakens, she says, "You won't believe what I

found."

"With you, I'd believe anything."

She takes his hand and leads him to a small, locked open-air affair off the pool to one side. Flowers surround it and a flowery perfume greets them as Angelica turns the key and opens the door. In the center of the room is a hammock chair.

"Our first exercise is called Joy in the Womb," she reads as she takes off her bathing suit and sets down two illustrations. Then she strips off Mitchener's bathing suit and takes it to a nearby chair under an umbrella. She throws back her hair, holds the two white, heavy ropes of the chair, lifts her legs and finds herself floating in mid-air. She motions Mitchener toward her body cuddled on it, as she wraps her legs around Mitchener's butt. She shows him how to hold the ropes apart while she swings away a little and then back a little against his erect welcome.

Angelica reads, "As you swing and rotate slowly there is a feeling of support unequalled by anything other than the womb. This is a recreation of the envelope of life."

"I like it," she says as he pulls her body against his in rhythm as she leans back and works her hips. Then she jumps out of the hammock chair and reads, "Your hammock is the limit in discovering new ways to use it."

After she leaves the hammock chair, Mitchener says, "I'm old fashioned; I prefer a bed. My exercise with this apparatus is exhausting. Let's return to the pool and my bedroom for my promised pleasuring."

Soon they are out of the pool, and Michener's excitement builds while they return hand in hand to his room. Comfortably in bed she sweeps her long, curly dark hair across his face and down his shoulders and stomach before her head disappears between his thighs. Her lips stroke him in a steady rhythm as her mouth, tongue and delicate fingers work their rhythmic wonders. She feels his passion mounting as he moans. Soon his silver stream erupts in a shower, covering her body.

"You're my lovely Jungle Jane. Thanks for being such a

good guide. With you I need no hammock chair. But I hope you enjoyed my loving in it," Mitchener says as he pulls her against his slippery body.

Mitchener contacts Christopher and they all agree to meet in Angelica's room that night at 10 p.m. When they've had a couple of beers, Mitchener goes over what they did on their mission during the day and how they managed it. Christopher agrees and Brunel says, "I didn't realize that adventuring would be this arduous. Frankly, I prefer the pool, but once I start something, I'm in it all the way."

CHAPTER THIRTYFOUR

At midday Brunel and Christopher set off. There is no mist. They've eaten a good hotel breakfast and are wearing their khaki outfits, hiking boots and have sprayed each other with mosquito bombs. They head down the trail as the jungle canopy rises about them.

"What are you doing with that thing," Brunel says sarcastically.

As she turns away, he hits her in the ass with the flat side of his machete.

"That's what I'm going to do with it," he says as the two thread their way through the lush, humid rainforest. Scents of flowers overpower them in a low area.

Christopher follows Mitchener's plan after many wrong turns, but they finally reach the tomb.

"Thank God, this will soon be over and we can return to the pool," says Brunel. "You've taught me a valuable lesson. Someday it may save my life. Avoid adventure. It's OK in the movies, but a true pain in the ass in the real world, don't you agree?"

"It's not a Sunday picnic," Christopher replies as sweat drips off his forehead and into his eyes in an open stretch of the trail before the smaller trail leads off to the tomb.

"Let's take a short break here. We're covered with sweat," says Brunel, who finds her anger hard to hide. Then Christopher hears a branch snap and turns to Brunel.

"Did you hear that?" "What? A cold shower?"

"A branch fell or was snapped." "Do you want to go back?"

"Let's get it over with," snaps Brunel.

Nearby a Mexican in a sombrero, dirty shirt and pants covered with sweat hides behind the trunk of a 100-foot Ceiba tree that reaches to the top of the jungle canopy and blocks much of the light. A machete hangs from his belt on one side and a pistol rests in a weathered holster on the other. A swarm of insects attacks him and moves on. He decides this is the perfect place to complete his mission after days of spying and waiting. The woman is the target, but he decides to shoot them both, pull them off the trail into the wilderness, strip their corpses and let the rainforest and its inhabitants do the rest. The trail is never used, hard to follow, and he could not have found it if he had not followed the gringos from the hotel.

He rechecks his pistol and ammunition. In his hip pocket is a small camera to provide evidence that he's done his job. There will be nothing left of their corpses in a month, he decides while moving forward to get a better field of fire. He thinks that I'll pump a couple of bullets into each one, drag them off and be out of here by dark.

While Brunel swats a fly, a mosquito bites her ear. She swaps it, trips and falls onto the forest floor. Two shots ring out. She can hear the bullets whiz past and crash into the brush. Christopher lunges into the bush and screams with pain.

The Mexican steps back onto the trail for a better shot. As he raises his pistol a branch crashes down on his wrist and smashes violently into the back of his head. His pistol drops and a woman dives to the ground and grabs it. Another blow to the head stuns the Mexican and knocks him off his feet. Regaining his balance, he turns and dashes off down the trail leaving his sombrero behind.

"Don't!" screams Angelica as Mitchener scrambles to his feet. "He's got a machete and knows how to use it. Maybe another pistol."

"Thank God that dead limb was nearby or I couldn't have clubbed him that fast," says Michener gasping for breath. Angelica, breathing normally, gives Mitchener a hug.

"My jungle hero."

Nearby, Brunel cries hysterically and rolls away from the entangled vegetation into the clearing. Christopher, bleeding from the hands, races over and embraces her. To Brunel the return trip through the jungle is a blur of insects, heat, humidity, mud, undergrowth, vines that entangle her boots and branches that smack her.

Mitchener walks silently with Christopher as they follow the trail back to the hotel, their minds pondering the attack.

As Angelica walks with Brunel, holding her hand and comforting her, she suggests that Brunel practice deep breathing as they walk. When they return to the hotel, she tells Brunel to take a shower and a sleeping pill. Things will be better in the morning.

"I have a feeling that you're in a mild state of shock. Rest is the best thing for you after this traumatic event. We'll meet in the morning to decide what to do next."

Christopher agrees to meet with Angelica and Mitch for drinks and dinner after a couple hours once they get back to the hotel.

In a familiar environment, Brunel turns up the air conditioning and takes off her dirty khaki apparel and boots.

"I'm in heaven with that blast of cold air," she says, smiling for the first time. "I needed that. I'm so glad you're in my room with me. And thanks for the adoring glance at my naked curves. It gives me a peaceful feeling."

She looks at her dirty clothes in a heap on the floor, and enters the shower and pulls the curtain as water splashes all over the bathroom. Then she sits in the shower on a plastic chair as water drenches her.

Christopher strips off his dirty khaki outfit, shorts and takes off his boots. The blood on the slight cuts on his hands is covered with dirt.

"Come over here and give me a hand, Brunel shouts from behind the shower curtain. As the water splashes off her clean body, she reaches out and pulls Christopher into the shower.

"Easy," he says laughing as his dirty nude body falls against hers. She pulls him to her, kisses him and rubs her full breasts against his body. She picks up a bar of soap, says, "Shut your eyes, handsome," and soaps his hair, face, arms, chest and suds his pubic area until his manhood is pubescent and he's moaning softly and breathing harder. Then she takes a sponge, cleans off the soap and towels him down.

"Please come to bed and make love to me. After all this madness, I want to enjoy your love. I don't want to eat. I don't want to drink. I want to share my love with you. That's all."

As they slip into her bed, she kisses him while her soft fingers softly pump his tumescent flesh.

"It is so exciting to know I arouse your passion for me. I can see it in your adoring eyes. I'm going to love you with all my body and heart."

Brunel rolls her body atop his, kisses him wildly, throws her long, blonde hair over his head and kisses his neck, shoulders, chest and chews on his nipples. Her breasts excite him as they lovingly move down his body. Lower, her lips part and her soft, long blond hair sweeps up and down his body while he moans and her mouth caresses him. Then he lifts her head, pushes her body back, suckles at her breasts before entering her and slowly, rhythmically thrusts while her back arches to meet him.

He finds he's been transformed into an expert lover. Now he knows how to satisfy her while his rhythmic thrusts thrill her and meet her rising hips, until sweat runs off her steaming flesh and she writhes in ecstasy, moans wildly while urging him on. She rides him until he is spent and then she collapses, her passion spent as she rolls off him.

"You know I love you through all these lifetimes. Hand me my sleeping pills from off my desk so I can drift off into paradise." After Brunel slips off into dreamland, Christopher knocks on Angelica's door and the three retreat to the remote, quiet end of the pool. As they slip wine, Christopher says, "What a welcome site you two were. What a great team."

"Congratulate Angelica, not me. After we left the bar the other night she whispered to me that man who bought us drinks is evil. Now I know his vibrations. When I feel them I'll know danger is near. When you set off today, Angelica talked me into following you both. I thought it was unnecessary, but she convinced me. So, we followed you until your rest stop. We were going to surprise you, but events changed."

Angelica interrupts, adding "I didn't get the man in the bar's vibrations. This was a different Mexican. It wasn't until he took out a gun that I pointed toward a nearby fallen branch and Mitch picked it up and clubbed him in the head. When it hit his head I heard a crack. As soon as his pistol hit the ground I jumped on it, raised it and was set to shoot him as he turned to flee. It was an easy shot. He was a big target. Then, for an unknown reason, my finger eased off the trigger and he escaped. Mitch brought his pistol back in his knapsack. He'll have someone at the hotel buy us some ammunition, just in case."

"In case of what?" asks Christopher.

"We're not done with our mission for the Mayans," says Angelica with an innocent smile.

"Maybe we should get a couple of Mayans with rifles to join us," suggests Mitchener, although I feel safe with a pistol and sharp-eyed Angelica. He raises his eyebrow and winks at Angelica. "Don't wrestle with her. She's beautiful and strong."

"Any ideas why he set out to kill us, Christopher?"

"If the attack wasn't connected with the treasure, there are only two possibilities, Marsha's ex-husband, who has only to pay alimony as long as she's alive, and my wife, Susan, who's got a $350,000 life insurance policy on me. I always said that I'm worth more dead than alive. But she's not the type."

~~~ CHAPTER THIRTYFIVE ~~~

The morning dawns full of sunshine; a North wind eases the humidity. Brunel and Christopher sit by the pool and enjoy a breakfast alone. Christopher wears small bandages on his bruised hands from his dive into the brush. Brunel decides to read by the pool and relax in this serene setting while Manuel, Mitchener, Christopher and Angelica complete moving the Mayan relics with their help to the secret cave.

"We discussed a number of possibilities concerning the attack last night," says Christopher and one concerned your former husband.

"I've long forgotten about Rick. I don't like to discuss that dark period of my life. We met in church and he seemed kind and generous. We both liked to dance and often went to bars with large dance floors. One night he surprised me by asking me to marry him. I was young and inexperienced. He was good looking, rich and good in bed. All my friends were getting married and it seemed like the logical thing to do.

"Our first years went well until one night one of his friends invited us to their home for some cocktails with the Explorers Club. There were four other couples there, all good looking and rich. We had a couple of drinks and then a hashish pipe was passed and I inhaled too much of it and got stoned. I had never smoked hashish before. Things started to seem like a dream. Soon we were all naked, put on masks and someone embraced me and started making love. Later, we went to the luxurious lower floor of the home and a nude, masked woman was handcuffed, hung by a chain from the ceiling and a masked man whipped her as she screamed and moaned. Then she whipped him. They seemed to take pleasure from experiencing pain.

"Soon, I was handcuffed in the same manner and whipped. It hurt and I screamed loudly, but experienced only pain, no pleasure. Then I was handed another hashish pipe and my memories faded. I do recall that the man I was whipping kept urging me to whip him harder. He loved it, but I hated whipping him. The following day I hurt all over and felt terrible. Rick thought it was thrilling and that the club tried many other sexual things as a group. I said I wouldn't go with him to the club again. Later, he asked if he could go with another female companion so he could remain in the club. This club also met with other clubs.

"I didn't like anything about the club or its activities. We drifted apart and I moved in with a girlfriend, left him and later divorced him. I thought the settlement was huge and he didn't seem to mind much. I never saw him again. I saved my money, left my job and came here."

"I'm sorry; it's such a sad tale," says Christopher and kisses Brunel on the shoulder.

"Don't be. The money rolls in monthly and I'll never have to work again as long as I don't remarry. And I met you."

"Do you think Rick would have you killed to stop the alimony?"

"No. He seemed to think it was peanuts. He has a lavish home, sports cars and money never was a problem. We were infatuated with each other when we wed, but I never felt I loved him or he me. When we parted I told him I hoped he'd find a loving S & M partner. He does not know where I am and doesn't contact me. I haven't seen or talked with him since the divorce. Don't worry about me. I'll read and relax by the pool in this little bit of paradise."

***

After the blow to the head, the would-be Mexican assassin makes his way slowly and painfully back to his shack in the jungle and falls into bed. For days afterward he has hallucinations, dizziness and feels disoriented. He checks in with the boss of his gang, gets his cut and tells a small lie: "I killed her and some guy with her. Didn't want witnesses. Lost my camera on the way back to my place. Sorry."

He'd killed people before and found it easier after each murder. However, he did feel bad about losing his pistol. Murder? Big deal. Life was easy. Someone lived and died each day. He didn't worry about the lie. These damn Yanks will flee, tell no one because of their fears and no one would be the wiser.

The following morning his girlfriend comes for a visit to satisfy his sexual needs. She ponders raising her rates as she enters his shack. Young, beautiful, with a winsome body, long, curly black hair and flashing eyes, she yells hello, gets no answer and finds his dead body in bed. After overcoming her shock, she goes through his pockets, every possible hiding place in the shack, finds $10,000 stashed away and disappears.

~~~ CHAPTER THIRTYSIX ~~~

Handcock fills two champagne glasses in his bedroom after Susan slips back into bed beside him after playtime.

"Viva, Mexico! My contact said earlier today your husband is dead. He's going to pay off the gang the other half of our bargain today. As your lawyer, I'll report him missing soon. I'll check with a legal colleague and find out how long these missing persons cases usually take before insurance companies pay off."

Susan, sitting on his chest, sighs and embraces him. Then her pendulous breasts fall temptingly near Handcock's lips. She smiles, lifts one and sucks her nipple.

"See how happy I am. My breasts are blushing. I can feel my blood rushing into them."

He takes her breast nearest him in both hands and lifts it to his lips. Her breast fills both his palms. An erotic electric charge shots between his legs and his manhood stiffens. He massages her breast with both hands, as Susan reaches between his legs and begins a familiar soft pumping motion that he never tires of. Handcock continues worshipping one breast, and then the other, lost in her bounteous flesh and welcoming nipples.

Handcock's member enters her while she pushes her hips forward. Soon her body arches, and she clenches her teeth while convulsing in spasms of pleasure.

"Don't stop, darling, please. You're my magic man."

"You're my magic woman, darling."

She decides to tell Charlene the good news later.

～～ CHAPTER THIRTYSEVEN ～～

At her hotel the next morning, Brunel decides she must get out of Mexico after she screams during a nightmare of her murder. Her screams awake Christopher who agrees that she's still in shock and they'll drive to the nearest airport after breakfast. He notifies the desk clerk to have a rental car brought to the hotel and they'll leave after lunch.

The clerk calls the gang leader and says Christopher and Brunel have asked him to rent a car for them and will be driving to the local airport after lunch ending with "I'll call when they leave."

"How are you doing, darling? Christopher asks as he hugs Brunel.

"To say I'm tired is an understatement," Brunel says, managing a slight smile.

Soon Christopher has packed the car, checked out of the hotel and paid the bill. The bags are in the trunk as the car drives off. All Christopher can think about is we have to get the hell out of here.

Brunel sits in the front seat, looks blankly ahead and thinks this can't be happening while Christopher starts the car and kisses her on the cheek. Soon, she's asleep. An hour later a car comes down the road going in the other direction. Christopher forgets it until he sees two headlights flash from the car behind them. While his foot pushes the gas pedal to the floor, a bullet crashes through the rearview mirror and more hit the trunk. He slows down as a car races around them and swerves in front of them.

He is forced to stop. All I can do is stop, he thinks. I'll give them money.

Brunel awakens in a state of shock and says nothing.

"Hello, again, my friend," says the bandit who smells of rum. "Please get out of the car for a photo."

Another car pulls up behind them, pulling a beat-up old trailer while the other bandit smiles, takes the camera and points it at Christopher's face. Then he walks over to Brunel, standing in a daze next to Christopher, and says, "Smile, pretty lady, for the camera."

Brunel looks blankly ahead. This can't be happening she repeatedly thinks.

"You both look tired. Please follow me to the trailer and lay down."

In a trance, Christopher and Brunel crawl into the trailer. Christopher places his arms behind him, ready to spring. No sooner has he thought it than three pistol shots end his life and three more ring out, ending Brunel's life.

"Bueno. Bueno," says the leader. "We'll bury them and sell the car. Our boss will be satisfied at last. No survivors. No one to identify us. Better ask if he wants us to bury their luggage. Or should we sell it."

~~~ CHAPTER THIRTYEIGHT ~~~

Susan returns home and immediately calls Charlene. She cannot contain her joy. On her way home she stops at a liquor store, picks up two bottles of the most expensive French champagne and decides not to mention her recent unplanned playtime with Handcock. She decides to skip snacks as she's slimmed down on her diet, improving her already attractive figure.

"Hello, darling. It's your next-door neighbor with a surprise for you. Throw on a robe and come over to the patio."

"Give me 15 minutes to freshen up."

Susan puts the two chaise lounges close to each other and places the ice buckets of champagne nearby. She feels joyously nervous as she fixes her hair, puts on a new, sexy robe and sandals. She places a gift next to the champagne tied with a red ribbon.

Charlene knocks on the tall, fenced patio's gate. Susan is relaxing on a chaise lounge, her body tanned and perfumed, her stomach flat after her recent workout at the gym and her nipples rouged. Her eyes sparkle with excitement. Her suntanned skin shines in the afternoon sun.

"Throw off your robe," Susan says smiling. "What about my sandals?" Charlene teases.

Susan is again overcome by Charlene's flaming red hair, now curled and hanging over her full breasts, as Charlene's nipples peek out from an opened robe. She jumps up and pulls the cords, revealing Charlene's oiled body. Susan thinks for a second, Charlene's full breasts have become even bigger since we met. She pulls Charlene's warm body against hers and they share lingering French kisses.

"I feel electricity shooting from your crimson rouged nipples."

"Try one," says Susan as she kisses the pulse in Charlene's throat.

Charlene takes Susan's full breast it both hands and licks and suckles one long nipple and then the other. Susan looks up into Charlene's adoring eyes and says, "You set me afire."

Before they decide to adjourn to Susan's bed, she pours two more glasses of bubbly, they click glasses and Susan says, "To us and my secret. Handcock called minutes ago with great news. My husband has disappeared in Mexico. Handcock's contact called him to confirm it. I'll file a missing person's report or have Handcock do it. I'm so happy for us. That's $175,000 for me. I'll owe Handcock the same amount."

"This is a welcome shocker," says Charlene. "Handcock tends to exaggerate, but this means I can put my house up for sale and move in with you, with your permission."

They click their glasses and Susan says, "To our new life together."

"It's a dream come true for me," says Charlene seriously as she sighs and relaxes in her chaise lounge. She examines Susan's body and marvels at the transformation. She always had shapely legs, an attractive face, delicate fingers that she is so familiar with, and wonderfully full breasts with long nipples that stiffen to greet her fingers and lips. And she's so kind and giving.

Impulsively, she rolls on her side and pulls Susan's hips to her lips and kisses her hairy mound.

"I don't know what I'd do without you."

They chat about cruises and foreign places they'd like to visit and lay back and watch the clouds.

"Open your gift."

Charlene carefully unties the ribbon and opens the box. Inside is a diamond necklace that sparkles as the sun dances off its facets as she holds it up. Tears stream down her cheeks and she kisses Susan tenderly.

"I do love you. Put this treasure around my neck."

Susan fastens the catch, kisses Charlene's tanned shoulders and then turns her body to face her. "It's perfect with your crimson hair, tanned shoulders and tempting breasts. You truly look like a goddess."

"I'm your goddess, my queen," says Charlene taking Susan into her arms. Then Susan describes how she negotiated a fair prize and waited until the perfect time to present it.

"Handcock is right. You are a red-haired, big breasted goddess."

Later, Susan asks, "What do you want to do about our arrangement with Handcock?"

"Let's make it once a week for each of us," says Charlene, "unless we're vacationing."

Then Charlene leads Susan by the hand into her bedroom and notices the red satin sheets.

"To show off your diamond necklace."

Charlene strikes a number of poses, pushes Susan gently into bed and then whispers in her ear, "I'm going to think of every possible loving way to thank you until you beg me to stop giving you pleasure."

CHAPTER THIRTYNINE

In the morning, Mitchener and Angelica leave even earlier on another jungle hike. Everything goes as planned. The tomb has not been looted; most of the pottery vessels and artifacts have been secreted away in the camouflaged Mayan cave.

Angelica says as they leave the small clearing to hike back to the hotel, "Let's have the shaman and their Mayan helpers finish the portaging of the sacred pottery vessels containing their codices. I feel we have done our part."

Then the earth shakes violently, throwing them to the ground while tree limbs and tropical plants fly through the air. Monkeys scream in horror. Stunned, Angelica and Mitchener lie on the ground for many minutes awaiting powerful aftershocks, but feel only one slight one. Then Angelica gets up ashen-faced.

"Are you OK?" Mitchener says as he takes Angelica in his arms and holds her.

"Don't worry, my love. I am all right."

"You look like you've seen a ghost," Mitchener says, examining her pale face closely.

Mitchener looks up. Two Mexicans, wearing dirty clothes and covered with fallen jungle debris from the tremor point their pistols.

"Climb it so we can enter it," says one as the other points his pistol at Angelica, who remains calm. Mitchener carefully climbs the pyramid tomb, now revealing new cracks and fallen and broken stones at its base. Most of the camouflaged branches have fallen away. One bandit motions for Angelica to follow Mitchener up the pyramid to the opening. Then the four work their way down the crumbling staircase to the room covered with crumbling, peeling stucco walls; all shine their lights into the darkness except Angelica. Then to the right a further narrow passage descends into the burial chamber.

One man shines his flashlight on a skeleton surrounded by four skeletons with the remains of long hair. Other artifacts wrapped in dilapidated textiles stand upright. The Mexican sneers at Mitchener while the gringo reaches for his handkerchief to whip the sweat off his brow.

Both pistols swing toward Mitchener, who says, "Ever see a handkerchief before, amigos?"

Just then a rolling rumble rocks the earth, sending rocks bouncing down the stairway and into the room. The Mexican turns and fires at a bouncing rock. Mitchener knocks his arm up and the bullets pierce the ceiling, knocking debris down on the other gunman. Angelica grabs his right arm and throws him to the ground while Mitchener wrestles with the other bandit and they both fall to the floor.

Another shot echoes off the walls and blood spatters the room while Mitchener and the other man's legs and arms remain entangled. Within seconds, one flashlight beam bounces crazily off the walls as one bandit races up and away. Angelica can hear him working his way up the stairs after fleeing the burial chamber.

Mitchener, covered with brains and blood, frees himself from the other bandit, whose body has gone limp. Stunned by the rapid flow of events, he tries to catch his breath as Angelica finds his flashlight on the floor and turns its beam on the grizzly sight of a bandit with half of his head blown off.

"God, what a horrible sight," says Angelica.

"I pushed his arm away from me as he pulled the trigger, blowing his head off, the bastard. I barely recognize him. It's a ghastly sight. Point your flashlight on his body again while I search him."

Mitchener rolls his body over and pulls a small pistol from a holster on his ankle. On his other ankle is a knife in a scabbard.

"The guy is a walking arsenal," says Mitchener, who turns away and vomits from the smell of the brains and blood covering his body.

"This is what I feared when we returned," says Angelica. Mitchener reloads the dead man's pistol as Angelica holds her flashlight beam on it.

"We can't stay here. Who knows when his buddy will return?" A violent aftershock shakes the burial vault as they dive toward the walls and cover their heads with their arms. The tomb is shrouded in the darkness as the earth quivers. Then a crash echoes in the room as the rocks in the entryway collapse and roll across the room. One hits Mitchener in the leg and he screams in pain.

Both fear they are being buried alive.

Meanwhile, fearful that Mitchener and Angelica might be trapped in the tomb, the shaman and his son check at the hotel, find that their friends are not there, but have not checked out, and decide to return once again to the Mayan tomb. For hours, they hike the jungle trail, in a search for the tennis shoe, marking the short path to the tomb. At sundown, they end their search, deciding to return in the morning with armed Mayans. The shaman marks the tree with a bandana.

In the tomb, sweat pours off Angelica and Mitchener as they hoist block after block and pile them against the far wall as the beam from Mitchener's flashlight grows weaker.

"We've got to take a break," says Mitchener, "or we'll be dehydrated in no time."

They sit down and soon fall sleep in each other's arms.

In the morning, they awake to a stench-filled tomb. Mitchener rechecks the dead Mexican's clothes in the beam of his flashlight and finds nothing. Then he notices a canteen that has rolled way from the dead man. It's covered with blood. He shakes it, smells it and dips a few drops on the palm of his hand and decides it's all right to drink.

"Gargle it, and spit it back in the bottle."

He turns off his flashlight to save the batteries. "Did you sleep?"

"A little. Thanks for holding me in your arms," says Angelica. "I'm so sorry this had to happen."

"I want you on my side in any fight. You're not only strong, but quick. Sorry, I can't serve you any breakfast."

Soon, the entry way to the tomb is cleared and they continue hauling stones away to the main burial chamber. No light shines in the darkness except Mitchener's flashlight beam.

"Thank God, we haven't encountered any huge rocks."

"These are big enough for me," replies Mitchener. "I could use a beer."

Nearby, Mayans, following the shaman and his son, search for the tennis shoe marking the trail to the tomb. After hours of fruitless searching, the shaman's son whacks away underbrush revealing the tennis shoe and the Mayans make their way to the pyramid ruins. The shaman and his son notice the earthquake has scattered the pyramid's ruins widely. After the Mayans hand down stone after crumbled stone, the entry is once again uncovered.

"Hello," shouts the shaman's son repeatedly. Leaning against the rubble, he hears Angelica's scream, "Hello, we're here. Help."

After a day of hard labor eight Mayan men remove the last of the rubble blocking the stairway and descend into the burial room. Farther on, the elderly shaman shines his light into the blood-spattered room with the body of the dead Mexican and then turns his attention to the blood-soaked clothes of Angelica and Mitchener. The shaman and his son hug the couple and apologize for bringing them so near to death.

"I grabbed his gun arm when he tried to murder us and then the tremor hit," says Mitchener. "I didn't blast that hole in his head. He accidentally shot himself in the struggle."

Mitchener reaches in the pocket of the dead man, pulls out a piece of Mayan jewelry and hands it to the shaman's son.

"This belongs to your people. Thank you for saving us from certain death."

Angelica and Mitchener crawl hand over hand up the stairs and into the fresh air. They look up into the blazing sun while their lungs fill with the fresh, humid air. The Mayans pour water from their canteens over the couple's heads before they gulp down water.

"His companion escaped before the second tremor," Mitchener says.

"We'll bury the body, clean the tomb and camouflage it after hiding the codices once again," promises the elderly shaman. "My son will lead you to a nearby stream where you can bathe before returning to the hotel."

~~~ CHAPTER FORTY ~~~

Once back at the hotel they take their wine to the pool, go to the far end and pull up their chairs. Angelica gives Mitchener a kiss on the cheek and tears stream from her eyes.

"I had hoped this would happen later. My people say they cannot stop the coming cataclysm. Earthlings will not change. The people from my planet, you would call them extra-terrestrials, warned me that an earthquake will be the harbinger. When this happens, a pole shift of the Earth is imminent. Millions will perish in this cataclysm."

Mitchener shakes his head in disbelief, realizes that she has been given many hints of her almost mystical powers, but that does not prepare him for this conversation.

"We will have a short time together or a long time together. It is up to you."

"What do you expect me to say?"

"It depends if your heart speaks or your rational mind speaks."

"Here is my story. My people have made a great discovery during our sojourns here. In conversations and dreams and other channels we have concluded that we have been searching for a missing part of ourselves, emotion. So, we have been searching for emotion. We realize that we have cloned and bred emotion out of our species to accelerate our development.

"Your genetic material is close to our original species. In some ways, we are brothers. Our so-called abductions are one way to observe you. You have taught me through your love how to become emotional again. Perhaps it is the exchange of our bodily fluids when we make love. Your love has changed me. This I never expected. When I met you, my mission was nearly over. Soon, I would have left the Earth.

"Because of our organic discoveries we can recapture the neuro-chemical secretions of emotion. I have achieved this with you, although it surprised and enchanted me. For me, I achieved this by loving you.

"Who would have thought a journalist, the most cynical of your species, would have an open mind? I discovered this from your resonations at the party. You did not know it, but it was to be my farewell party on Earth.

"We found that your idea called curiosity is an emotional, not a mental, response. One of our focuses here has been sexuality. As you know, I have done more than observe it with you. Imagination is not a myth, but a realm of reality. You allow communication that you could receive no other way. Strangely, it is the unknown that you fear, yet it drives you. I never invaded you. All my actions were based on love and your openness to my love."

"Are you from the Pleiades star system," asks Mitchener. "I think I read that this alien race or planet has been observing us?"

"We work with those from the Pleiades. There are no stars so widely acclaimed by Earthlings. Their beauty and grace are spoken of in literature from all cultures, past and present. No other area of space has been investigated as often and as closely as that containing the Pleiades. Located in the constellation of Taurus, the Bull, the Pleiades,—Plee ya dez as Earthlings pronounce it—look like a small reproduction of the Big Dipper and are often mislabeled the Little Dipper. They are about 500 light years from the Earth.

"The Great Pyramid is riddled with Pleiadian mysteries. It has seven mystical chambers to honor the seven visible stars in the Pleiades. It's seven mystical chambers commemorate the seven visible stars of the Pleiades. Amazingly, the figured time of the rotation of our solar system around the Pleiades, 25,827.5 years, was worked into four places in this massive stone structure.

"As I said we are studying the relationship between sexuality and biochemistry."

"Are you using me in this experiment?" asks Mitchener.

"Did you ask that question with your heart or your mind?"

"I apologize," Mitchener says, knowing it deeply hurt Angelica.

"Before I resonated with an idea, not a person. Then I met you. My physical state can be permanent or altered."

Mitchener kisses her and runs his hands over her body as his passion grows into a powerful force.

"When we leave here, I will give you a chance to express your passion for me while I express my passion for you. I can feel my strong emotions responding to your love as I speak. Your resonance answers my questions for me without your words. Do I have to step down my vibrations sometimes when I make love to you? Yes. But as our love grows, your love is allowing stronger vibrations from me. I hope the thought excites you."

Mitchener winks.

"You earthlings will always draw to you what you want or need to experience. You are as curious as we are. Some of us seek sexual contact to see what it's like. I experienced it with you before I thought about it. We just seemed to flow into each other.

"As you know we can stimulate organs through the focus of thought. You create the physical sensations through my stimulations. I guess you could say we dropped emotion out of our physical bodies rather than suppressing it," says Angelica.

"Will I ever understand you?"

"Your heart does now."

Mitchener takes her hand, looks into those bottomless brown eyes, and says, "Thank you for sharing your secret. I understand why you said nothing before. It answers some old questions and arises some others."

"Oh, and I forgot to tell you that I quit my job before I returned to you. The answer to your next unspoken question is "Yes, I have saved a good deal of money. If we must part and I must return to my home planet, I will give it to you."

When they get to Angelica's room, she goes into her bathroom, showers, retouches her makeup, sprays on perfume and fixes her hair.

"My God, your extraterrestrials are beautiful."

"Do you mean, my God, Angelica you are beautiful."

"Yes, forgive me," he says as his heart melts.

Earlier, Mitchener, while lying naked in bed and pondering Angelica's revelations, finds his passion for her is even more aroused. He smiles and then wonders if she is focusing it on me from behind those doors?

When she returns, she says, "I wish to share some of the things I've learned about emotion before we part."

"Your life forces should be aimed to broaden aims and purposes. This will bring you more joy and harmony to your body. Breathe deeply and slowly and your anger will disappear. Water soothes the mind and comforts the spirit. The breath moves the consciousness on all levels. Soothing sounds alter the emotions.

"Life in its manifestations is vibration. Vibration that is creative is a good thing. Surround yourself with the light of God, of goodness. This will fight off any harm to yourself or to the emotions of your body. It will end fear of mental or spiritual forces used by the dark influences.

"The subconscious mind is in your body along with the conscious mind. It is the bridge to the God consciousness. This releases the powerful hormones of the endocrine glands that cause life-giving reactions within you and change your life.

"Budget time for meditation. Emphasize uplifting energy and light. Emphasize love, mercy, forgiveness, patience, faith, meekness, humility, gentleness, peace, joy, goodness and love."

"That's a big order," says Mitchener.

"There's one more thing. Knowing your body and mind have a great capacity for pleasure is invaluable," says Angelica smiling. "Absorb frequencies of light and turn them into heat as I do. We enjoy a wonderful feeling of coming together, of union, a great feeling of love."

She slides her curvaceous body next to Mitchener's, leans

on one elbow, and says softly, "I love to have you shut your eyes and envision the stars. My body is a dazzling star, sparkling with light. It's dazzling you with its warm orbs, its secret, welcoming places, its mesmerizing flesh. Feel my love awakening new emotions and unknown passions. Feel the warmth of my presence drawing you into me. Now, you are so open to me that when I say this, it thrills me and stimulates me to a higher degree. There is no blockage for me to overcome, only your welcoming love."

Angelica brushes her lips across his and kisses him tenderly and deeply. He pulls her against his body and then tenderly kisses her forehead, behind her ears, on her closed eyes and softly licks her neck as her pulse pounds. He weaves his fingers in her hair and pulls her face closer. He opens his mouth and his lips welcome her warm tongue. He probes with his tongue and feels lost in her warmth. His supple fingers softly knead her back; he cups her warm breast, sending tingling feelings throughout her body.

She is lost in his loving energy as it sweeps through her body, excites every cell, and enflames her desire. She moans softly as he lowers his head to her warm, erect nipple, and suckles it as she pushes it deeper into his warm mouth. He massages and caresses it.

Mitchener suckles and tongues her full breasts and his hands caress her thighs. Moments later she whispers, "You shall have your bliss as I am filled with joy. Visualize how you wish to experience perfect pleasure with me."

Mitchener pulls Angelica to him and embraces her while she massages the aura that surrounds body, thrilling him with new sensations as his breathing rate increases, his heart pumps faster and each nerve thrills. His manhood blazes.

New pleasures thrill him, tingling, pulsing, recharging, stirring him deeply and satisfying all longings. Angelica fulfills each of his desires, while he is fulfilling her new found secret desires. She feels at one with Mitchener. A sense of transcendence envelops her.

Angelica fulfills all the pleasures that he seeks as her

voluptuous body rises and falls above him. She, too, is awakening unknown physical pleasures. Their bodies rise and fall, move in and out rhythmically stimulating her nerve endings; his fingers, his mouth, his lips, his tongue, his magic wand excite her. She amplifies his passionate energies, lovingly, erotically and more powerfully than she dared earlier.

Occasionally, he opens his eyes to thrill to the motions of her superb body as it rises and falls rhythmically above him. His desires are fulfilled by her mystical, yet animal, magnetism. She pleases him in all ways.

Neither wants this loving union to end yet her flesh becomes warmer, her hips move faster and he is drawn deeper. Her strong, warm interior muscles milk his manhood as he moans before her hips rise to meet his thrusts. She moans quietly, then to her surprise, louder, as a wild passion overcomes her. He enters the gateway to female consciousness as a reverie, an interior passionate pulsing, carries their bodies into a transcendent, blissful union.

His silver stream erupts as she arches her back and pulls him deeper. She cannot stop, whispering softly, "More! More!" Then she climaxes in a transcendent reverie again.

Time stops. Both lie quietly and feel they must part soon. "When you make love to me, you're making love in the fourth dimension, Mitch. Each time it grows easier for you to enter the fourth dimension with my help."

"You are my magic, my love," Mitchener says.

~~~ CHAPTER FORTYONE ~~~

When Angelica and Mitchener arrive at the chilams hut, they are greeted warmly and invited to have cups of cocoa. As they sip it, the aged Zak-kuk says, "The great change is coming soon. We feel it will restore our ancient powers. This will be the fulfillment of the new Mayan age we are now in.

"We pre-Inca peoples knew that the stars were inhabited and the gods came down to them from the constellation of the Pleiades, changing their lives for the better.

"We believed our gods were avatars of certain stars, notably Orion and the planets Mars, Venus, Neptune, Jupiter and Saturn. Our religion, like that of the ancient Egyptians, was extraterrestrial in outlook. We believed that the First Father of the human race, the maize god, came from and later returned to Orion.

"Your Bible (Revelation, chapter 21) offers a prophecy of the opening of the bottomless pit, which is followed soon after with the appearance of a new heaven and a new Earth.

"This connects with the Mayan prophecy for the start of the fifth sun. On Dec. 21, 2012, the Mayan calendar ended its long count calendar date of the thirteenth baktun since creation day on August 12, 3114 B.C. Then the sun was positioned at the southern Stargate. The constellation of Orion was the birthplace of their two father gods. This will signal the tribulation mentioned in the Bible and the beginning of a new age. This ends the cycle of 5,125 days."

"Father speaks the truth. The time has come. We welcome it with our hearts," says Katu-Quila smiling. "We are glad that you have come. Today, our trusted Mayan friends are removing the last of the sacred texts in their pottery vessels, the sacred skeletons and burial goods from the tomb and our first hiding place. Soon, others will discover the burials in the pyramid but the sacred items will be gone. We will close its entrance so it will be difficult to reopen. It will be revealed at the proper time. That time is not now. We Mayans thank you for your help in saving our history."

Zak-kuk bows his head slightly and hugs Mitchener and then Angelica and says, "I feel this will be our last time together. It is sad, but our spirits will join again. I know it. I feel that Angelica knows this too."

"It has been a great joy for me to know you and your people. I have said little, but my heart has filled with love for you and your son. I feel as you do that a great change is coming. And very soon."

They all smile and Mitchener and Angelica bow and leave. "In my wildest dreams I could never have imagined these things would happen upon my return to Palenque. Life is truly unbelievable."

He takes Angelica's hand as they walk through the rainforest track that is now familiar. They both are lost in thought as Mitchener says, "It was a good idea to walk this time. One sees and feels so much more."

Angelica slaps a mosquito on Mitchener's check and blood runs down it.

"It hope I don't feel too much more of this," says Mitchener, smiling.

That evening the two, tired from their walk, go the hotel bar in search of Brunel and Christopher. The bartender says, "I heard your friends checked out late yesterday. You gringos are always in a hurry. Allow me to buy you two beers on the house."

He pours two draft beers in mugs as foam rises to the top and dark thoughts cloud Angelica's mind. She decides to say nothing and raises her mug, "To our friends, may their trip home be safe and all their wishes come true. We know their unspoken wishes have come true. They have found new loves."

Even Mitchener begins to feel a flicker of finality in their events here, but the cool beer is so welcome after the long hike that these thoughts soon fade.

~~~ CHAPTER FORYTWO ~~~

In the middle of the night, Mitchener feels Angelica get up, but quickly goes back to sleep. He seldom is able to read Angelica's emotions because she is so happy all the time, but she offers a slight indication at breakfast when she says, "Maybe they will take you with me if you wish."

Mitchener dreaded this moment when Angelica discussed it with him.

"I could never forgive myself if I did not go with you," he says solemnly and embraces her. He is tempted for a half second to say, "What a story!" but the impulse flickers past.

"Will I die if I remain on Earth?"

"Yes. Few will survive. Cataclysms are not hard to predict, but the results are," says Angelica. "I would ask that you keep this as our secret. To tell this secret would serve no purpose. My people say they cannot stop the pole shift. Earthlings will not change. This has happened to Earth before."

Mitchener hears the words, but finds it hard to believe this is happening. He thinks I suppose this is what severely wounded soldiers feel on a battlefield before they die.

"There will be a slight, brief earthquake. Later, I will be contacted and taken from a spot I will show you this afternoon. It was shown to me when I was alone here. Maybe my people will allow you to go with me. I cannot say."

As the morning passes Mitchener feels as though he is in a state of suspended animation. Time has stopped. His only wish is to be near Angelica. Then they return to their rooms, put on their jungle duds, and Angelica takes his hand and leads him down a trail to a spot where a small trail leads off to a clearing. It looks like it was once a swamp, but the earth is now hard packed and the brushes and grasses are pressed flat.

"This is the spot where I will be picked up. I was directed by a cooling spot on my forehead that the spaceship would soon arrive. Look around so it does not seem strange to you. My people landed here to prepare the spot. This was a swamp before the landing. This must be obvious to you."

"Right."

"First you will hear a low, throbbing, humming sound. Then you will see a circular, gleaming silver, disk-shaped craft circling slowly above us. When the craft lands, birds will fly off and other animals will scurry away, then you will hear a high vibration, a humming sound. The craft will come from that direction, the west, where it will race down from the heavens in seconds and then its speed will slow quickly over this spot. It will set down gently on the ground, become completely silent and its earlier sounds will be replaced by silence.

"Do not advance toward it. Stay where you are. If you move toward it, you will feel paralyzed. We don't want that. Then a young, attractive, long-haired blonde, who will appear human in all respects, will come from behind the craft. The earth's atmosphere is suited to her. She likes it better than our homeland. You will think her beautiful, but not as beautiful as me. Right?"

"Of course," Mitchener says, as he lifts her warm hand and kisses it.

"Say it again," Angelica says in a commanding voice and then smiles and nods her head.

"I love you," Mitchener says easily and thinks she's right. We Homo sapiens are such fickle, changeable creatures, we need reminding. Our ways and thoughts wander with the circumstances. We are easily deceived by flesh, money and other attractions.

"She will walk toward us with easy, natural grace, but she will be even stronger than me. You know my strength. She will greet me in our usual way and then shake hands with you. Her grip will be strong and sure. She is accustomed to our language so she will understand all you say. Our conversation will be short. I will do most of the talking. However, you must give your permission to her to join me on the ship.

"We will walk with her into the craft, enter it and sit down. It will disappear in seconds. If you look out the window, you will see that everything will change colors in seconds. That is caused by radiation. Your body will not experience pain during the incredible acceleration.

"Although Earthlings have taken the first step into space, it is a primitive step. You have only been able to fly to the moon. To go into deep space, Earthlings need a propulsion system that is able to produce a so-called hyperspace velocity so vast distances are overcome by non-space and non-time. Through this technology fractions of a second are enough to travel light years.

It took me seven hours to travel from my planet to earth, three and one-half hours to your solar system and another three and one-half hours to slow down to reach planet earth. Our beam ship goes from the speed of light to the speed of thought. We call it null time or spiritual energy. This way the spaceship steps out of time and later materializes.

Our forefathers were like your forefathers and practiced peace and love. Life on our world is similar to life on your world. We grow up, get married and have families. Our ancestors are similar to your ancestors. Some were nine feet tall like ancient skeletons you have found. However, we live from 700 to 1,000 years. We have lived peacefully for 50,000 years.

"We also have the ability to time travel. I revealed this when you dreamed of me. I was a priestess of Hathor.

"I'll tell you more after we enjoy lunch. From now on you must consider this an adventure, a loving adventure, and think only positive, loving thoughts. If you do not, you will be thinking in terms of last things, the last breakfast, the last morning, and more. These memories will repeat themselves in your mind and be difficult to erase. We must use our energies for loving. I don't want my lovemaking with you blocked.

"And one more thing. My people are waiting for a shift of your poles, that is a shift of your planet Earth on its axis, a cleansing, and a turning point for the evolution of mankind.

This, too, is a positive, not a negative, event.

"The Mayans were not the only ones who tracked and explored the meaning of end times. Other civilizations, including the Egyptians, Babylonians, and Hopi, Aztec and Eastern Indians knew of this era and viewed it as a period of transformation and renewal.

"Some Mayan elders say the veil between the living and the dead will dissolve and communication with those on the other side will become unremarkable. Others associate this time with wisdom, harmony, love, consciousness and the return of natural order. We are still creating the future. We must raise the global spiritual vibration.

"Be glad that you have the opportunity to be alive at this time and be part of that preparation for the coming of a spiritual nature that must rule the world. Be happy of it and give thanks daily for it".

As they walk back through the jungle, Angelica takes his hand and kisses it. "Isn't it wonderful to treasure each moment like this, to live in this moment?"

"Yes, it is. My life has been a race against time, deadlines, appointments, only busy-ness or busi-ness. This is the first time in my life that I am living for the moment, each moment with you."

They enjoy a light lunch of salads and each has a glass of wine. They chat about their joyous times together and return to their rooms for their bathing suits.

Then Mitchener relaxes in a chaise lounge at the pool under a splendid sun and is cooled by light breezes as Angelica graceful walks toward him, a curvaceous vision in her blue swimming suit.

"Your eyes are focused on my flesh, which will always welcome you," says Angelica. "I see your pulse is pounding and your flesh is rising beneath your swimming suit. My ardor is rising, too."

"Making love to you is my greatest pleasure. I feel it is an honor how your flesh responses to my flesh after a glance."

She sits down on a chaise lounge next to him and reaches

across with her hand and grasps his swimming suit with her fingers. She smiles as she feels his stiff flesh under his swimming suit.

He moans softly. She smiles.

"I was just checking. It was an impulsive gesture. I feel the same way, but you must save your strength for if you are allowed to accompany me. If we make love now, I will forget myself and when we are finished your dreams will be fulfilled and your energy will be spent. I would never tease you with my body. If you just wish relief, I will give it to you, but I will not make love to you at this time. Wait. You will not regret it."

He rolls over onto her wide chaise lounge, slips the strap of her bathing suit off her shoulder and his hand cups and then massages her warm, gorgeous breast and twirls and plays with her nipple. He says nothing for long minutes and sighs.

"You are right," he says. "I must save my strength for the coming days. I know you would love me and thrill me as no other woman if it was the perfect time. It is not. As the saying goes, the flesh is weak. I needed to hold and feel your flesh and let it thrill me. I will hold you tonight in my bed," he says and realizes that he is smiling. "We men haven't changed much since our days in the caves."

"I'll tell you what I know, Mitch, before I leave and then you can ask questions. If you cannot say goodbye to me, you must trust me. I have to keep it simple. The answers are merely clues. I'll do it point by point."

The following day is like a dream to Mitchener as he treasures each moment with Angelica, whose beauty seems to grow each precious moment. After breakfast Angelica takes Mitchener's hand, squeezes it and says, "I have wonderful news. It is not certain, but it looks like they will take you with me when I leave."

In the early, quiet hours just after dawn Angelica tries to answer more of Mitchener's questions concerning the propulsion of the spaceship.

"We don't travel from Point One to Point Two in a straight line at the speed of light, some 670,000 m.p.h. When we deal with space-time operating in an intense gravitational field, we bend or warp space-time between these two points, bringing them close together. The more intense the gravitational field, the greater the distortion of space-time and the sooner we get there.

Our super drive generates a million-fold the speed of light, thus the speed by which super space is penetrated. So, time and space collapse or become zero time and zero space. Space and time don't exist. We travel distances of light years is a fraction of a second. There is no time lag and you can turn the gravitational field off and on. That's all I know. As I said it took me seven hours from my planet to Earth.

Oh, we have a reactor that uses a special element as fuel to create our power source. I forget its number. Our disc will be about 40 feet in diameter and is very sleek. A beam screen will protect our craft in space.

Our spaceships are protected by a screen of energy which automatically rejects any kind of resistance and every bit of matter. The projective screen is identical with the specific gravitational field which we build up around our ships. With this gravitational screen, we are able to neutralize the gravitational field effect of any planet.

We are similar to human beings on earth, but we have more knowledge, wisdom and have made far more technological advances. It is much easier for us to learn all languages spoken on Earth. We learn, as you do, in classes. I learned English in about 30 days.

We are still far removed from perfection and have to evolve constantly, just as you do. We are not super-human nor missionaries. However, we do try to supervise the developing of human life in space to ensure a measure of order. We do this by selecting some individuals and instructing them. We do this only when a race is in a higher state of evolution. Then we prove to them that they are not the only thinking beings in the universe. Creation, by itself, is a law and every form of life must conform to it.

It might be necessary to transfer us to a larger ship, perhaps big enough to hold a city of 150,000 inhabitants. Hopefully, we can go to the dark side of the moon and reside in one of its inhabited craters which hold thousands. It depends on the length of the cataclysm.

Thought transmission is the purest form of thought communication. I'll teach it to you, Mitch. I am telepathic. Our society is 30 centuries ahead of yours in various ways. You know this is true. You are learning to love me in the fourth dimension.

We do not reach to an end of the universe, for such does not exist.

Space travelers have visited your Earth from other stars, more than 100 civilizations, sometimes from distant civilizations as myself. In the 16th century before the industrial revolution your air was much cleaner, the sky bluer, and the grass greener. The earth had a fresher feel.

We are 30 centuries ahead of earth cultures in knowledge, social structure and science.

A spiritually developed being as part of creation acknowledges creation in all things, even the smallest microprobe. Leading a creative life causes fears and doubts to vanish. By creative thinking man acquires wisdom and a sense of unlimited strength which releases him from the limitations of convention and dogma.

We think of the universe as a creation, follow the universal laws of creation and use reincarnation to evolve life after life. We seek truth, wisdom, love and understanding.

We can look into the future and also change it with our free will. Prophecies we consider to be warnings. We will never interfere with earthly events as long as you do not go beyond your solar system.

Material life on Earth is only a passing event. Before and after life there continues to exist the creative presence of the universe."

～～ CHAPTER FORTYTHREE ～～

Angelica awakens, nudges Mitchener and kisses him awake. She pulls his warm body to her naked body and says, "I've a surprise. I've hired a cab to take us to Bonampak. Remember when I surprised you by dressing as a Mayan priestess? I said to you in my room, I see your sword is erect, warrior. Your homage is welcomed. On your knees, warrior.

I drenched my body in perfume and a powerful scent filled my room. Then I poured my bottle of myrrh causing your head to spin dizzily. I commanded you to worship my blue, painted body.

I wore feathered plumes and flashing tiara to accent my dark brown eyes, high cheekbones, wide smile, pouty lips and curve of my neck and you know the rest. You were mesmerized. You kissed my flesh from head to foot with love until you were exhausted.

I wore a colorful, loose blouse and long skirt with Mayan patterns. The fanciful designs in blacks and greens stood out against the pink-orange cloth like those worn in festivals by modern Mayan women. I'll never forget my headdress of plumed pink, crimson and bright yellow feathers tucked into a jade and turquoise encrusted tiara. I loved those golden-colored earrings studded with diorite and turquoise.

What a night. Unforgettable. It took me days to recover. Today we're going to see murals picturing that Mayan costume I bought to enchant you."

The 95-mile cab ride from Palenque to the ruins of Bonampak passes slowly along a bumpy road which is slowly being encroached by the ever-intriguing jungle. The unknown seems to lurk around each curve in the gravel road. With a captured audience, the cab driver delivers his history of the ruins.

The Yucatan Peninsula is the largest continuously inhabited part of Mexico. The Mayan inhabitants came as early as 2500 B.C. They used solar and lunar cycles to develop their highly accurate calendar and had a complex mathematical and hieroglyphic system. But the art, it's incredible. You will see it today.

This rings true as they enter the Temple of the Paintings where the walls and vaulted ceilings of these three chambers are decorated with brilliantly colored murals. Here, the courtly life of the nobles is depicted in all their riches. The colorful pageantry surrounding Mayan warfare comes to life in radiant colors. As they read a fuller understanding of the Mayan way of life, methods of warfare, customs, beliefs and costumes comes to life.

"See, Mitch, there are the feathered plumes, the ear flares and the other colorful parts of your costume," says Angelica. There are few people around them so there are few distractions as they look back hundreds and maybe thousands of years of Mayan history.

"There have been many tourists who have visited these small temples and ruins but none of them have had its rituals come to life as we have," says Michener, giving Angelica a hug. "Because of you, a deep feeling for these ancient people and their ways of life and their incredible rituals has filled my mind, and more importantly, my heart."

"Bonampak, meaning painted walls, has been a visual and artistic experience which has touched our hearts," says Angelica. "And we're to stay at a small hotel and tomorrow we'll kayak the Usumacinta River."

That night as they lie in an uncomfortable bed the unforgettable images flash before their minds—the vivid scenes of haughty Mayan lords, splendidly attired in jaguar-skin and quetzal-plumed headdresses, well-dressed ladies, bound prisoners with their fingers ripped off and blood spurting from their wounds, severed heads, musicians playing pipes and trumpets, lords in jaguar robes, a lord's wife preparing to prick her tongue on paper to be buried in ritual for Mayan gods and groups of magnificently dressed Mayans dancing on the temples steps, their eyes looking dazed after taking hallucinogenic drugs.

The scene triggers powerful emotions in Mitchener. He pulls Angelica's soft, curvaceous body against his as her breathing becomes more rapid and he suckles at her breasts and her hands reach down and caress and pump his manhood. His kisses cover her warm flesh, seeking her secret areas that thrill her and enthrall him. As her lips leave his shaft, her back arches and he enters her body, riding them both into ecstasy. He cannot image life without her.

The following day Angelica and Mitchener, saturated with mosquito repellent and wearing tennis shoes, swimsuits and sombreros slip their kayaks into the wide, meandering Usumacinta River that forms part of the border between Mexico and Guatemala. The mists have lifted from the encroaching jungle and the sun warms their suntanned bodies covered with suntan lotion. The river, named after the howler monkey, flows through one of the largest protected wetlands in the world and passes through towering canyons.

The river and its tributaries were once important trade routes for the ancient Mayans and the jungles lining their banks seem shrouded in mysteries and the unknown. Along its banks rise the ancient Mayan cities, now in ruins, of Yaxchilan and Piedras Negras. As the current slowly carries the kayakers and their guide along the river's warm waters and its banks lead only to impenetrable jungle, an otherworldly feeling and quiet serenity overpowers them.

Even with the current, Mitchener's muscles tire and he welcomes their luncheon picnic on huge, warm rocks. The vast spectacle of seemingly unending river and jungle enraptures them as they munch on their simple taco meal and drink their welcome water. In the late afternoon towering canyons shoot up as the river narrows, their speed increases and small rapids challenge them as they follow their guide.

At last their kayaks arrive at Yaxchilan that rises 65 feet above the fast-flowing river and is one of the most dramatic of all Mayan sites.

"Situated in the heart of the Lacandon rainforest, it was

built between 350 and 800 A.D. and rose late to prominence under famed rulers "Shield Jaguar" and "Bird Jaguar,'" reads Michener to Angelica at a remote bar as they sip cool, welcome beers and then enjoy a dinner of rice, beans and tamales at their simple hotel.

After dinner, they relax in bed before climbing the steep hills behind the ruins in the sunset to watch the last rays of a waning sun lend a magic to this superb natural setting. That night the only sounds are those of moaning howler monkeys as they drift off to sleep.

"What a magical place," Angelica whispers as she drifts off to sleep in Mitchener's arms.

In the early morning, they rise and walk beneath giant trees that keep the ruins shady as the temperature begins climbing with the sun. They feel the timelessness of the spot as later they take a branching path leading up to the little plaza surrounded by the ruins of 13 buildings. A lintel of one building depicts a ruler, Escudo Jaguar, with one of his warriors. Throughout the ruins, small paths lead off to unidentified ruins that are lost in history. Then they go to Edifice 13 that overlooks the site's most famed site. Known as the Palacio, its superb lintels preserve fine carvings, one of Pesaro Jaguar IV. In ancient times, it was a political court, and thereafter a religious site for the Abandon Indians.

They wind up their visit at the Grand Plaza as the sun shines through the roof comb and huge tree roots climb the stairs of an ancient ruin reminding them of cities lost in remote jungles around the world. There are splendid paintings, relief carvings, and steles showing rituals and other scenes.

Angelica works her magic with ferries and taxis and combis and by dinner they are back in Palenque at their old hotel where they swim for awhile, take naps in their chaise lounges and decide to have another glass of wine at the bar before they climb to the rooftop to watch the sun spread its golden-magenta rays across the jungle's treetops.

Then the stars spread across the skies and Angelica points and says, "There's a shooting star. What a wonderful harbinger."

"Truly it is and you saw it first."

"It's our star," says Angelica.

That night they fall asleep in each other's arms.

The days slip by as in a dream. One day they return to the Parque Nacional Agua Azul to once again enjoy some of the most majestic falls in Mexico with its more than 500 falls ranging from 10 to 100 feet in height and a series of aquamarine colored rock pools. Angelica finds a rickety bridge that crosses the river and eventually they reach an impressive gorge where a tributary explodes out of a jungle-enshrouded mountain. Flocks of butterflies greet the interlopers.

"Perfect! I love it here," shouts Angelica over the roar of the plunging water. Now to find a cool pool where we can cool off."

Farther on appears a shallow, shaded pool shaded by tall palm trees.

Sweating profusely after a stiff climb, Mitchener strips off his backpack filled with water bottles, then tosses his sombrero, his shirt and shorts onto a nearby rock, spreads a towel and bows.

"Welcome to my kingdom, your majesty."

"You forgot to take off your socks and hiking boots, peasant," says Angelica, who rapidly disrobes and sprays Mitchener's sweat-covered, tanned skin that shines in the sun.

Angelica slips easily into the cool pool and Mitch grabs her in a wet embrace.

"I've learned my lesson, strong Amazon woman. I will not embarrass myself by trying to dunk your beautiful head."

Soon a water fight breaks out as the cool water splashes cover their naked bodies.

"This is how I like you, beautiful one. Naked. In all your beauty," says Mitchener. Soon they are embracing, slipping into a shallower area and Angelica lies back, spreads her legs in a V and his throbbing shaft slips into her warmth as her practiced muscles squeeze and pump him into ecstasy while he suckles at her breasts and covers her shoulders with kisses.

"I've been practicing, my love," says Angelica as her powerful female muscles milk his member and his body responds. Time passes until his body is swept in pleasure again and again and he moans, "enough, enough" while convulsions take over her writhing body.

I don't want to stop until he is completely satisfied, she thinks, and every cell of his body is enflamed with bliss and overpowering pleasure. I want him never to forget this precious time of love.

Soon, the lovers float lazily upon the pool's placid waters before returning to their blanket for a nap, exhausted and full of love.

When Mitchener awakens with Angelica's warm body pressed against his, he smiles and says, "I'm in paradise. This is no dream."

An arduous hike along jungle paths returns them to a taxi after hours of hiking through remote paths. Mitchener continues to marvel at Angelica's energy, which he now sees as a cosmic force that she somehow draws into her body.

The following day the two take a pleasant public transport to Misol-Ha with its 80-foot falls, fern-lined trails and a wide pool that they share with families. They pack a picnic lunch and Angelica continues reading about the ancient Mayan while Mitchener enjoys his serenity and wonders why he spent all those years in the madness, the busy-ness of New York City chasing dreams.

Another day, Angelica leads Mitchener to a small temple down a seldom trod trail. Vines crowd its entrance, but Angelica pushes them out of the way and Mitchener shines his flashlight against the walls. Sweat pours off Mitchener.

"Is this the ruin you wished me to see?" asks Mitch.

"This is the temple with the beautiful ceiling depicting the brilliant blue sky holding the constellation known as the Pleiades. The inscription states `Deity, taking pity upon the children of the Earth, sent one of the divine sons to live among them and instruct them," says Angelica, pointing at the ceiling. "My people were here long before the Conquistadors bringing peace and wisdom," says Angelica. "May God bless them."

The two visit the temple after hilltop temple as Angelica wonders what wonders are yet to be excavated.

"I love that Temple of the Sun," says Mitchener, "so well preserved, so perfectly sited on that four-level pyramid crowned by a roof comb. Inside, is that massive carved stone slab with glyphs, and stucco friezes that show the sun."

They walk to a quiet spot in the courtyard of the palace and rest their tired feet and drink deeply from their water bottles. Angelica recalls with a smile, "I wanted to make love to you when I was an Egyptian priestess, not in a dream, but in the flesh. I had a hint then that I could love you if given the chance, but I did not have a chance. I had to wait a long time in your time, not mine. It was worth the wait. It nearly did not happen. I focused on your vibrations, your resonance for 24 hours to get you to that damn party.

"Once I met you I could not keep my hands off you. My heart was drawn to you. My whole being was drawn to you. I was so anxious to share my body with yours. My heart had such a strong desire to unite with you in the flesh and in spirit. Then you fulfilled all my desires."

"You mentioned that story briefly before, but I love to hear it. It always excites me and reminds me of my love for you."

They embrace, kiss and then glaze at a quiet corner of the courtyard. A mysterious, luminous female figure appears and walks toward them. Her eyes shine like laser beams directly at Angelica. Mitchener is stunned at this vision. Then she disappears.

"She says the beam ship will land tomorrow morning at the spot shown me."

"I didn't hear anything," says Michener.

"She was speaking through thought transference. She is a guide from another dimension who has appeared to me during my missions in the earthly realm. She sends cosmic wisdom along a golden laser beam. I rested here because I could feel the magnetic field here is so strong."

CHAPTER FORTYFOUR

As the morning passes Mitchener feels as though he is in a state of suspended animation. Time has stopped. His only wish is to be near Angelica. They have a light breakfast and then Angelica, looking radiant in her comfortable jungle apparel and carrying a small backpack, takes his hand as he throws his small backpack over his khaki outfit, and leads him down the small jungle trail to the clearing that Angelica has earlier pointed out. In this swampy area, the earth remains hard packed and the brushes and grasses are still pressed flat.

"Remember, first you will hear a low, throbbing, humming sound. Then you will see a circular, gleaming silver, disk-shaped craft circling slowly above us. When the craft lands, birds will fly off and other animals will scurry away, then you will hear a high vibration, a humming sound. The craft will come from that direction," she says, pointing to the west. "Then it will race down from the heavens in seconds and then its speed will slow quickly as it hangs over this spot. It will set down gently, become completely silent and its earlier sounds will be replaced by silence.

"Do not advance toward it. Stay where you are. If you move toward it, you will feel paralyzed. We don't want that. Then probably the young, attractive, long-haired blonde, who will appear human in all respects, will come from behind the craft.

"She will walk toward us with easy, natural grace. She will greet me in our usual way and then shake hands with you. She is fluent in English, accustomed to our language so she will understand all you say. Our conversation will be short. I will do most of the talking. However, you must give your permission to her to join me on the ship.

"We will walk with her into the craft, enter it and sit

down. I assume it will disappear in seconds. If you look out the window, you will see that everything will change colors in seconds. That is caused by radiation. Your body will not experience pain during the incredible acceleration."

Mitchener wears his light khaki clothing, carries a light backpack with items Angelica has chosen, and wears comfortable hiking boots. She whispers, "Are you ready to go with me, to leave your planet, your way of life?"

"Yes, you will outlive me by centuries, but my time with you will be my treasure. A shared treasure. I will try to fulfill your wishes and your love."

Soon Angelica feels a cooling spot on her forehead and says patiently, "It's coming."

Mitchener finds he is not anxious as Angelica has explained that her ancestors are the same as those of earthlings and he can expect many meaningful conversations if all goes well. He knows they come in peace and love.

Then he steps forward, forgetting that Angelica has told him not to do this. Instantly an unseen force stops him, paralyzing any movement. She whispers, "You will be allowed to walk forward and board the beam ship once permission is given."

Then a tall, dark-haired handsome cosmonaut in a tight-fitting suit comes forward from behind the beam ship and walks with stern grace toward Angelica and embraces her. A long exchange of words takes place in a language unknown to Michener and a frown crosses Angelica's face.

"There must be some mistake," says Angelica calmly. "I had no idea that you planned to ask me to be your wife. You gave no hint that you hoped for this."

A fierce look crosses the cosmonauts face as he motions her forward, takes her arm and they walk around the silver disc and disappear. Within seconds there is a low, throbbing, humming sound. Then the craft rises and silently vanishes in a flash.

Mitchener is speechless. The beam ship raced into the heavens and disappeared in seconds with a high vibration, humming sound. If he hadn't seen it, he wouldn't have believed it.

Thoughts of the disappearance of Sara slip into his mind.

Is it happening again? Am I cursed, he thinks. Now what? He drops his knapsack and sits on the ground and waits. The bent grass reminds him of his loss.

Then a vision appears in his mind, a beautiful face with dark sunglasses, high cheekbones, dark brown piercing eyes and his heart beats faster. A wide, attractive smile crosses her face. There's only one smile like that, Angelica's. Her lips do not move but the message is clear:

"Do not leave the spot. I will return. Remain here until sunset. I will return if possible. Do not despair. I love you. I can feel your heart beating faster, your pulse pounding with the vision of my face reflecting my love for you. Go in peace."

Momentarily, Mitchener feels his rational mind questioning his vision, but then his heart takes command and he feels hope as he picks up his backpack and moves under a giant Ceiba tree for shade. He decides to think about various things that Angelica has told him about her planet. They flash across his mind as each statement brings more visions.

He recalls her statements:

"My planet has enjoyed peace for the last 50,000 years."

"My planet is alive as its systems continually evolve. Like your planet we have evolved after each Ice Age. After each one its inhabitants evolve, its animals evolve, even its soil and rocks evolve. Everything is evolving."

"We are ruled by Kings of Wisdom who are in the form of spirits from a far more advanced planet. We are part of the family of man in these vast universes."

"Our planet is 10 percent smaller than the Earth, but the two are alike in many ways. However, our skies are more blue, our air cleaner and our waters purer. We never had an industrial revolution such as yours."

"This beam ship is a small. Our mother ship can accommodate up to 1,400 people. Amazing? It is amazing for me to experience or think about too."

"We believe in the laws of creation."

He remembers she smiled when she made the following statement: "We understand each other's thoughts and feelings, not just their words. This encourages goodness and loving thoughts."

Many anecdotal visions follow this thought to clarify this statement.

"One-third of earthlings have our genetic seeds. In so many ways we are alike, although technically we are far ahead of you."

"We understand that the future is not fixed. We have the ability to go 100 years into the future in visions based on our current thinking. This helps us not to make mistakes. In other words, we are seeing the results of our present thinking. This is a great advantage. As you know the future is ever changing because God has granted mankind free will. With it, we can create wonderful things and events or terrible catastrophes."

"We are 100 percent responsible for ourselves."

"We constantly seek wisdom, truth and love, while devoting 70 years solely to our education."

"Our aim is to be friendly, helpful and delightful. We do not have the dark forces of some worlds."

"We consider the partnership of men and women offers an opportunity to learn and discover. We do not seek mates that are like us. This would limit our opportunity to discover things. Have you discovered things loving me, Mitch? I think so. A man and woman who are extremely different can discover more. Versatility is a good quality."

"People on our planet always attempt to be friendly, helpful and delightful. Was I not delightful around you, Mitch? You made me delightful, Alien Man."

"Often you earthlings refuse to accept that men and women are different. Would men enjoy pregnancy? Many women find it a divine state."

"In the future many races will come to your country as many alien beings have come to your planet over the millenniums, maybe hundreds of thousands of years."

Mitchener finds time is slipping by rapidly while each thought produces many visions that seem to flash across his mind. He feels a sense of excitement concerning the new world that he will discover if Angelica can command the beam ship to return for him.

Then a light rain falls, later changing to fierce winds and then to booming thunder as bolts of lightning flash across the sky. He becomes sopping wet and his rain drenched clothes cling to him. His thoughts darken as the clouds turn day into a thunder-filled night.

He thinks sarcastically of his great preparation for the trip. No umbrella. No rain jacket. Then he spots a large hole in the trunk of a towering Ceiba tree and his spirits rise. Soon, as in many tropical storms, it passes and the sun becomes a flaming, radiant gold and then magenta as it prepares to slip under the horizon.

Then, a bit of Mother Nature's magic appears, a shining ark with its magnificent bands of color. This rainbow, a spectrum of hope, slowly becomes more radiant as a silver disc appears below it and streaks toward the landing pad.

Within seconds there is a low, throbbing, humming sound. Then Mitchener sees a circular silver, disk-shaped craft circling slowly above the landing field. When the shining beam ship lands, Mitchener hears a high humming sound as it hangs over this spot before gently setting down on the ground. A deafening silence follows.

This time Mitchener remembers not to advance toward the craft as a young, attractive brown-haired vision races from behind the disc, trips and falls face first into the swampy muck. Mitchener is so captivated by the rainbow he fails to identify the mud-covered Angelica until she covers his face with muddy kisses and screams "Mitch, it's me. Follow me, we have only seconds to board the beam ship."

Mitchener throws on his wet backpack and races after Angelica. The two disappear behind the shining beam ship. Inside Mitchener hears nothing, but in seconds the craft is airborne. As Mitchener embraces mud-covered Angelica, he looks out the circular porthole and down on the Earth far below. Light from the rainbow seems to circle Angelica's smiling face.

THE END

VICTORIA VERITAS AND ASTARA, NOVELISTS

Men find me attractive, I've been called voluptuous, but I'm shy and have never sought the spotlight. As a very private person I chose the pen name of Victoria Veritas because of a wild dream I once had. I've worked in public relations, fashion and been an author, screenwriter, newspaper reporter and editor, critic, reviewer, free-lance writer, photographer and worked overseas for Reuters.

I've lived for periods of time in four foreign countries, speak fluent French, and have traveled since I was a young backpacker. During those travels two women came to fascinate me—Hatshepsut, the ancient Egyptian queen, who usurped the throne, became pharaoh and ruled as a man, and the brilliant, beautiful French courtesan Diane de Poitiers, who became the mistress of French King Henry II, who was 20 or so years, younger.

From these fascinations emerged my two novels, "Egypt's Erotic, Esoteric Female Pharaoh Hatsheptsut" and "The French King's Mistress: Diane de Portiers."

I was introduced to Diane de Portiers at the Sound and Light show at the unforgettable castle of Chenonceau in France and to Hatshepsut at her famed Mortuary Temple up the Nile and across from Luxor, Egypt. Luxor, which has had other names over the centuries, is often chaotic and dusty, but holds a vivid, lovely place in my memories.

The Valley of the Kings lies over a cliff beyond Hatshepsut's temple. When the Egyptian sun sets, an ethereal, crimson-magenta spreads across Luxor, and beyond it the silver Nile and the rosy cliffs of the Land of the Beyond. Below those intriguing cliffs lies the vast, empty Great Western Desert. In climbing the hills around the Valley of the Kings, descending into the rock-cut tombs of nobles and pharaohs, and riding feluccas up and down the Nile, Egypt slipped deeply, silently into my soul. I confess I've illegally entered these tombs with secretive, funny young guides who traded cigarettes for secret, illegal entries.

I did my research, didn't believe many of my guides' stories and Egyptologists' claims. However, with Hatshepsut and Diane I followed my intuition where choices had to be made. After all, a writer writes for herself, first, and her readers can make their choices.

The trick is to make historical characters come alive. Scenes spread before my imagination and came to life in my mind. I typed them up. Simple, challenging, and oft times frustrating.

There are always gaps in history. Usually writers choose the scenario that makes the most sense to them. Sometimes writers go for surprises. Diane de Poitiers destroyed all her letters to King Henry II before she died. Hatshepsut disappeared from Egypt's historical records.

Arguably, I tried to stick to the historical records, but often there was none. I took everything I knew or read about the times and the worlds my heroines lived in and made my best guess concerning controversial events.

Both periods were provocative. In Hatshepsut's period at the height of Egyptian power, common women had more power than in many ancient societies. However, female slaves served without question. In Egyptian palaces, courtesans, royalty, slaves and servants battled fiercely for power and position, often using sexual favors to further their ambitions.

In Diane's time, women had much more freedom than earlier. An anything goes atmosphere prevailed in the court of the French king Francois I, who loved women. It was also the time of the Reformation with its trials and tribulations.

One character in "Mistress" is typical. Her father had three wives and 30 children. She learned early that she had three ways to make her way, the convent, marriage or the beds of rich men. As she says to men, "What do you want of me?

What arouses your passion? How can I best fulfill your fantasies in bed and in life? I have grace, honor and a jewel box … If we understand each other, I am yours. A kiss to begin our adventure?"

In "Hatshepsut" the queen's humor matches her beauty when it becomes time for her to produce an heir with her masked lover, a commoner disguised as the god Anubis.

"Any trouble slipping through the palace, Anubis?"
"None, your Majesty. I'm a god, remember?"
"It's your lucky night, Anubis."

"Senenmut removes his mask, looks down on Hatshepsut's fine, rouged facial bones. Her welcoming breasts are thrust forward; her nipples are hard and pointed. She slips off her golden sandals; her golden bracelets, finger rings and earrings accent her beauty. Her lithe hips move gently under a sheer linen gown. The fragrance of myrrh announces her elegance."

Each heroine's beauty is matched by her intelligence. Alas, I'm no match for my heroines but I do play better badminton.

This novel took me into new territory, UFOs, aliens, the Mayans, the year 2012 and a coming apocalypse. Oddly, I returned to old sources and ideas that have fascinated me for years in this novel.

In "Apocalypse" Angelica has powers which Earthlings can only imagine, but she must exercise care not to overpower Mitchener's earthly body. First, she has him envision his desires before she can fulfill them with her body and unearthly powers.

After inviting him for dinner on their first date, she meets him at her apartment door wrapped only in a bathroom. After handing her a bottle of wine and his gift this scene unfolds:

A tear slips down Angelica's face. After a long pause, she pulls Mitchener to her warm body, embraces him, parts his lips and her tongue explores his mouth in a deep kiss. Then she turns, drops her white bathrobe to the floor and says softly, "Please put this treasure around my neck."

Mitchener, surprised by her nakedness, touches her soft, warm shoulders and takes the golden clasp and gently fastens it while he looks down on her soft skin, the slope of her shoulders, her legs, the welcoming curves of her back and the curve of her buttocks.

"This loving gift touches my heart. I want to savor every moment tonight."

"You say that as if this is the end, not the beginning."

"Shut your eyes. Envision the stars. My body is a dazzling star, sparkling with light. It's dazzling you with its warm orbs, its secret, welcoming places, its mesmerizing flesh. Feel my love awakening new emotions and unknown passions. Feel the warmth of my presence drawing you into me."